GRAVE DIGGER

Roland Winsall

Also written by Roland Winsall

Asylum

ISBN: 978-1-923078-11-6
Published by Vivid Publishing
A division of Fontaine Publishing Group
P.O. Box 948, Fremantle
Western Australia 6959
www.vividpublishing.com.au

 A catalogue record for this book is available from the National Library of Australia

For Robyn – (in Corowa)

Acknowledgements

I would like to thank the following people who have helped me enormously when writing this story:

Robert Knox – an old friend and confidant whose comments and suggestions are always helpful and insightful, and gratefully received.

Robyn Renner (in Melbourne) – a friend and talented reviewer of my manuscripts. Her comments and contributions are much appreciated.

Sisters: Sherry Hodson (dec'd – gone but not forgotten) and Janine Sabec - two of my greatest supporters.

Friends and valued readers of my stories: Peter Renner (Robyn's husband), Chris & Sue Munton, Ray & Jan Thomas, Carol Shaw, David Drill and Esther & Cecil Hamer.

Special thank you to Jason Swiney and staff of Fontaine Publishing Group.

1

COURT ROOM NUMBER two, Law Courts Building, Sydney, New South Wales, and Daniel Wainwright, known to everyone as 'Danny', was being sentenced for a murder he'd committed some six months ago. He'd exhausted all his legal appeals, and now it was time to face the music. His defence lawyer had pleaded with the judge not to sentence him too harshly. He stressed that Danny, although he had made a foolish mistake, was still a young man and had excellent prospects for rehabilitation. But the judge, who had a reputation for imposing lengthy sentences, pointed out that murder was hardly what you could call a foolish mistake; it was the worst crime a person could commit. So Danny had resigned himself to doing a long stretch, a stretch that would see his better years fading away as he stared out through the metal bars of a prison cell.

He sat with his counsel and gazed despondently at his surroundings: the highly polished panelled walls that reached from floor to ceiling, the faded red-and-blue carpet that had been walked on by thousands of accused and accusers alike, the visitors' gallery filled with people waiting to hear his fate – some he knew; some he didn't – the stenographer wearing glasses far too big for her, the cops sitting together and quietly chatting, the judge resplendent in his robes. And then there was the witness box where he'd sat while the prosecution pummelled him with questions and accusations. In the end, it was clear he was guilty and the jury had an easy decision to make.

He craned his neck around and searched the faces of the people sitting behind him. He wondered if his mother would be there, but she wasn't. He hadn't seen her now for a long time. Once again, he was on his own. He swung back around and faced the front. Off to the side, an ancient electric clock hung on the wall; it whirred away, counting down the hours, minutes, and seconds until he found out his fate. Doing a stretch in the slammer was a given. It was just a matter of how long and where.

Looks like you've really stuffed it up this time!

The courtroom remained quiet as everyone waited while the judge bent down from his lofty vantage point and spoke to his young female assistant in whispered tones. Finally, they both nodded and smiled at each other. The assistant took her seat in front of the bench while the judge sat back up and adjusted his glasses. He glanced down to his papers, cleared his throat, and, assuming a solemn expression, stared at the young man. Danny's lips became dry and his stomach stirred as he peered up at the judge and wondered just how it would go.

Outside, lightning flashed as dark storm clouds gathered over the harbour. Thunder rumbled in the distance and briefly rattled the windows. The carnival music at the back of Danny's brain began playing away again. It was always there – sometimes loud, sometimes soft, but always there. It was a psychological problem that had plagued him for a long, long time – ever since that fateful meeting at the showgrounds, the time when he decided he was no longer going to back down.

The judge cleared his throat and began.

'*Daniel Edward Wainwright. On the 27th of March ...*'

Danny listened as the judge droned on, but despite his best efforts to concentrate, his mind wandered. He leant back in his seat and wondered how it had come to this. From being just an ordinary boy to someone who carried a knife, then a handgun, and watching as a man's head split open like a watermelon hit with an axe the instant he pulled the trigger.

He never guessed for a moment it would turn out this way, but his life had taken many unexpected twists since his childhood. In fact, so many twists … he'd lost count.

2

ON THE OTHER side of the courtroom, in amongst the small group of police, sat Detective Senior Sergeant Presley Cooper, known in the cop shop as 'Elvis', but not to his face; he wasn't someone who could take a joke. He was the man who would benefit most from the sentencing of Danny.

Cooper came from a long line of police officers. His father and grandfather had both served in the force and had careers that were solid without being exceptional. The best rank achieved in the family before him had been by his father, who'd made it to Sergeant. As a Senior Sergeant, Cooper already held a superior rank, but it didn't stop his old man from telling him how difficult it had been back in his day, when he was the boss and ran the cop shop down in the Cross.

'All sorts there, boy. You really had to have your wits about you! I suppose you have to namby-pamby them these days. Well, we didn't! We had real tough buggers to deal with. Crims of all sorts. Violent, vicious men ... you young blokes got no idea what it was like!'

Cooper listened while his father raved on. The older his father grew, the more often he drifted back to yesteryear. Cooper would just sit there and suffer in silence. He hated it when his old man told him how hard it had been back then. He suspected that it was even more difficult *now* with the cities and suburbs flooded with drugs and guns, but he knew his father would never accept it. Well, with

Danny Wainwright in the bag, things would be different. With this arrest and conviction, he would pass the final hurdle for promotion to Inspector, the prestigious rank he so desperately craved.

Cooper looked across the courtroom at Wainwright and contemplated when the ceremony would take place. He could picture himself receiving the Inspector's badge and epaulettes from the commissioner. He'd make sure his father was there; that would shut the old bastard up. There would also be a big crowd of his fellow policemen to shake his hand and slap his back. He would be the centre of attention. And there was a rumour doing the rounds, but only a rumour, that with Wainwright in the slammer, he could also be in line for the Police Medal. It was going to be a good day – a very good day.

It had all fallen into place for Cooper with the murder of a bikie. A police phone tap had fingered Wainwright as the hitman, and Cooper jumped at the chance to arrest him. His team caught up with him in a rundown motel room. They surrounded it, and Wainwright gave up without a fight. Cooper was the arresting officer, and so the honour went to him. Once they had Wainwright on remand, Cooper worked with the police prosecutor for months to make sure he was convicted; in the end, it was a slam dunk. And so Cooper was in court today to witness the final two steps he needed to secure his elevation to the lofty new level. He was going to call the commissioner and tell him in person the sentence Wainwright received and the institution he'd be banged up in. He could hardly stop himself from smiling.

3

DANNY SAT QUIETLY as the judge continued. His mind drifted back to the time when, as a young boy, he'd suffered his first incarceration.

At home it was just Danny and his mother. He never knew his father, a lorry driver who was killed in a motor accident shortly after Danny was born. But he knew what he looked like. There was a photo of him in his mother's bedroom. It sat on her dressing table beside her bed. Danny noticed she dusted it every day. Attached to the frame was a faded, curled-up piece of paper.

It read: '*To Miriam – love Maurice*'

Danny often wondered what he would have been like, the tall man with the smiling face.

The house they lived in was a small two-bedroom weatherboard situated in an inner suburb of Sydney. He went to school with lots of other kids but only had one or two he could call a friend. But that was okay; he preferred being home by himself with the books his mother brought him from the local library.

To make ends meet, his mother worked in a textile factory. It was a struggle, but she managed to make sure she was always there to greet him when he arrived home. Danny knew she loved him, and he loved her, but he also knew she was lonely. Sometimes he'd hear her crying in her bedroom late at night. But worse than all of that, he noticed she'd started drinking, and when she did, things changed. It was like the alcohol put an invisible barrier between them.

At school Danny was quiet and reserved. He wasn't a big kid, and this made him a target. He tried to stay away from the bigger kids but was constantly bullied. As the years went by, his main antagonist was Luke Brennan, a much bigger boy who took great pleasure in beating him up. Things really came to a head one day at high school when he was cornered near the assembly hall. He was surrounded by Brennan and his mates. The bully pushed Danny over and punched him every time he went to stand up. Danny attempted to ward off the blows, but they came heavy and fast. He left school with two black eyes and blood on his shirt. He was a mess.

By the time he arrived home, one eye had closed over completely, but at least the blood from his nose had stopped running and was starting to congeal. Relief washed over him as he pushed open the front gate and walked up the path to his house. His mother came out of the front door, and her expression changed from a smile to a look of horror.

'Oh, Danny, what happened?' She rushed forward and held him at arm's length, staring at his battered face.

Danny didn't answer.

'Did that horrible boy at school hit you again?' she said as she took him in her arms and hugged him tightly.

Danny remained silent.

'I'm going straight back there now to sort this out!'

'No, please don't, Mum!' Danny pleaded. 'It'll only make things worse!'

His mother sighed and hugged him again, her face full of both love and pity. She wanted to go to the school and confront the teachers, and also the boy who did it, but she didn't want to upset Danny. And perhaps he was right – maybe it would make things worse.

'All right,' she said and hugged him even tighter. 'You'd better get inside, and I'll bathe those eyes.'

His mother told him he could stay home for the rest of the week to give his bruises time to heal.

In his bedroom Danny picked up one of his favourite books – 'Boy's Adventures'. He loved to read the 'Exploits of Billy Rainbow'. Billy was a hero; he was never bullied, and Danny loved seeing what he got up to and how he managed to get himself out of tight places.

It was in one of these stories that he saw a picture of a raging bear towering over Billy. The title of the story was 'Billy Kills a Bear'. In the picture, Billy didn't seem scared – he was never scared. Danny read on intently, fascinated to see what his hero would do next.

The bear came at Billy on its hind legs, slashing claws out-stretched, ready to strike. Its enormous jaws opened wide, showing teeth that could tear him to pieces. Billy stood his ground and waited for the hulking beast to advance. When it pounced, Billy thrust a knife into the bear's upper stomach. He made sure it missed the rib cage so it didn't get caught on bone, then he thrust the blade upwards, penetrating the huge thumping heart. Billy was crushed underneath the massive animal as it fell. But he could feel it dying on top of him. He waited until it no longer moved, then slowly climbed out from under the mammoth body and wiped the knife clean on its thick brown fur.

Danny read and reread the story, fascinated with how his hero had overcome such a powerful adversary. It caught his imagination, so much so that he stole a six-inch carving knife from his mother's knifeboard and stashed it in his room just in case he too ran into a raging bear. After a few weeks, he started carrying it with him, tucked into his sock. Soon, putting it there was part of his ritual when he dressed, and after a couple of months, some of the time, he even forgot he was carrying it.

It was a bright April day when Danny and a friend went to the

Sydney Royal Easter Show. They bought show bags and decided to walk down Sideshow Alley. Noise from the rides and sideshow booths dominated the soundwaves. Spruikers were calling out, trying to drum up business. The rides were in full swing, each with their music blaring out as loud as it would go. The dodgem cars raced across the smooth, polished floor, electric arms sparking away in the wire ceiling above. The Ghost Train was roaring, ghouls were crying out, and girls were screaming. It was almost impossible to hear what anyone was saying. And as Danny and his friend turned a corner, they ran straight into Luke Brennan and his mates.

'Hey, look what we got here!' Brennan yelled as he walked over and grabbed Danny by the shirtfront.

Brennan's large square head was topped off with a spiky crew cut. His blue eyes bulged large, as though they were going to jump out of his face. He was going through puberty, and numerous ugly pimples shone a fiery red. He pushed Danny backwards and grabbed his show bags. Danny held on, but Brennan ripped them out of his hand.

'Give them back!' Danny protested and made to grab them.

Brennan held them out of reach and punched Danny in the face. He emptied the contents of each bag onto the ground and kicked them away, smiling as he did it.

'Come and get 'em, Wainwright!'

Before Danny could move, Brennan launched into him, raining blows on his face and body. Danny fell backwards and landed heavily. He tried to stand up, but Brennan hit him again. Tears started in Danny's eyes. Brennan looked back at his friends and laughed.

'Check out the crybaby!'

He came back at Danny, who was still on the ground. As Danny started to get up, he felt a sharp jab to his foot. It was the knife. It must have moved downwards and pricked him. It jogged his memory; he'd forgotten he had it. Danny ran his hand down his leg and took the blade out of his sock as he stood up. He hid it from sight as Brennan came closer.

Don't back down! Not again! Whatever you do! Don't – Back – Down – Again!

Adrenaline surged through Danny's body like an electric current as he gripped the knife and waited for the next onslaught. Brennan came forward and towered over him like the bear Billy Rainbow had encountered. Danny wore another punch, but this time he didn't fall back. Instead, he forced himself forward. His body was shaking as he leant into Brennan. He pointed the knife at the bully's solar plexus and shoved it in. He heard Brennan gasp as the knife split his skin. Then Danny thrust it upwards as hard as he could, just like Billy Rainbow had done. Brennan screamed out in pain and stepped backwards as a small trickle of blood leaked out of his light-blue tee shirt.

'Shit! Look! He's been stabbed!' one of Brennan's friends yelled and pointed.

Brennan held his stomach and stared down at his own blood. He tried to wipe it off, but as soon as he did, more took its place.

'Oh, Jesus!' Brennan snarled at Danny. 'You bastard!'

Danny stepped back and held the knife out. Brennan went to go at Danny but stopped as blood streamed through his shirt. The bully grimaced as he pushed hard against his chest, trying to hold together something deep inside himself. He lurched forward, and a long low howl burst from his lips. Now the blood oozed through his fingers much faster. He turned to his friends, his face a ghostly white. He looked like he was going to cry. Then, as though a water main had burst, his chest exploded and he was covered in his own blood. It surged out between his fingers as tears started in his eyes. He squinted in agony as the strength left his body. Within moments, he dropped to his knees, toppled over, and died in the dirt at Danny's feet. Danny stared down at the bloodied knife, hardly believing what had happened – how easily it went in, how devastating the end result.

But just like Billy Rainbow's knife had done, Danny's knife had found its mark. It punctured the left ventricle of Brennan's heart, and with every move the bully made, with every beat of his heart, the wound split open just a little bit more, until eventually, Brennan's heart simply ripped itself apart.

Danny stood there with the bloodied knife still in his hand, the carnival music screaming in his head. The rides whirled faster than before. He thought of running, but didn't. A black-cloaked ghoul from the Ghost Train ran over to where Brennan lay.

'What've you done?' he shouted. 'Give me that!' He wrenched the bloodied knife out of Danny's hand.

Danny couldn't move. The man was in his face, yelling and gesturing, but Danny couldn't make out what he was saying. It was as though his ears were blocked with wads of cotton wool. His head was flooded with the insane noises of the carnival. He glanced across at his friend, who just stood there open-mouthed. A huge crowd gathered, and it wasn't long before the police arrived and took Danny away.

* * *

The case was reasonably clear-cut, but his lawyer was able to argue that Danny was provoked and acting in self-defence. His charge was reduced from manslaughter to unlawful and dangerous stabbing. He pleaded guilty, which gave him a further reduction, but the judge noted that he was carrying a concealed weapon, and this went against him. His mother stayed every day in the Children's Court and begged that he be given home detention, but her desperate plea fell on 'deaf ears'. The judge sentenced Danny to a control order of seven years with a non-parole period of four.

He was just fifteen years old.

4

THE JUDGE PLOUGHED on:

'... acting alone, you did wilfully ...'

But Danny wasn't listening. His mind was fully absorbed in recounting the scenes from his troubled past.

He was terrified as the authorities drove him and four other boys to the juvenile justice centre on the outskirts of Sydney. The van slowed at a high perimeter fence and came to a brief stop while the gates opened. Danny shuddered when he heard them slam shut behind him once they were through. He peered out through a small window in the van as it bounced along and could see a drab two-storey concrete building in the distance.

Inside, they were ordered to strip. Danny stood there naked with the other boys while a guard placed their clothes in separate black plastic bags with their name tags attached.

The grim-faced guard stood in front of Danny. 'You have any personal effects?'

'No,' Danny said softly and gently shook his head.

'No, *sir!*' the guard shouted.

'No, sir,' Danny said and shivered in the cold.

The guard stood back and inspected the naked boys. A sly smile crossed his face as he checked out their shrivelled genitals. After a full minute of ogling, he yelled at them.

'Get dressed – your clothes are there!' He pointed to a large cardboard box containing prison-issue tracksuit pants and jumpers.

Once they were dressed, the boys were called together. The head guard notified them of their rights and the rules they had to follow while in the centre. Danny watched as each boy's personal property was recorded and taken away. They were told they would receive their things back at the end of their sentence. The guard also said they could use the telephone once a day to call relatives or caregivers. At the end of the instructions, guards were assigned to show the boys to their rooms. One of them motioned to Danny to follow him, and together they walked down a stark, lonely corridor. Danny's mind was racing as he wondered what his room would be like. They stopped at No. 7.

'This one's yours,' the guard said and stepped aside so Danny could enter.

Danny noticed there were two beds in it.

'We're overcrowded at the moment,' the guard said. 'You're bunking in with Ainsworth. He's older than you and been here two years already. Once we free up some rooms, you'll get your own. Put your stuff over there,' he continued and pointed to one of the beds. 'You've missed lunch. Dinner is five thirty … sharp!'

The guard turned and left, leaving Danny by himself in the small room. It had a toilet, shower, desk, and shelf. On the shelf there were folded sheets, a blanket, a pillow, and some basic toiletries. He sat on the bed and started to cry. A few minutes later a tall boy entered the room. Danny quickly wiped his eyes.

'What's your name?' the tall boy asked.

Danny looked at him, worried.

'Danny. Danny Wainwright.'

'You been cryin'?'

'No,' Danny said and wiped under one eye with his wrist.

'Don't cry in here, mate! They see you cryin', they'll pick on you.'

The boy gazed down at Danny.

'I already know your name. The guard told me. I'm Dillon. Dillon Ainsworth.' He held out his hand, and Danny shook it.

'Limp-wrist handshake,' Ainsworth said. 'You better toughen up quick.'

Ainsworth walked over to the shelf and threw Danny the sheets and blanket. 'Make up your bed. The guard will be doin' his rounds soon.'

Danny started to unravel the sheets. He'd never had to do it before; his mother had always made his bed up for him. He hoped he'd get it right.

'You're the kid that did the killin' in the showgrounds, aren't ya?'

Danny stopped momentarily as the carnival music kicked in and took over. With an effort, he pushed it into the background and continued tucking the sheets under the thin mattress.

'Yes,' he said.

'You stabbed that kid in the heart?'

'Sort of,' Danny replied.

'What do ya mean … *sort of*?'

Danny took in a deep breath. He wondered how this boy knew so much about him already.

'I got him in the stomach first, and then shoved the knife up into his heart.'

Ainsworth, a bit perplexed, stared across at Danny.

'How'd you know to do that?'

'Read it … in a book.'

Ainsworth nodded and frowned; he'd never read a book in his life. He took a long look at Danny and said, 'I run a gang in here, the Outlaws. You wanna run with us?'

Danny was worried and unsure of what to say.

You have no choice … say yes!

'Sure,' Danny said, his voice shaking. 'What do I have to do?'

'Nothin' yet. I'll let you know soon enough. First, I'll introduce you to the others in the gang in the 'chow hall' when we're havin' dinner tonight.'

* * *

That evening, just before 5:30pm, Danny and Dillon Ainsworth entered the spacious room. The sign over the entrance read – Dining Room.

Ainsworth led Danny to one of twelve trestle tables. Each had bench seats on either side where a total of ten boys could sit. Within minutes a large group of boys started filing into the room, talking at the top of their voices while they found their seats. Danny took a seat next to Ainsworth and two other boys, while five boys sat on the other side. A guard waited until everyone was seated and the room slowly became quiet.

'Boys, please stand while we say the Lord's Prayer.'

There was a general rumbling on the wooden floor as they got to their feet. A guard stood out the front of the room and commenced the prayer.

'Our Father …'

Each boy mumbled their way through the prayer until, finally, it was over.

'All right, boys. Starting with table one, please move over to the canteen, grab a tray, your plate, knives, and forks. You others, sit down and wait until I call your number.'

Danny sat and waited in silence while the boys on his table whispered to each other. 'Who's he?' he heard.

'What's his name?' another boy said and pointed at Danny.

Ainsworth spoke up. 'This is Danny Wainwright. He's joining our gang. He did the killing in the showgrounds.'

The boys were impressed, and one by one they introduced themselves. Danny followed them when it was their turn to get food. He returned to his seat and saw that a new boy had taken the empty spot next to him.

'Hi,' the boy said in an effeminate voice. 'I'm Miles, Miles Lonigan. You're new, aren't ya?'

'Uh-huh,' Danny said as he placed his tray of food on the table and sat down.

Lonigan smiled at Danny and said, 'You wanna be my friend?'

Danny looked over to Ainsworth to see what he'd say. Then he felt Lonigan's hand run over his leg. 'Get lost!' Danny yelled.

'Hey, Lonigan, fuck off! Get off our table … now!' Ainsworth shouted and stood up. 'He's not one of you lot. Piss off!'

'What's going on?' a guard said and walked over to the table.

'Nothing, sir,' Ainsworth replied. 'Lonigan's on the wrong table.'

'Lonigan,' the guard said, 'beat it.' He pointed his finger at another table.

Lonigan stood up, grabbed his tray, and sauntered over to a table on the other side of the room.

The guard gazed down at Danny and the other boys. 'Eat your dinner,' he ordered and walked off.

'Don't talk to him,' Ainsworth said to Danny as he pointed over to Lonigan. 'He's a queer! He has plenty of queer mates in here.'

Danny didn't need to be told but took Ainsworth's advice nevertheless. During dinner, he found out the Outlaws were mainly involved in petty theft and that Ainsworth and a few of the older members of the gang also ran a protection racket. They stood over the younger inmates and demanded payment in the form of the supplies those kids received from their parents every now and then.

* * *

A few months into his sentence, Ainsworth gave Danny a shiv. It was made from a toothbrush and had one end filed down to a nee-dle-sharp point.

'Keep it. We might want you to use it. You can hide it here.'

Ainsworth showed Danny a place where there was a gap between the leg of the bed and the bed frame.

'Thanks,' Danny said. He flicked it around in his hand and tucked it in his sock. Ainsworth smiled his approval.

It was only a couple of weeks later when it came in handy.

5

___

ONE OF DANNY'S assigned chores was helping in the laundry. It was early afternoon, and he was in the laundry by himself. The room was stifling hot as the huge dryers turned and rumbled. Danny was loading clothes into one of the washing machines and didn't hear two boys walk in. One was Lonigan, but Danny didn't know the other one.

'Hi,' Lonigan said in his mincing, effeminate voice. He smiled at Danny, then twirled his hand above the head of the other boy and said, '*This* is my friend, Zacaria Adelman. Say hello, Zac.'

'Hello,' Adelman whispered with a slight lisp. 'You look nice,' he added and smiled sweetly. He walked forward and stood beside Lonigan, blocking Danny's path to the door.

Danny was immediately on edge.

Lonigan stepped closer.

'Zac says he likes you … so do I,' Lonigan said as he reached out and touched Danny's arm.

'Piss off,' Danny hissed and pushed his hand away.

Danny tried to shove by them, but Lonigan held him. Adelman stepped forward and held his other arm. He fought Lonigan off, but Adelman ran his hand down Danny's stomach towards his groin.

'You're really cute,' Adelman said and exposed a mouth full of rotting, yellow teeth.

'Get lost,' Danny yelled and struggled to free himself.

He was fast losing any chance of escape. The boys were holding him tight. Lonigan pushed Danny's head down towards his crotch. Danny was desperate. He was about to yell out when he remembered the shiv. He dropped to his knees and freed his arms.

'Oh … I think he really likes you, Miles,' Adelman said.

Danny fumbled around on the ground trying to grab the shiv while Lonigan started grunting and groaning as he loosened his tracksuit pants.

'Hold him, Zac,' Lonigan said breathlessly. 'He has such a pretty mouth.'

Lonigan was groaning loudly and began removing his underpants. Finally, Danny found the shiv and rammed it upwards at Lonigan's groin.

'Ahh, shit!' Lonigan yelled.

Lonigan lurched backwards, holding himself between his legs. Adelman moved in and grabbed Danny's hand, trying to get the shiv.

'Give me that, boy-bitch!' Adelman yelled.

Adelman tried to yank the shiv out of Danny's hand, but Danny held on tight. Lonigan screeched and rolled sideways, clutching at his bleeding groin. He fell onto Adelman's leg and caused him to stagger. It was all the advantage Danny needed. He wrenched his hand free and aimed the shiv at Adelman's head. It hit home not far from his eye.

Adelman lurched backwards with blood spurting from his temple.

'Oh hell! You nasty boy!' he shrieked and held his hand to his forehead. 'You … you horrible boy-bitch!'

Danny saw his chance and forced his way through the door. He hurried to his room. Within minutes, a guard walked into the laundry and noticed both Lonigan and Adelman there.

'What are you two doing here?'

Neither boy answered, but the guard noticed Lonigan pulling up his pants. 'Why are you here? You're s'posed to be in the kitchen!'

The guard stared at Adelman. 'Why are you bleeding?'

Adelman held his hand to the side of his head. 'I slipped and hit my head.'

Unconvinced, the guard stared at him. 'Where's Wainwright?'

'Don't know, sir,' Lonigan said.

'He's s'posed to be here in the laundry!' the guard roared. Then he saw Lonigan hobbling and asked, 'Why are you limping?'

'Sore leg, sir,' Lonigan said as he held his crotch and hobbled out of the laundry.

Back in his room Danny ran his hands under the cold water and washed off the blood. He hid the shiv just as the guard entered the room.

'What are you doing here, Wainwright?'

Danny was startled. He wondered if he knew what had happened in the laundry. 'Nothing, sir.'

'You're not supposed to be here. You're meant to be in the laundry!'

'Yes, sir. I know … I … ahh … needed … needed the toilet. I don't like to use the communal ones.'

The guard seemed sceptical. There was something going on, but he didn't know what.

'Lonigan and Adelman were both in the laundry when I was there just a minute ago.'

Danny didn't speak.

'Why were they there?'

'I don't know, sir.'

The room became silent as the guard stared at Danny. He knew it was odd that Lonigan and Adelman were in the laundry. He knew they were both aggressive gays and wondered if they had put the 'hard word' on Wainwright.

'Did those boys speak to you?'

Danny hesitated; he would have to lie. 'No, sir.'

The guard looked at him unconvinced, then said, 'Get back in the laundry now!'

'Yes, sir,' said Danny and walked past the guard.

To Danny's great relief, there was no sign of either Lonigan or Adelman when he walked through the laundry door.

Back in his room that night, Danny told Ainsworth what had happened.

'Did they touch you?' Ainsworth asked.

'Not much. They tried to hold me, but I broke free. I stabbed both of them!'

'Good,' Ainsworth said. 'Don't worry about them anymore. We'll take care of 'em.'

And so Danny was free of Lonigan and Adelman from that day on. Two days later, there was a ruckus in the dining room. All the guards were alerted and raced to sort it out. The distraction had been organised by Ainsworth. He made sure both Lonigan and Adelman were alone in the kitchen when he and three other members of the Outlaws surrounded them. The bashing those boys received was significant; not so much around the head, where it was noticeable, but their ribs and groins were black and blue when the beating was over.

And despite random searches of the rooms, the guards never did find the shiv. Danny made sure he carried it during the day; it was his insurance policy. It reminded him of the knife he'd carried in the early days. And despite being groped by Lonigan and Adelman, things turned out well for Danny. Word went around that he could defend himself, and with deadly effect. Ainsworth was pleased also. He knew he had recruited someone valuable for his gang, someone he could call on to enforce the rules if anyone stepped out of line.

Danny made the most of being in the gang, and to prove he was one of them, he also became involved in the petty thefts. Being a gang member made it safe for him inside, but as it turned out, it was the wrong crowd to mix with. He didn't learn any life skills while he was in there. What he did learn was how to survive as a criminal once he was released. He was soon to find out his days of 'killing the bear' were far from over.

6

THE JUDGE CLEARED his throat, and Danny snapped back to reality. He looked out of the courtroom window at the approaching storm and then down at the floor. But it didn't take long before his mind slipped back to that cold June morning, four years after the start of his custody in the juvenile centre, when he was released. He'd just turned nineteen.

Grey clouds hung overhead and a cold wind blew as he waited for the guard to unlock the perimeter gates. He was tall now, as tall as the guard. In fact, he was one of the tallest boys in there. And he was much stronger than previously, but more important than that, he now had a streak of confidence about him that he'd never had before. His time inside had put a hard edge on him. He'd learnt how to swear, and he'd learnt how to fight. He told himself he was never going to be bullied again.

Thoughts flooded his mind as he waited for the guard to unlock the gates. He wondered what it would be like to get back home, back to his room. Would it be the same? Would the stack of books he loved to read still be there? Would his mother still be the same? Would she still love him, even though he'd done a stint inside?

The gates opened, and the guard said goodbye, but Danny ignored him. He just walked straight ahead to where he could see his mother standing by her car in the car park. She had visited him only twice in the time he'd been in there. He desperately wanted to see her more often and told her so, but both times she smiled a sad smile and said that she'd had to take on extra hours at the textile factory and work had prevented her from seeing him more often. She told him she'd do what she could, but it was clear to Danny she didn't want to be there. He guessed the embarrassment of visiting her only child in a jail for kids was too much for her. Danny walked over and put his arms around her.

'Hi, Mum,' he said.

'Hello, darling,' she replied and hugged him tightly.

He could see she had changed. Her face was drawn. There were dark lines around her eyes. She was thinner than he remembered. But more than this, she seemed distant, as though she had moved on with her life.

The drive home was done mostly in silence. When they arrived, Danny saw how right his suspicions had been. He was greeted at the front door of his house by a man – a stranger. The man put his hand out and said his name was Edison. Danny shook it but disliked him from the instant they met. He wondered who this person was and why he was here with his mother. He was devastated when he found out that Edison was living with them and that he shared his mother's bed. The grunting and groaning coming from her bedroom at night was torture to him. He also learnt that his mother no longer worked; she had lost her job and was now living on welfare.

Edison and his mother spent most days drinking, and by the late afternoon, they were both dead drunk. The house that used to be so clean was now squalid. Danny hated it. He hated everything about it. He stayed for only a month, then he left home – for good.

7

THUNDER RATTLED THE courtroom windows again and re-verberated along the city streets. Danny gazed up at the bench and shifted uncomfortably in his chair as the judge rambled on. Once more memories from his past came flooding back.

After being released from the juvenile centre and then leaving home, things got worse for Danny. He had little money, and what he did have was quickly disappearing. However, things started to look up when, on a hot day in Sydney, he decided to have a drink. He walked into a bar in The Rocks and recognised some young men who were there. They were from 'juvie', and Dillon Ainsworth was among them. He walked over to him.

'G'day, Dillon.'

Ainsworth's smile lit up his face when he recognised Danny. 'Danny! How are you?'

'Good, thanks,' Danny said, but Dillon could see he was not happy.

'It's great to see you again, mate. What have you been doin' since you got out?'

Danny paused before answering.

'Not much. Just tryin' to stay out of trouble.'

Ainsworth smiled and took a sip of his beer. 'You got work since you got out?'

'No, not really.'

'Oh!' Ainsworth said and nodded.

The noise of the pub burbled away in the background as Ainsworth swirled the dregs of his beer around in his glass. He stared across at Danny and put his glass down on the bar.

'You … ahh … you wanna earn some cash?' Ainsworth asked before picking up his glass and tipping the remainder of his drink down his throat.

Danny hesitated for a moment as butterflies stirred in his stomach. 'Yeah, sure,' he said and wondered what Ainsworth had in mind.

'Well, perhaps I can help. I'll introduce you to someone who's always searching for new talent.'

'Okay,' Danny said and tried to sound pleased, but the doubts were really starting to kick in.

Ainsworth picked Danny up the next day, and they drove to Bankstown, a tough outer area of Sydney. They cruised into a deserted industrial area and stopped in front of a featureless row of factories. Broken-down and weed-ridden cyclone wire fences ran parallel to a busy highway. The noise of cars and trucks rushing by filled the air. Rusted car bodies were parked haphazardly in front of a panel beater's shop that looked like it hadn't been open for years. The roads were streaked with black tyre marks, evidence of hundreds of burnouts.

Danny glanced over at Ainsworth. 'Where are we?'

'Nowhere,' Ainsworth said solemnly as he got out of the car and started walking.

Danny followed him, and they soon came to a factory and stood in front of a wide roll-up door. Ainsworth waited without knocking. A cold gust of wind swept through, and pieces of battered corrugated-iron roofing banged and rattled overhead. Danny heard the whir of an electric motor. He looked up and noticed a CCTV camera pointing directly down at them.

Ainsworth turned to Danny. 'I'm going to introduce you to

Assad. He's the main man here. He runs a gang that controls a large chunk of town,' Ainsworth said and waved his arm around at the desolate expanse behind.

The carnival music stirred in Danny's head.

'He's always searching for new people; I reckon you'll fit in well.'

Danny gazed around. Soon the door lifted, and a stocky Middle Eastern man stood in front of them. Three gold chains swung and jangled around his neck as he held out his hand to Ainsworth. His muscular arms were covered in tattoos.

'Dill,' the man said and smiled.

Ainsworth shook his hand and smiled back at him. 'Assad, how are you, bro?'

Assad didn't reply. His eyes shone like dark mirrors as he eyed Danny suspiciously.

Ainsworth added, 'Assad, this is Danny ... Danny Wainwright. He was in juvie with me.'

Assad looked Danny up and down.

'Hello, Danny,' Assad said and held out his hand.

Danny shook Assad's hand. Ainsworth shuffled uncomfortably.

'Danny's good value, Assad. You said we needed someone we could trust and ... ahh ... someone to sort things out for us. I think Danny would be perfect.'

Assad eyed Ainsworth carefully. 'Okay, Dill ... okay,' Assad eventually said and then smiled broadly. 'You boys better come in.'

Assad led Ainsworth and Danny into the clubhouse. He stopped at a makeshift bar and took a seat. Danny peered around at the clubhouse walls. The place was unremarkable and sparsely furnished, with just a few tables and chairs randomly spread around. A number of motorbikes leant up against a wall. To Danny, it appeared to be a place that could be vacated very quickly if the need arose. A group of men playing cards on an upturned cable spool stopped and stared at them. The place fell silent as Danny and Ainsworth stood beside Assad at the bar.

Assad held up his hand to the men who started walking towards them. 'Boys, Dillon has brought a friend … this is Danny. Let's have a drink and get to know him.'

Assad smiled at Ainsworth and Danny. 'You'll be okay here,' he said and then gave the thumbs-up to one of his men who walked around the back of the bar and started pouring drinks.

During the afternoon, Danny learnt that Assad's gang was a major supplier of pot and pills to the locals. Assad had built up a significant clientele throughout Bankstown, and to ensure there was a steady supply of drugs, he employed a number of trusted dealers. They picked up their supplies from the clubhouse and had specific areas where they could sell. Assad paid them well and collected the proceeds of their sales on a weekly basis.

The drinking session lasted a couple of hours, until eventually, Ainsworth suggested to Danny that they should go.

* * *

It was a week later when Ainsworth met up with Danny again. 'Danny, good news!'

Danny looked at Ainsworth and felt a sense of unease.

'I saw Assad this morning, and he said you're in.' Ainsworth's smile spread across his face.

Danny, perplexed, looked at him. 'The gang?' he asked.

'Yeah,' Ainsworth said and smiled and nodded.

'Oh … okay,' Danny said and looked worried.

Ainsworth noticed Danny's hesitation.

'It'll be good, Danny; you can make some cash.' Ainsworth's smile started to fade. 'But I'll be honest with you … there's something that needs to be done first, sort of an initiation, but don't worry. It's right up your alley.'

'What's that?' Danny asked.

Ainsworth hesitated before he went on. 'It's one of Assad's dealers.'

Ainsworth didn't elaborate. Instead, he handed Danny an envelope. Danny opened it and counted out two hundred dollars in cash. He felt apprehensive as he held the notes, but he was stony broke, and this was the first money he'd seen in weeks. He decided that no matter what Assad wanted done, he was willing to do it.

'It's from Assad,' Ainsworth said, pointing to the cash. 'A sort of starting pay. There'll be more once you've done the job.'

'What does he want done?' Danny asked as he slipped the notes into his pocket.

Ainsworth's smile disappeared altogether.

'He's found out a dealer is stealing weed and pills from the storeroom and selling it for himself.'

'Oh,' Danny said.

'Yes,' Ainsworth said and nodded. 'He wants to put an end to it … real soon!' Ainsworth paused before he went on. 'And he wants you to do it!' There was a deadly silence as Ainsworth gazed directly at Danny.

Danny's mouth went dry, and the carnival in his head stirred into life.

Ainsworth continued, 'The guy's name is Whelan; they call him 'Wheels'.'

Danny nodded, trying to fight away the persistent carnival noises as they got louder. 'How long has he been stealing the stuff?' Danny asked.

'Not sure,' Ainsworth said and shrugged unconvincingly as he averted his eyes.

Danny had a feeling Ainsworth was lying. He'd been suspicious all along as to the reason Ainsworth had introduced him to Assad, and now things were starting to make sense. In juvie, Ainsworth would point out people who needed to be dealt with – those boys who had become a problem to the gang. It was then up to Danny and the others to sort the situation out; it appeared that this was a similar circumstance. He wondered if Ainsworth had seen the opportunity to fix Assad's problem on that first day when they'd met in the pub. Danny suspected it had been a convenient coincidence for Ainsworth when he'd turned up. And now that he'd found a solution to Assad's problem, Ainsworth would look good in Assad's eyes while it would be Danny who'd be doing the dirty work.

'Don't worry,' Ainsworth said. 'I'll help you. Be at the clubhouse around six tonight. I'll point Whelan out to you.'

Danny nodded slowly and eyed Ainsworth but didn't speak. His heart started beating like a bag of ferrets thrown into a river.

* * *

In the early evening Danny met Ainsworth at the clubhouse door. Ainsworth explained that the gang met every Saturday night for pizza, girls, drinks, and drugs. The door was already half open, and Danny and Ainsworth ducked under and walked in. There were at least thirty men and women inside. The music was loud, and the drinks were flowing. A fire basket burnt brightly in the middle of the huge expanse, and the smoke from it hung in the air. Men and women sat on wooden stools arranged haphazardly around the fire. Danny sat down while Ainsworth brought back a couple of beers from the bar. A thin man with a wispy goatee walked past. He held a stubby of beer in one hand and hunched his loose-fitting coat around his shoulders with the other hand. His shifty dark brown eyes darted nervously from side to side. He stared at Danny momentarily as he passed by.

'That's him,' Ainsworth whispered to Danny as Whelan took a seat on the opposite side to them. 'Remember his face.'

They stayed until around 10:00pm, when Ainsworth said it was time to go. They saw Assad and said they were leaving and walked back to Ainsworth's car. Ainsworth started it up, and they sat in the dark with the car idling. Ainsworth reached into his pocket and took out a handgun. Butterflies took to the wing in Danny's stomach.

'You ever use a gun before, Danny?' Ainsworth asked.

Danny felt like saying he was a crack shot but thought better of it. Besides, it wouldn't be too long before Ainsworth would see he had no idea how to use it.

Don't lie to Ainsworth! Whatever you're thinking, DO NOT LIE TO AINSWORTH!

'No, just the knife …' Danny said and rubbed his brow. 'And the shiv,' he added as an afterthought.

Ainsworth ignored him and fingered the handgun lovingly.

'I've had this gun a long time now. It's good, but I got a new one recently. You can have this … you're gonna need it!'

He handed the gun to Danny.

'Thanks,' Danny said as he took the gun and felt its weight. It was now clear how far he would have to go to do what Ainsworth and Assad wanted.

He closed his fingers around the butt of the gun and had to admit it was a very satisfying feeling; it felt like he'd found a new strength – a potent and deadly strength. Ainsworth smiled when he saw the look on Danny's face. It reminded him of when he gave the shiv to Danny in juvie.

'I'll show ya how to use it. Meet me at the southern entrance to the Police Paddocks, ten o'clock tomorrow morning.'

'Police Paddocks!' Danny said worriedly.

'Yeah, don't worry. It's got nothing to do with the cops; it's just a name. The place is generally deserted. There's heaps of bush and lots of trees. It's a perfect spot to be by ourselves … no one will bother us.'

Danny nodded but didn't respond.

Next morning Danny was there early. When Ainsworth arrived they walked out into the scrub until they were well out of earshot of anyone who might be around.

'You need to practise. Practise until the gun is like part of your hand. You never know how many times you're gonna have to use it,' Ainsworth stressed.

He stared at Danny intently before he went on.

'And, Danny ...'

Danny took his eyes off the weapon and stared back at Ainsworth.

'Do your homework, just like when we were in juvie. Know everything there is to know about the target. Where he goes, what he does, and who he hangs around with. Never take anything for granted. People are unpredictable. Be ready for them to do something you don't expect.'

Danny's mind started to race. The carnival music cranked up, and memories from the juvenile centre – the fights, the guards, the small boys being bullied, and the stabbing of Lonigan and Adelman – all came flooding back.

'Okay,' Danny said and nodded his head as he snapped out of it. 'Okay.'

Danny practised for days, shooting various trees and the cardboard targets that Ainsworth had supplied. He got better; in fact, he was so good that after only a couple of weeks, he was an expert shot from a ten-metre distance.

The judge's voice briefly floated around the edge of his thoughts.

'... *your reputation as a hired gun* ...'

But Danny wasn't listening. His eyes glazed over as he remembered his first hit. It would be something he'd never done before, and something that would once again put him on the wrong side of the law. But he was cash-strapped and desperate, and had no other real prospects. He decided if he was going to do what Ainsworth and Assad wanted, then he was going to do it well.

8

WHELAN PROVED TO be an elusive target. Danny saw where he lived, but it was in a busy block of flats, and he knew he couldn't deliver the hit there. So he started following him. He noticed Whelan would leave his flat carrying a duffle bag as night approached and would make his way into town. Once on the busy streets, he would walk down different lanes and arcades, sometimes turning back the way he'd come as though trying to shake off a tail. Danny followed him several times but invariably lost him in a maze of walkways. It wasn't until Whelan left later than usual one night that Danny was able to follow him to a rundown café on the outskirts of town.

The café was the only place open on the deserted road. A tired neon sign blinked sporadically claiming the right to 'Best Eatery in Town'. A large front-facing window made it possible to see into the café's interior. Dull lights from the inside spilt out and lit up a small section of the cracked and uneven footpath. Out on the street, on one side of the café, vacant shopfronts stood in a row. Faded signs showed where a butcher, real estate agent, and dressmaker had once traded. On the other side ancient crumbling-brick and rotting timber-clad factories stood silent and empty. Tags and ugly graffiti covered the walls. Iron bars stood out on every window. Heavy chains and padlocks secured doors that would likely never be opened again. Danny guessed that somewhere in the distant past the café owners may have had a thriving business selling lunches and coffee to the factory workers and general public, but clearly those days were gone. However, despite the seeming loss of a regular clientele, and the obvious decay in this deserted part of town, the owners had somehow kept the business running.

Danny stood in the dark on the opposite side of the road in an empty kids' playground and waited. He looked across and could see the place was almost empty; just two couples were dining there, and they were sitting well away from the door. He noticed a lane that ran next to the café. It was not lit at all. He checked the neighbouring buildings and power poles; unsurprisingly, there was no CCTV.

As Danny stood in the playground, he idly pushed one of the swings back and forth. It reminded him of the times when he was a young boy and his mother had taken him to the park. In those days it was just him and her. He felt safe, and things were so much simpler then. There were no bullies. No knives. No guns. No need to hunt people down. No killing. He found it hard to believe how much his life had changed. Not only had he lost his mother to drink and some stranger, but he'd also lost a way of life that he could never get back. Now it felt like he was walking a narrow path on a high precipice; one wrong step and over the edge he would go.

But that was how things had turned out, and he had to deal with it. He had to be ready. He had to make the most of what came next. He didn't want to let Ainsworth down, even if he had set him up and introduced him to Assad's gang just to get rid of Whelan. But it really didn't matter; Dillon had been good to him in the past, and he wanted to repay him. The only problem in all of this was the terrible consequence. Somebody would soon lose their life, and it would be him, Danny Wainwright, who would cause it to happen.

Danny followed Whelan to the café for another two weeks, and by now he knew his routine off by heart. At the café, Whelan would sit near the door, order a drink, and wait. Then around a half hour later, he would get up, pay the bill, and leave. Whelan would walk down the lane carrying his duffle bag and stand in a side entrance of one of the abandoned factories. Once in the tiny alcove, he couldn't be seen from the road. He noticed that Whelan's clients always approached from the north, the entrance closest to the café. The southern end was no good at all as it was well-lit and opened onto a major road. Whelan had a good stream of customers and usually finished selling to them around 11:00pm.

Danny had done his homework.

9

ONE WEEK LATER, Danny arrived early and waited in the empty playground as light rain fell. He pulled his soft-peaked cap down, trying to cover his ears. He stuffed his hands into his pockets as a wind from somewhere near Antarctica gusted through.

It wasn't too long before he saw Whelan arrive at the café. He watched him take his usual seat near the door, put the duffle bag under his chair, and order a drink. Around twenty minutes later Danny watched as Whelan checked the time and paid the bill. Danny moved behind a kids' slide as Whelan walked out the front door and peered up and down the road. When he was sure it was clear, Whelan entered the lane.

Danny waited across the road in the freezing cold as Whelan's clients came and went. Every so often he took his hands out of his pockets and rubbed them together to keep the blood flowing. After about two hours he saw a man he recognised as Whelan's last client walk out of the lane past the café. He waited another couple of minutes, but no one else came.

It was close to 11:00pm and time to move. He strode through the playground, crossed the dark road still glistening wet from a recent shower, and entered the alley. He kept his footsteps as quiet as he could on the damp cobblestones. He could hear Whelan zipping up his duffle bag.

'Wait up!'

Whelan was pleased; it looked like he had another client. He unzipped the bag. 'What? You wanna buy?'

'Sure,' Danny said as he approached. 'I wanna buy!'

Danny's heart started beating at a million miles an hour. Finally, the culmination of all his planning had come together, and now the time to confront Whelan had arrived. His fingers tingled as he gripped the handgun. The music in his head was ear-splitting; carnival rides rotated madly. He drew the gun out of his jacket and flicked the safety off. Whelan's eyes grew wide.

'No! Wait! Wait!' Whelan said. 'No need to do that! Here, you can have this ... for free!'

Whelan knelt down and began scrabbling around in the bag but kept looking up at Danny and the handgun. Danny hesitated and waited for him to pull out the handful of drugs he was sure would be coming.

What are you going to do? Don't stuff this up! But WHAT are you going to do?

Danny's mind was racing. The adrenaline was surging through his body. Perhaps there was no need to go through with this, he thought. Maybe he could convince Whelan to simply walk away. He'd tell Ainsworth and Assad that Whelan had run and left the bag behind. Maybe they'd believe him.

'Wheels ... stop!' Danny said. 'I don't want the drugs. Just leave the bag there and walk away. I'll tell Assad that when you saw me with a gun, you just left.'

'What?' Whelan said. 'Assad ... what about him?'

'Yeah ... Assad knows you're stealing from him. He wants me to ...' Danny hesitated before he went on. 'Just leave the bag and go!'

Whelan stared at Danny, perplexed. 'How does he know 'bout me and the drugs?' he asked, and a deep frown furrowed his brow.

'I don't know ... I just know he does,' Danny said.

Whelan stopped fossicking around in the bag as he considered what Danny had to say. His eyes were fixed on the gun. At the southern end of the lane, a car roared past, and light rain began to fall. Danny took his eyes off Whelan for a moment and peered down the lane towards the noise. Whelan continued to feel around inside the bag.

Danny looked back at Whelan. 'Assad wants you gone,' he said. 'Just walk away and never come back, and everything will be fine.'

Whelan didn't move. Danny decided to press the point. 'Wheels, he sent me to …' Danny glanced down at the gun.

It was the moment Whelan needed. He pulled his hand out of the bag and stood up. 'Fuck you!' Whelan yelled and raised a pistol.

Danny dodged instinctively as Whelan fired. Two shots exploded out and sprayed Danny's head and neck with bits of brick as the bullets ploughed into the wall behind him. He recovered, and with successive reflex shots, pumped three bullets into Whelan's chest. Lung, heart, lung, just like the preferred method of the mafia he'd read about in *Boy's Adventures*. Whelan's mouth fell open and a long trail of blood smeared the wall behind him as he slowly slid down and collapsed in the lane.

Danny watched, waiting to see if Whelan would move. After a few seconds he kicked Whelan's gun away. He quickly picked up the bag as a pool of blood began to spread out on the slick black cobblestones.

'Oh, Jesus,' he said to himself as he stared down at Whelan. 'Why the hell didn't you run? You could have just left and this would never have happened!'

He turned and walked back in the direction of the café just as a dishevelled young couple came down the lane towards him. He shoved the pistol into his jacket and pulled the peak of his cap further over his face as he passed them. He was angry at himself.

You idiot! You nearly got yourself killed. Think! THINK! You can't afford this kind of slip-up! All that planning, and you still made a mistake! People like Whelan are never going to walk away – they're always going to pull a gun!

He swore silently to himself as he turned out of the lane and paced along the darkened street. Then he heard a woman scream. He looked back and noticed the café owner step out of the front door and peer down the lane. Danny clutched the bag to his chest and started to sprint into the night.

10

ASSAD WAS PLEASED. The hit had gone well. Whelan had been removed, and when Danny handed him the duffle bag Whelan had been using, he got what was left of the drugs. News of the shooting made the papers, but predictably the cops had no suspect and could find no witnesses. Danny's standing in the gang soon grew, and he became the 'go-to' man when there was a problem that needed to be fixed. But reports of his expertise as a hitman also spread quickly throughout the underworld. His confidence increased, and his destiny was laid out in front of him when he decided to set himself up as a hired gun and work for a fee upfront. He would help the gang when needed, but now he worked freelance and reported to no one. There were lots more targets. Business was brisk, and the cash started to roll in.

The judge's voice briefly broke Danny's concentration.

'... *your target was a man best described as a member of an outlawed motorcycle gang ...*'

Danny gazed out the courtroom window and could see the storm getting closer. He was not concentrating on the proceedings at all. His mind kept returning to the same thing.

Didn't do all the homework! You didn't do all the homework!

Danny had been hired by a man whose main business was

conducted in Kings Cross, a suburb of Sydney with a violent and lawless history. On the surface the job sounded easy, just another shooting. However, he had been blindsided by the man who paid him for the hit; this was the same man who had landed him here on this day in court. Danny had trusted him, a stupid mistake that looked like costing him plenty of years in jail.

The man Danny was paid to terminate was Lex Draken, the sergeant-at-arms of the Western Sydney chapter of the Tarantulas Motorcycle Club, a notorious gang of thieves and stand-over men. Draken was well-respected in the gang was a good helper and organiser. However, on the streets, he was a loose cannon and a terrifying figure. He ran the drug distribution and sales for the Tarantulas and personally handed out many vicious beatings and shootings to those who didn't pay on time. He finally overstepped the mark when he decided to rob a local tobacco store in central Sydney.

On this particular day, ten bikies rolled up to the front of Haverlock's Tobacco and Accessories shop on a busy road in the Cross. They meant business. Draken took off his helmet and hung it on his bike's handlebars.

'Come on!' he shouted to the other bikies. 'This prick's been holdin' out on us. Let's do some collectin'!'

The other bikies followed him inside.

'Hey, Haverlock! You fuckin' owe us!' Draken yelled.

Bernie Haverlock stood behind his counter, startled, as the bikies stormed into his tiny shop.

'What do you mean?'

'You know what I mean, old man!' Draken said and jumped the counter.

Haverlock reeled backwards as Draken approached.

'Get out!' Haverlock yelled. 'I don't owe you anything!'

'Bullshit!' Draken yelled. 'You fuckin' owe us, all right!'

Draken grabbed Haverlock and punched him in the face.

Haverlock went down hard. Sean D'Arcy, Haverlock's assistant, raced to the end of the counter away from the ruckus and hid behind some disued supply boxes. Draken continued to beat Haverlock. He was clearly enjoying himself. The other bikies ransacked the till and scooped up boxes of cigarettes and shoved them into bags they'd brought along for the job. After a few minutes, they were all finished – except for Draken!

'Hey, Lex, we got everything,' one of Draken's bikie mates yelled, but Draken took no notice. 'Lex! Lex! We've got it all. There's nothin' left!'

But Draken continued to punch and kick the unconscious man. Finally, one of the bikies pulled him away.

'Come on, Lex. He's half-dead. Let's go!' the bikie said as he pointed to the prone body of the shop proprietor.

Finally, Draken left the shop, followed by the others. They kicked their bikes into life and roared away through the city streets. When they'd gone, D'Arcy came out from his hiding spot and crawled over to his boss. He checked for a pulse, then rang triple zero straight away.

The ambulance arrived at the tobacco shop five minutes before the cops. The paramedics took one look at Haverlock and quickly loaded him into the back of the ambulance. They rushed him to the nearest emergency department while the police questioned Haverlock's offsider. D'Arcy told them it was a bunch of bikies who'd done it but couldn't elaborate on who they were. However, he did notice the colours they wore. He said he felt like a coward as he hid in the shop while his boss was being beaten, but he was terrified of suffering the same fate.

At the hospital the medical team worked on Haverlock for a full hour. They did everything they could, but he never regained consciousness. The hospital contacted his wife, and she and her two children rushed to be by his bedside. A doctor took them to a private room where he explained to her that her husband was brain dead and there was no hope of recovery. But she refused to believe him.

She said she would pray for her husband and hope for a miracle. It was a further three days before her kids convinced her to stop, and together, they finally pulled the plug on Bernie Haverlock's life support.

But there was a major problem with the robbing of the tobacco shop – it was Haverlock's connections. Haverlock happened to be a cousin of Jimmy 'The Noose' Gagliano, the man who ran the Kings Cross underworld. Gagliano was involved in drugs and also shifted a large amount of illegal 'chop-chop' through Haverlock's store. He was livid when he found out the place had been robbed and Haverlock had been killed. He was further enraged when he found out who did it. Gagliano had a loose but convenient relationship with the Tarantulas motorcycle gang as he used them to deliver drugs to various locations throughout Sydney. He wanted to keep the connection but knew Draken was bull-headed and virtually un-controllable. He had a bad reputation and had made things difficult for Gagliano in the past. Things finally came to a head when Haver-lock's family, his wife and eldest son, saw him and said something had to be done. Gagliano agreed. This was the final straw, and he knew Draken had to be removed. He told Haverlock's people that he would see to it. He assured them that retribution would be swift and only an 'eye-for-an-eye' would suffice.

Gagliano had a number of nasty people on his books who could take care of this matter efficiently, but he had heard of Danny and wanted to distance himself from the hit as far as possible. He made a few discreet enquiries and contacted Assad. Assad called Ainsworth, who gave Gagliano Danny's number.

Danny picked up the burner phone. 'Yeah?'

'Danny Wainwright?'

'Who wants to know?'

'Gagliano. Jimmy Gagliano.'

Danny had heard of him. He was a big deal in the Cross and had made newspaper headlines more than once, generally when other criminals were either found dead or had gone missing. Danny knew he wasn't someone to be messed with.

'How'd you get this number?'

'I have contacts.'

Danny paused before he spoke, wondering why a big shot like Gagliano was contacting him.

'What can I do for ya?'

'I've got a job I'd like you to do. It pays well.'

Danny was sceptical but interested.

'Okay, so what's the deal?'

'Meet me at the Vegas Hotel in the Cross tomorrow at two in the afternoon … lounge bar.' The phone went dead.

* * *

Next day Danny arrived at the Vegas and entered through the front door. He walked through the main bar where two lone drinkers were watching a horse race on an overhead TV. He walked out into the lounge area and could see a man sitting by himself. Danny recognised him straight away. He guessed Gagliano was in his mid-fifties. He had a shock of wavy grey hair and piercing blue eyes. His face was set like a block of stone.

Gagliano spotted him and raised his hand.

'Wainwright?'

Danny nodded his head as he walked over to him.

'Have a seat,' Gagliano said and pointed to the empty chair on the opposite side of the table.

Danny glanced around warily, then pulled the chair around so his back faced a wall before he sat down. A waiter arrived at the table, but Gagliano waved him away.

'So, what's the deal?' Danny asked.

Gagliano wasted no time. He pushed a newspaper cutting across the table. 'You remember this?'

Danny read the first couple of lines and peered at the picture. It showed Haverlock being loaded into an ambulance. The story was vaguely familiar to Danny, but before he could answer, Gagliano went on.

'He's a cousin of mine. This man killed him.'

Gagliano pushed another cutting across the table. It was an older one and showed a group of bikies brawling outside a strip club.

'Tall one there.' Gagliano pointed at the grainy picture. 'That's the one who did it. He's the target!'

There was silence as Danny stared down at the newspaper cuttings. The carnival music started up at the back of his brain and his fingers tingled as the reality of what he was being asked to do was laid out on the table in front of him.

He stared out through the hotel window where the sun streamed in. Tiny flecks of dust floated and spun in the sun's rays. He could hear cars driving past and the general hubbub of the city. People were out there going about their ordinary lives. He wondered what it would be like to live one of those lives, working from nine to five for a regular pay packet, coming home to a wife and kids – living, loving, and dying in the suburbs. Being anonymous – just being normal.

Forget it! That life's not for you! You've turned too many wrong corners! Been in too many violent backstreets! That life you're dreaming of – it'll never be for you!

He was jolted back to reality when Gagliano spoke.

'Well, what do you say?' Gagliano bit the words off and stared at Danny.

'Okay,' Danny said and pulled the cutting of the bikies around to get a better look at the quarry. 'Yeah, all right, but I work for a fee upfront.'

'I'll pay half now and the other when it's done.'

'All of it … upfront!' Danny repeated, slightly agitated.

He pushed the cutting to one side and met Gagliano's eye. Gagliano, not used to being spoken to like that, glared at Danny. He shook his head.

'I know you get paid between ten and twenty grand for a hit.'

Gagliano's knowledge of his business shouldn't have come as a surprise to Danny, but it did. Gagliano continued.

'This pays double … forty … twenty now, and twenty when it's done. I don't welch!' There was another moment's silence. 'I know you didn't get paid for the Arlo hit. You still chasin' that?'

Danny frowned when Gagliano mentioned this. Again, he was surprised by how much Gagliano knew about his work.

'The guy who ordered the hit drinks at the Rooty Hill RSL. Gonna visit him soon. He'll either pay or he won't be drinkin' there, or anywhere else, much longer!'

Gagliano gave a half-smile and pushed a shopping bag towards Danny. 'There's twenty in there. Count it if you like.'

Danny opened the bag and peered in. It was full of bundles of fifty-dollar notes. Danny nodded his head and closed the bag; this payment would be bigger than anything he'd had before.

'All right,' he said and took the bag off the table. 'So, give me some details about this guy.'

'His name's Lex Draken. He's a big deal at the Tarantulas, a bikie gang.' Gagliano pulled a folded piece of paper out of his jacket pocket. 'Here's the clubhouse address and Draken's mobile number.'

Gagliano got up.

'Call me when it's done, and I'll organise the rest,' he said and pointed at the bag of money.

Gagliano walked out of the hotel and into the brilliant afternoon sunlight. Danny watched him leave, then ordered a beer. He waited ten minutes, scooped the newspaper cuttings into the bag of money, and left by a side door.

11

DANNY WATCHED THE Tarantulas' clubhouse for the next two weeks and got to see Draken in the flesh. He followed him from a safe distance, searching for the best place to deliver the hit. As it turned out, it would be at a pub in Balmain.

The bikies' local haunt was the Halifax Hotel, situated close to the Parramatta River. The pub was tired and rundown. What little accommodation it did provide was sparse and hardly ever used and so the place had become a simple watering hole, gradually giving way to the years. But this was where the bikies drank and played pool every Friday night. They usually rolled in around 6:00pm and stood their bikes in the gravel car park out the back. Danny had checked the place out previously. Despite having plenty of car spaces, it was not a well-used entrance to the hotel. The area was poorly lit and covered with dark shrubs and scrawny trees – an ideal place to deliver the hit.

Danny arrived the next Friday a bit before six in the evening. He parked outside on the main road and sat in the car and waited. The rush-hour congestion was beginning to thin, and traffic was flowing a little better. The whoosh of cars passing by had a calming effect on him as he watched dusk slowly start to fall. The sun continued its deep decent to the west in a blaze of oranges and reds. The tips of tiny waves on the river shone like sparkling diamonds. Streetlights began to flicker on as the dark fingers of night steadily crept across the landscape.

A car horn blared, and he was jolted back to reality. He stared out along the highway and waited. Draken and the other bikies would come from that direction, and he had to be ready.

Soon he saw a dozen or so single headlights making their way along the black bitumen road. The carnival music started up again, and he squinted in an effort to push it into the background.

Be ready! Check everything! BE READY!

Danny felt for the handgun in his pocket. He took it out and slid the magazine out of the handle. He checked to make sure it was full, then pushed it back into place. He flicked the safety off, then flicked it back on again. He was ready!

Within minutes, Draken and his mates rolled into the car park, Harleys' roaring. Danny waited while they parked their bikes, switched them off, and entered the hotel by the back entrance. He gave it a couple of minutes, then got out of the car. The stones in the car park scrunched under his feet as he walked to a dark recess and hid. He took the burner phone out of his pocket and called Draken's number.

Lex Draken was standing at the bar when his mobile vibrated and rang. He checked the screen – it said: '*No Caller ID*'

'Yeah! Who's this?' Draken yelled into the phone, trying to make himself heard over the racket in the main bar.

'Someone's touching your bike,' Danny said in a hoarse whisper.

The music in Danny's head played louder. It threatened to unnerve him. He fought it off and pushed it into the background.

The phone went dead in Draken's ear.

'What? Who is this? … Fuck!' Draken grunted and put his beer down and turned to the closest bikie.

'Just gonna check on the bikes!'

He pushed open the back door of the pub and walked out into the car park and over to his Harley. Danny moved out of the shadows and came up behind him. The carnival rides swirled fast in his brain, and the music played louder than ever. He put the gun to the back of Draken's head and pulled the trigger. The noise of the shot burst out like a cheap firecracker. The front of the bikie's head split open. Part of his forehead broke off and flew out into the dirt as the bullet ripped through his skull. The carnival music was now deafening. Draken pitched forward and toppled over his bike, sending it crashing to the ground. Blood from the bikie's head began to form in a giant pool. Danny was staring down at him as he lay on the ground when a man stepped out through the back door of the pub.

'What the fuck!' he said as he ran over to Draken. 'Lex … Lex!' he yelled.

The man grabbed Draken by his jacket and turned him over. The hole in Draken's forehead yawned open. Danny noticed a red spider tattoo on the back of the man's hand. This was no ordinary man. The tattoo, no doubt, meant he was also a member of the bikie gang. He eyed Danny.

'What the …!' He stopped momentarily when he saw the gun in Danny's hand.

Danny turned and began to sprint out of the car park. The gravel burst out from his feet as he raced for the exit. He chanced a look behind and saw the bikie running back into the pub. No doubt he would tell the other members of the gang, and they'd be after him. He reached the car, reefed open the door, and slid in. The tyres screamed as he hit the accelerator. The car fishtailed for a moment until he got it under control, and then he sped away.

The carnival music began to recede as Danny flew along the suburban streets. He headed for his usual haunt, a ramshackle motel just on the outskirts of Sydney. His plan was to stay there for a day or two until things settled down. He checked the rear-vision mirror, but there was no one following. He fumbled around in his pocket, took the phone out, and rang Gagliano.

'Yeah?'

'Job's done – target's been eliminated,' Danny said.

'Good,' said Gagliano.

'The other twenty … same place in the Cross?' Danny asked.

'No,' Gagliano replied. 'The heat's on at the moment; too many eyes on the street!' Gagliano paused, waiting to set the trap. 'Can we meet somewhere near you?'

There was silence on the line as Danny didn't answer.

'Somewhere away from the CBD?' Gagliano tried again, waiting for Danny to speak.

Danny didn't like this. He didn't want anyone to know about his hideout in 'the sticks', but the lure of another twenty grand was too hard to resist. Eventually, he spoke.

'Meet me tonight at the Truck Stop Motel in Bankstown. It's on the Hume.'

Danny hung up. He waited until he was crossing a bridge, then pitched the phone out the car window and into the river below.

But the phone call turned out to be a serious mistake. Once Gagliano found out Draken had been killed, he needed to distance himself from the murder. He contacted the president of the Tarantulas and told him that Wainwright was probably the hitman. He said he'd seen Draken and Wainwright arguing some time ago, a straight-out lie but a good one. He also told him where Danny would be hiding. This would work out well for Gagliano as it would mean the end of Wainwright and also save him from paying the other 20K.

But the phone call caused a further problem for Danny. Unbeknown to Gagliano, his phone was being tapped by Detective Senior Sergeant Presley Cooper and his police mates. So the cops also found out where Danny would be hiding and raced to the motel. They beat the bikies to it and cordoned off the streets.

Danny's heart sank when he heard the police sirens. He pushed the cheap curtains to one side and could see the place was surrounded by police. The red and blue lights from their cars swirled around the room, making him feel like he was in some weird amusement game. It was clear that escape was impossible. At first he wondered how the hell they knew he was there, but it soon dawned on him that Gagliano had probably double-crossed him.

A voice from a loudspeaker split the air.

'Wainwright! This is the police! Come out with your hands up!'

He sighed heavily and pushed the curtains back. He gazed around the room to see what he might be able to take with him. There was a photo of his mother. He removed it from the frame, folded it, and stuffed it in his pocket. He thought of hiding the handgun but knew that would be a waste of time as there was nowhere to put it. Then he remembered a trick he'd learnt in the juvenile centre.

He took a knife from a kitchen drawer and cut a couple of the strands of cotton holding the cuff of his pants together. He took a fifty dollar note out of his wallet, folded it numerous times until it was small enough to slide between the lining, and then pushed the cuff back together as best he could. With a bit of luck, they wouldn't see it when he was being processed, and it might come in handy when he was inside, if he could get to it. Otherwise, at least he'd have some money when he got out, whenever that may be. He scanned the room one more time and then opened the door. He was greeted by four burly policemen, all brandishing huge pistols.

'Don't shoot! Don't shoot!' he said and held his hands high.

He slowly walked towards them. The police holstered their guns and frog-marched him to a waiting police car. He was handed over to the main copper with sergeant stripes on his sleeve. His name badge said 'Cooper'. The cop handcuffed him and pushed his head down as he put him into the backseat.

'Who gave me up?' Danny asked.

'What makes you think we didn't just work it out?' Cooper said and smiled back with a cheesy grin.

'Come on, you bastards are too dumb to do that!'

Cooper's smile disappeared. 'Well … it was someone you, *and we*, know very well! He likes to think he's a big deal in the Cross!'

Danny nodded his head without speaking. Now he had no doubt it was Gagliano who'd stitched him up. The police car sped off, and Danny watched as the scenery flashed past. Thoughts flooded his head.

Looks like it's all over for you – you're goin' away for a very long time!

12

AND SO DANNY was put through the court system, and it had come down to this day. At least he wouldn't be killed in a threadbare motel room by a gang of vicious bikies, but there were plenty of patched members of the Tarantulas in jail who would love to get revenge for Draken's killing. He wouldn't be safe in there either.

Once again, he was wrenched back to the present as the judge's voice got louder.

'*And therefore, I sentence you to twenty years in jail with a non-parole period of seventeen years and three months.*'

The judge paused for a moment to let the sentence sink in. Danny glanced across to his counsel, who patted him on the shoulder and whispered, 'Don't worry. It'll be okay. We'll appeal the sentence.'

Danny peered around the courtroom and saw the detective who'd arrested him. Cooper was on his phone, and as he was speaking, he looked across at Danny. The faintest hint of a satisfied smile crossed Cooper's face as he spoke into the phone.

In his best theatrically authoritative voice, the judge added, '*Guards, take the prisoner away!*'

PART TWO

TWISTS OF FATE

run … hide … lie …

13

TWO BEEFY SECURITY officers grabbed Danny by either arm.
They escorted him downstairs to a holding area where five other
men were all waiting to be processed at the Silverwater Correctional
Complex. They stood together in the tiny cell and waited. No one
spoke. Danny's heart was pounding, but at least he felt a little more
comfortable now he was briefly out of his prison greens. For sentencing, prisoners were allowed to be dressed in their street clothes.
He glanced down at the shirt, pants, and shoes he'd been arrested
in and wondered just how many years it would be before he could
wear them again.

Back in the courtroom, two men remained seated as the visitors'
gallery slowly emptied. One of them picked up his mobile phone
and made a call.

'They've taken him down. Transport van should show up any
time now. You boys get that scumbag before the cops get him to jail!'

Outside, lightning sizzled and lit up the enormous dark storm
clouds covering Sydney town, followed immediately by a crack of
thunder that boomed and echoed along the city streets. Then, with
the clouds no longer able to hold their burgeoning load, it started
to bucket down. Huge drops of rain smashed onto the footpaths,
filling the gutters to overflowing. Water surged along the streets.
People caught outside were darting and ducking under whatever
shelter they could find.

Across the road from the court building, six men on motorbikes took cover under an awning, blocking the footpath. A man in a business suit trying to stay out of the rain complained.

'Can you please get off the footpath?'

'Walk in the rain, fuckwit!' one of the bikies shouted back.

When the bikie threatened to get off his bike and confront him, the man quickly moved on and was soon soaked to the skin as he hurried out onto the road.

A couple of minutes later, the bikies watched as a roller door slowly lifted and the prisoner transport vehicle inched its way up the steep incline from the underground cells. James McMahon, the young driver who was reasonably new to the job, leaned forward and peered around to see if the footpath was clear. The van's windscreen wiper blades flung back and forth manically in a hopeless attempt to clear the water cascading down the windscreen. The driving rain thumped down on the van's metal roof, making it almost impossible for him to be heard.

'How's it look your side?' he shouted to his partner in the passenger's seat.

Tinsley, a veteran guard of ten years plus, and lazy enough to not want to be the driver, squinted out the window through the thundering deluge. 'Yeah, looks clear!' he said unconvincingly.

The van crawled forward and turned right onto the road, which was now quickly flooding. The six men on bikes waited for it to pass, then gunned their motors and rapidly caught up.

'Can't see a damn thing!' McMahon muttered to himself.

The busy city street narrowed, and the bikies made their move. One rode in front of the van and motioned for it to pull over while the others surrounded it.

'What the hell? … What's he doin'?' McMahon cursed under his breath as he slowed down to miss the bike.

'Jesus!' Tinsley yelled. 'Check it out. They're both sides of us!'

The young driver glanced in his mirrors and saw them. He

pressed on the accelerator and sounded the horn. The van gained speed and nudged the bike in front, causing it to slide off onto the footpath. A bikie riding on the driver's side banged on the door.

'Pull over!'

'Don't stop!' Tinsley shouted as he checked the driver's side mirror. 'I think he's got a gun!'

McMahon didn't need to be told twice; this time he slammed his foot down on the gas, and the van rocketed forward. The bikie aimed his handgun and motioned for him to stop. McMahon stared out at the road ahead, praying the traffic wouldn't close in. A shot rang out, and the driver's side window exploded. A thousand tiny chunks of glass filled the cabin, showering both men.

'Shit! Go, James, go!' Tinsley screamed.

A second shot followed, and blood instantly sprayed the inside of the windscreen as the bullet tore through the young driver's head. McMahon slumped forward, twisting the steering wheel violently to the right, and collapsed to the floor on the accelerator. The van hurtled ahead in a deadly arc.

'Oh no!' Tinsley shouted as he leant over from the passenger's seat and grabbed the steering wheel.

He attempted to straighten it up but overcorrected. Now the van veered hard to the left. He swung the wheel again, but in the wet, it was impossible to steer. He braced himself as the van lurched and eventually toppled over onto the driver's side and slid along the narrow road. It shuddered to a stop when it slammed into the corner of a building.

The men in the back of the van were screaming, and despite the torrential rainfall, a fire started under the bonnet. Tinsley wiped blood from his face and picked a large lump of glass out of his forehead. He reached over and grabbed the shoulder of the young driver and shook him.

'James! James!'

But there was no response. The young man's head was covered

in blood, and a large pool was beginning to spread the entire length of the inside of the cabin. Tinsley turned and managed to push open the passenger door. He slowly climbed out into the driving rain and worked his way to the back of the vehicle. He unlocked the doors and drew his pistol as lightning streaked across the sky, followed instantly by a deafening crash of thunder. He was saturated as he pushed the door open.

'Get out! Get out! Do not run or I *will* shoot!' he shouted at the men at the top of his voice.

The men, all yelling and cursing, began to crawl out. Tinsley wiped his eyes as the rain pelted down. He yelled at them again not to run and didn't hear the bikies as they converged behind him.

'Move!' a bikie yelled. 'We don't want you! Move!'

Tinsley turned around, not able to see who it was in the driving rain. 'Fuckin' move!' the bikie screamed again.

Finally, Tinsley could see the man was holding a gun. He panicked, raised his own, and fired. The bikie grabbed his chest and fell to his knees. The other bikies immediately returned fire. And in the confusion, Danny burst out of the prison van and ran to the side of the road. He hesitated for a moment, not wanting to get shot. Danny could see a bikie looking down at the security guard while the other bikies seemed to be holding the rest of the prisoners.

They're checking for you! Run! FOR GOD'S SAKE … RRUUNN!

Danny bolted. He entered an arcade. People started to come out of shops to see what was happening. He pushed past them and glanced behind to see if he was being followed, but no one seemed to be coming in his direction.

He turned a corner and came out onto a main street. He rapidly put as much distance as he could between himself and the pandemonium of gunfire, bikies, and the burning prisoner-transport van.

14

NOW OUT ON the streets, Danny forced himself to walk, hoping not to attract attention. He entered a crisscross web of roads and lanes, sticking as best he could to the verandahs overhead. He was not familiar with this part of the city but kept heading as far away from the crash site as possible. Buses and cars surged along the flooded roads, sending up heavy sheets of rainwater. He headed towards the harbour and ended up at Circular Quay. He noticed the railway station on the other side of a wide road and ran into the main entrance. Dripping wet, he rounded a corner, jumped a ticket gate, and rode the escalators up to the platforms. The headboard on the nearest platform read:

'*Next Train – Wynyard, Town Hall and Central – 2 minutes*'

He mingled with the crowd until the train arrived. He got on board, sat down, and stared out the window as it slowly pulled away. Part of Danny wanted to run and keep running, but he thought the train trip would give him a little bit of time to think and perhaps he could come up with a plan. He'd had to keep a cool head many times in the past, and this time should be no different.

As the train sped along, an idea came to him. He was pretty sure the XPT left from Central Station and ran all the way to Melbourne. His most pressing concern was to get out of Sydney, so maybe the XPT could be his best chance. If he was able to get on that express train, he might be safe down in Victoria for a while.

He waited for the train to pull into Central Station and then got off and mingled with the other passengers as they made their way along the wide walkways. The only challenge now was to find out which platform the XPT ran from and what time it departed. He walked up to a ticket booth. Inside, a tired-looking woman leant on the counter and gazed past him at the throng of people going about their business.

'Excuse me,' he half yelled to make himself heard over the rain pounding down on the station roof. She flicked her eyes at him. 'Can you please tell me when the XPT leaves for Melbourne?'

She didn't reply; she simply pointed to a large illuminated timetable board on the opposite wall. Danny turned and read it.

'XPT to Melbourne leaving from platform 1 – 20:42'

He noticed a large digital clock on the wall next to it showing 15:30, so he had a bit over five hours to kill.

'Thanks,' he said to her as he looked back, but she ignored him and walked off and made a phone call.

He searched around and saw a sign pointing towards the toilets. He found the gents and dried off as best he could. He located platform 1 and decided to take a seat nearby where he had a broad view of the station. He desperately hoped that the cops wouldn't check for him here and made himself as inconspicuous as possible. Thoughts flooded his brain.

Jesus, that was close!

They were bikies that shot the prison guard; Tarantulas – I saw their colours! No doubt, they wanted you!

The bullet that guard took was for you!

They were waitin' for the van to enter the street!

They knew you were in it! One of them looked familiar!

Danny ran his hand over his mouth and gazed down at the platform as a couple walked past.

Holy Jesus, that was close!

15

'I TELL YOU what, mate, Elvis is not gonna be happy!' sniggered Gibson, one of the two probationary constables manning the front counter of the Balmain Police Station.

'Yeah, I know!' said his colleague. 'Of all the cons who could have escaped, it had to be Cooper's ticket to Inspector!' A broad smile broke out on his face.

'Don't get in his way!' Gibson said and suppressed another laugh.

Meanwhile, Detective Senior Sergeant Presley Cooper was in his office on the phone – to the commissioner.

'Yes, sir, I understand. I'll head up the team. He won't get far!'

'He better not!' came the reply down the line. 'There'll be no promotion until Wainwright is caught and behind bars. Do you understand?'

'Yes, sir!'

The commissioner hung up in Cooper's ear. Cooper, red in the face, burst out of his office and addressed everyone in the station.

'I want to see all of you! NOW!'

16

LATER THAT EVENING, Danny's heart skipped a beat when he heard the massive rumbling of diesel engines filling the station as the XPT rolled in. He'd kept a low profile and his eyes peeled for any cops, but so far, he hadn't seen one. He waited nervously on the platform and joined the other passengers as they slowly boarded the train. He found a place where four people could sit either side of a small central table. He took a seat and watched. He needed a ticket; there was bound to be a ticket inspector doing the rounds during the trip. It could be all over if he got caught for fare evasion and they made a phone call.

At exactly 20:42, the XPT began to pull out of Central Station, Sydney.

Once it was on the move, Danny started walking up and down the carriages, looking around. Soon he spotted an opportunity. A man using his laptop had taken his jacket off and placed it on the empty aisle seat next to him. The jacket had fallen open, and poking out of an inside pocket was what appeared to be a ticket.

He walked past and saw a man a few seats back reading his newspaper. Danny caught the headline:

'Prison Van Break - 3 dead 1 escapee'

He walked back to the laptop owner. 'Hey, mate!' he said.

The guy looked up from his computer with a surprised expression. 'What?'

'That guy down there says you've stolen his laptop!' Danny pointed to the man reading the paper. 'I'm taking it back for him!'

With that, Danny yanked the laptop out of the man's hands and strode down the carriage.

'What? Wait! Give it back!'

Danny slammed the laptop down on the newspaper. 'There's your computer back!'

The newspaper reader was startled. Other passengers began to turn around and watch the action.

'That's the bloke who stole it from you!' Danny said and pointed at the laptop owner who'd marched down the carriage behind him. 'He says that's his!' Danny shouted and pointed at the computer.

'No, it's not!' yelled the man. 'The laptop's mine!'

'I know!' said the guy reading the paper. 'I never said it was mine!'

'Yes, you did!' shouted Danny. 'You called him an ugly, thieving bastard!'

'I never!'

'You called me a thieving bastard?'

The men started to gesticulate and argue. Danny could see the passengers nearby were also becoming completely absorbed in the confrontation. He waited for a strategic moment, then quickly walked back down the carriage, away from the action, and lifted the ticket out of the laptop owner's jacket pocket. He left the carriage straight away and moved through the glass sliding doors to the next carriage. When it looked like no one had followed him, he moved again to the next carriage at the rear of the train. He took a seat and curled up as best he could so he wouldn't be seen.

The train hurtled on through the night. The rhythmic sound of the wheels on the rails was mesmerising, but sleep only came to him in fits and starts. Early next morning, the ticket inspector arrived.

'Tickets, please!'

Danny handed over the ticket. The inspector checked and clipped it. Danny was relieved but knew there would soon be a problem, particularly when the laptop owner discovered his ticket was gone. Would he put two and two together and suspect who had stolen it and tell the inspector?

Danny's prediction proved correct. Within ten minutes the door at the end of his carriage slid open and the ticket inspector started to make his way towards him.

The XPT began to slow as it made its long crawl towards Southern Cross Station. Danny watched as Broadmeadows Station went by and thought that he must be close to Melbourne by now. He'd seen news reports in Sydney of trouble in Broadmeadows and knew it was a suburb on the fringes of the city. He hunched down in the seat and stared out the window at the dreary early morning. In the distance, the glass, metal and concrete towers of the Melbourne city skyline stood stark and resolute. He chanced a quick look back down the carriage. The inspector was moving towards him, checking every seat.

Danny knew he had to get out; staying on the train was not an option. He got up and moved over to the train door. He tried to open it, but it was jammed shut under the force of the pressurised gas. He tried again, but this time put his foot on the handle and his back against the nearest seat. Using all the strength in his leg, he forced the door open. The cold morning air rushed in. He pushed one arm through the opening and then shoved his body out and clung on desperately to the outside of the door. The wind grabbed his hair and ripped at his clothes. He glanced up just as the ticket inspector's face appeared on the other side of the glass window. They stared at each other for a moment. Danny peered back down at the tracks as they sped past, not sure whether to chance it or not.

Jump! You've gotta jump!

He picked a likely spot and let go of the door. He landed hard on the dirt and crushed rock scattered beside the railway sleepers.

'Ahh!' he yelled and grabbed his elbow.

He stood up and watched as the XPT rolled away towards the station. He was dazed, battered, and bruised – but he *had* made it to Melbourne.

17

HE LIMPED ALONG the tracks, following the XPT as it slowly pulled alongside a platform at Southern Cross Station. He stopped for a moment and rested. His elbow was bleeding, and his right ankle was killing him. He watched as the first passengers started to disembark, then walked towards the platform. He had to find a way out onto the streets, and had to do it fast.

Move! Now! Before that ticket inspector raises the alarm!

He crossed over from the tracks to a weed-covered path next to a broken-down cyclone-wire fence. Across the road, he could see a drab red-brick building with tall walls covered in razor wire. It made his mind up. He wouldn't chance going into the CBD.

He stopped a short distance from the train and waited while the last of the passengers disembarked. When the coast seemed clear, he climbed up onto the platform. He shuffled along until he found a deserted gate that led onto Spencer Street. Out on the busy street, he stopped and checked his ankle. It was starting to swell, but he thought he could force himself to walk without limping; he had to if he didn't want to bring attention to himself. He slowly made his way to the corner where Spencer Street met Collins Street and decided to walk up the hill bordering the station – away from the city centre.

A tram rattled past, and traffic raced by on both sides of the road as he struggled up Collins Street. He was halfway along when the smell of freshly brewed coffee and bacon and eggs drifted out from one of the station cafes. His stomach gurgled. He knew he should keep moving, but hunger got the better of him. He checked his pockets, but they were empty. Then he remembered the fifty-dollar note he'd hidden in the cuff of his pants. He bent down and slowly prised it out. He turned right and walked into the station proper. A short distance in front of him, a railway employee and two policemen were talking. They looked over in his direction as he approached, then casually returned to their conversation. Danny walked straight into the café, his heart pounding.

'Yes, sir. What can I get ya?' the café attendant asked.

'Coffee, black, and a toasted bacon-and-egg sandwich, thanks, mate,' he said to the young kid behind the jump and handed him the fifty.

'Okay, sir. Take a seat, and I'll bring it over.'

Danny moved to a spot where he hoped he couldn't be seen, but as soon as he sat down the two cops entered the café and walked up to the counter.

Oh, Jesus, what kinda luck is that? If they recognise you, you're done!

The cops ordered coffee and stood there chatting and occasionally peering out into the bowels of the station. Danny kept his head down. He had nowhere to hide. He was in plain view of them and knew if they recognised him he was a goner. He checked his elbow. At least it had stopped bleeding, but there was a tear in his jacket where he'd landed on the rocks. He straightened up his shirt and jacket and tried not to look out of place. The kid brought over his change, coffee, and food. Danny dug in straight away. He was starving; even being busted by the cops wouldn't stop him finishing breakfast.

The cops eventually got their coffees and casually strolled out of the café and rode the escalators down towards Spencer Street.

Danny pocketed the change, finished the sandwich, and drank the blisteringly hot brew. He checked there were no more police, then walked out onto Collins Street, over the hill, and into the Docklands precinct.

He trailed behind a few early morning suits walking towards an area dominated by office blocks and green parkland. He watched as they disappeared into coffee shops or office buildings. He kept walking until he reached the water and gazed out on the huge expanse of the Bolte Bridge.

Nowhere as good as the coat-hanger!

But then he saw something that grabbed his attention. On the other side of the river were the wharves with huge mountains of shipping containers. It might be a place to hide, and with a bit of luck, he wouldn't be recognised there.

18

HE FOUND A bridge that crossed a river, and he continued on to the docks. A sign read:

'*No Pedestrian Traffic*'

There was no footpath. Cars in multiple lanes of traffic sped past in both directions. He looked around, climbed over the bridge's low wall, and limped along, sticking as close to the edge as possible. The wind from passing cars buffeted him and threatened to send him over the side and into the water. A car horn blared out, but he ignored it and kept going until he reached the opposite side. He picked a likely spot, climbed back over the wall, and carefully jumped down while trying to protect his injured ankle. He headed towards the shipping yards. A little way along, he came up to a cyclone-wire fence with a metal gate. A sign clipped to the fence said:

'*Port of Melbourne Authority – Authorised Entry Only*'

A small unmanned guard shelter stood next to the gate. It was definitely not the main entrance. An open padlock hung on the fence next to a sliding bolt that held the gate in place. He grabbed the bolt, slid it back, and pushed the gate open.

'Hey, what do ya think you're doin'?' a voice called out from behind. A man in a guard's uniform walked out from some bushes doing up his fly.

Think! Think! THINK!

Danny managed a smile as he desperately tried to conjure up a believable excuse. 'I, ahh … I'm … I'm here to see the boss. I start today!'

The guard frowned. 'Didn't he give you a security pass? You don't enter here!'

'Nah … no … he said he'd get one organised for me.'

'Fuckin' typical. I s'pose it was Gallagher you saw?'

'Yeah … yeah, Gallagher.'

Danny started sweating as the sun broke through a curtain of dull-grey clouds.

'Oh, that'd be right! He's bloody hopeless when it comes to puttin' people on. Go through. His office is on the other side of those containers,' the guard said and pointed. 'And listen, mate!'

Danny had started to walk off but turned around, worried.

'When you see him, get him to give you a pass, okay? And show you where the main gate is.'

'Yeah, sure. Thanks.'

He'd come this far, and it could be all over very soon. He was sore and exhausted. Perhaps he should have taken his chances in the CBD. But what the hell, he had nothing left to lose except what little freedom he had right now. He decided to find Gallagher and see what might happen, but his hopes weren't high.

He turned a corner and slowly walked between towering stacks of shipping containers. Huge cranes moved noisily overhead. He could hear men talking and working. In the distance, blasts of foghorns echoed out as ships sailed towards the docks. Trucks drove along narrow wharf roads. A forklift driver tooted and waved him to one side as he roared past. He turned another corner and saw a small wooden shack with a headboard that read:

'*Mick Gallagher – Container Manager*'

He walked up to the open door and knocked.

'Yeah! … Yeah, come in! … Come in!'

Gallagher, an overweight man in his fifties, had his back to

Danny. He was on the phone and agitated. His desk was piled high with papers, and various shipping manifests were pinned to the walls, together with a partly covered girly calendar from years ago. The pretty blonde was smiling with her barely covered boobs hanging over a picture of a shipping container. The caption read:

'Just About Anything Fits In A Shipping Container'

The floor was wooden and covered in dust. A battered chair sat on the opposite side to Gallagher; the seat sagged in the middle, and one arm was missing. There were two windows, both covered with years of built-up grime.

'I'll get it done as soon as I can. I told you that yesterday. I'm under the pump here, you know! I'll call you tomorrow!' Gallagher slammed the phone down, rubbed his forehead, and swung around in his chair. He hesitated for a moment, and perplexed, he stared at Danny.

'Yeah … what can I do for you?'

Danny's mind was racing again. This guy seemed flat out. Perhaps he had one last chance. 'I was … ahh … I was wondering if I could apply for a job?'

Gallagher tipped his chair back until his head touched the office wall behind him. He folded his arms over his ample girth and stared at Danny incredulously.

'*What?*'

The butterflies started in Danny's stomach.

'I heard you needed some help and thought maybe I could apply.'

Gallagher shook his head, hardly believing what he was hearing.

'How'd you get in?'

'The guy at the gate … he said I should see you.' More lies, but what the hell.

'Morrison! He's s'posed to be running security for me! Jesus Christ! So, what's your name?'

'Danny.'

'You got a last name, Danny?'

Danny didn't answer; instead, he stared down at the floor.

Perhaps this is where it all finishes!

Gallagher sat forward and squinted at the ragged young man in front of him.

'You in trouble, Danny?'

'Yes,' he said softly, deciding that he might as well fess up.

'Where're you from?'

'New South Wales.'

'Bloody big place, New South Wales!' Gallagher snorted. 'Unless you give me a little more detail, we're finished here!' Gallagher stared suspiciously at him. 'You in *police-type* trouble, Danny?' he asked in a softer voice.

Danny's heart sank.

You might as well tell him.

'Yeah … the cops are lookin' for me,' Danny half whispered. 'I'm from Bankstown in Western Sydney,' he added despondently.

Gallagher tilted back in his chair as he considered what the young man had said. He sensed an opportunity. He rubbed his hands through his unruly, grey hair and smiled to himself.

'Well, it just so happens I have a few on me books who've had that sorta trouble. S'pose you've got nowhere to stay?'

'No,' Danny replied and gently touched his wounded elbow.

Gallagher smiled again and nodded his head slightly. 'The cops know you've come this way?'

'No … don't think so.'

Gallagher rubbed the stubble on his chin.

'Okay, Danny … *with no last name*, this might be your lucky day. I can give you a job, temporary like. It pays fuck-all, but I can put a roof over your head. But – and I mean this – you can't leave here!'

Gallagher gazed out through one of the dirt-covered windows, then back at Danny.

'I can't have employees in trouble with the police travellin' all over town … know what I mean?' Gallagher didn't wait for an answer. 'You blab your mouth off to the cops, and they track you back to me … won't be good for ya, Danny!' Gallagher shook his head and glared at the young man.

'Thanks,' Danny said, unsure where this conversation was headed.

Gallagher ignored him.

'Morrison out there is a shit security guard, but he is a crack shot. You try to leave, and he'll shoot ya, and I'll bury ya … at sea!' Gallagher paused to let what he said sink in. 'No one's ever gonna find ya out there!' he went on and jabbed a thumb in the general direction of the bay outside.

He gazed long and hard at Danny, making sure his threat had registered. Then he pushed a handful of papers off a huge ledger. He opened it up, and a pile of dust billowed off the desk as he let the pages fall.

'Sit down.'

Danny took a seat. It was instant relief as he took the weight off his throbbing ankle.

'For me to run a payroll, you gotta have a last name.'

He waited for Danny to give up his surname, but when he didn't, he stared up at the roof and then back at the ledger.

'You remind me of a friend I had in New South Wales a long time ago. He's dead now. Got himself shot. Name was Strickland. What do ya think … Danny Strickland?'

Danny couldn't believe his luck.

'Sounds good! Thank you … thanks very much.'

PART THREE

ON THE DOCKS

Gallagher's domain …

19

MICK GALLAGHER'S UPBRINGING at home was tough. He was the eldest of five siblings, and they basically had nothing. The family led a hand-to-mouth existence in one of the poorer parts of Williamstown and struggled from one week to the next. His mother stayed at home washing, ironing, and cooking, while his father, a tugboat captain, would get home late at night invariably reeking of alcohol and stale tobacco.

There were no backyards in the neighbourhood where Gallagher lived as the blocks were simply too small, so he and his brothers and sister played with the other kids out on the roads and in the narrow back lanes. Tied-up newspapers sufficed as footballs, and games of tag along the smooth, rounded cobblestones were among his favourites. And it was during one of these times when Gallagher learnt some hard life lessons.

Marty Ruebrick, a kid from the back blocks, and one step up from Gallagher's neighbourhood, accused Gallagher of cheating. He said that Gallagher was never 'it' for long because he always watched where the other kids ran when he was supposed to have his eyes closed. Gallagher denied it, but Ruebrick kept at him in front of all the others. He said Gallagher cheated all the time and that if he wanted to win so badly, they'd give him a 'charity' head start because he was so fat and slow. The other kids all laughed. Gallagher went red in the face, then punched Ruebrick so hard it sent him staggering back into a fence. He hit him again, and this time broke his nose. The kids all quit playing and told Gallagher to stop. They helped Ruebrick up. His shirt was covered in blood. They left Gallagher by himself standing in the street. He watched them go as they helped Ruebrick back to his house. Gallagher brushed a single tear from his eye and then sauntered back home.

So what if you cheat? … Everybody does!

But that day, Mick was confronted with a couple of very important truths. Firstly, people like the 'Marty Ruebricks' of this world are never to be punched. It turns out other people like them more than they like you. Secondly, and perhaps more importantly, if you're going to cheat, make sure you do it so well that nobody can see what you're doing! Mick never forgot what happened that day and carried these lessons with him for the rest of his life.

Gallagher was sixteen when he got a job on the docks. His father put in a good word for him when it was clear Mick was never going to be any good at school. It was a rude wake-up call for the young man, but he grabbed the opportunity with both hands. He turned out to be a good worker and got on well with the other men. He learnt from them and went the extra yard to help out whenever he could. He became trusted and slowly climbed the ladder.

He was two years into the job when his father became sick, so sick that he was eventually housebound and could no longer captain the tugboat. It was a savage blow to the family. Gallagher now found himself as the major breadwinner and regularly worked overtime to increase his take-home pay.

It was early one evening, after a long day at work, when Gallagher finally arrived home. His mother greeted him as he walked through the door and told him his father wanted to see him. Mick draped his coat over the back of a kitchen chair and walked into the small living room where his father sat. A single globe hanging from the ceiling threw a weak glow on the room's meagre contents. Dark-brown wallpaper, modern at the turn of the century, was giving way to the years and hanging in strips from the room's stark plaster-board. A picture of early Australiana hung suspended by wires from a dust-covered picture rail. The faded carpet was threadbare in front of each chair that faced the ancient television set.

His father looked up when Gallagher entered the room. Next to him stood a large oxygen tank connected to a plastic tube that snaked around the old man's armchair and poked into a facemask covering his mouth and nose. He took a deep breath and moved it away as Mick took a seat next to him.

'Boy ... I want you to take the tugboat.'

The old man exhaled loudly; the effort it took to speak was exhausting. He replaced the mask and sucked in as much of the bottled air as he could. Mick sat there listening to the death rattle in his father's chest. The room was quiet, the only sound being the gentle hiss of oxygen as it fed the old man's tortured and dying lungs. His father spoke again, but this time his speech was muffled as the words barely penetrated the mask. The effort required to remove it a second time was just too much.

'I want you to get a Captain's Ticket,' his father gasped.

Each sentence now took a monumental effort. Mick watched as the mask covering his father's face clouded over with condensation, then became clear again as his fight for life continued.

'Do what you have to do to get it ... it should pay better than the docks job!' The old man coughed and rubbed his throat.

'Okay,' Mick replied and watched as his father closed his eyes. A moment later, his father's chin collapsed onto his chest, and he fell into a fitful sleep.

Mick spent the next two months sitting with him each night when he got home from work. He watched as his father slept in his armchair and listened to his laboured breathing. It was a blessing when the time finally came. Mick was also dozing when he was woken by a loud, exhausted gasp for air. He saw his father open his eyes for the last time and look at some distant point. Perhaps he could see his place on the other side, Mick thought. Then, without taking another breath, his father simply slipped away.

Mick organised the funeral with the help of some of his father's cronies. It was a big affair with close to one hundred people packing the tiny church. The priest was rapt. Once the ceremony was over, he worked the crowd to see if he could convince any newcomers to attend Sunday Mass.

Mick kept his father's tugboat and got permission to tie it up at the wharves but was told to keep it well out of the way of the main action. He found a backwater a small distance away. Wharf 23 had become redundant long before anyone who currently worked on the docks could remember. Its rotten and rickety walkway was treacherous, but Mick saw that as an advantage; if anyone wanted to steal the boat, they'd be taking their life in their hands just walking down there. And despite the derelict surroundings, Mick kept the tugboat in good order. He taught himself how to pilot it but never did get the qualification his father wanted for him; he was simply too busy, and there was never the time.

20

GALLAGHER WORKED IN a variety of different jobs on the docks. But it was when he was put in charge of a section of the container-handling area that he met men who were making a little extra on the side. These men were expert in removing security seals on shipping-container doors and resealing them again after pilfering some, but not all, of the goods inside. It was dangerous and obviously illegal, but very profitable. The goods they stole were then on-sold to third parties for cash, with the proceeds being divvied up every Friday, just before knock-off time.

Barkly, the most experienced in the area and the man who would report directly to the new boss, took Gallagher aside on his first day and revealed what they were doing. He was worried Gallagher would put an end to their 'arrangement'. Barkly said they should meet in a disused workshop on the outskirts of the container yard.

'Mick … there's something I need to talk to you about. It's … ahh …' Barkly hesitated before he went on. 'The boys and me … we got a good little earner goin' on here.'

Gallagher had heard rumours of the area being less than above board.

'So … you're doin' something you shouldn't be?' Gallagher asked and couldn't stop a smile from crossing his face.

'Yes,' Barkly said. 'We were wonderin' if you want to be involved?'

The workshop became quiet. Barkly stared at Gallagher intently, waiting to see what he'd say or do. Gallagher slowly nodded his head.

'So tell me, what's goin' on? I guess it's not legal.'

Barkly ran his tongue around his lips. 'No … not exactly … well, Mick … it's not legal at all.'

'How long have you been doin' this?'

'About three years now!' Barkly said. He was becoming worried that Gallagher might give the game away.

Gallagher considered what Barkly had to say and was silent for a while. He could do the right thing and report Barkly and his men to Port Authority management and get a new team, but that didn't appeal to him. There was money to be made here, and if the pilfering had already run for three years without being detected, there was a good chance it could go on well into the future.

'So … exactly what do you do?'

Barkly explained the process of opening the containers, taking some of the goods, selling them, resealing the containers, and splitting up the cash proceeds.

Gallagher nodded before he spoke. 'Who else knows about it?'

'No one … only the boys and me,' Barkly said and clasped his hands together.

'How much are you makin'?'

Barkly could sense Gallagher was interested.

'About five grand a month.' Barkly swallowed hard. 'We hand it out once a week on a Friday.'

'What about security … like the CCTV?'

'Hasn't worked for years, Mick,' Barkly said and pointed outside.

Gallagher gazed out through a window and could see the cameras were covered in dust. One, supposedly covering a large section of the container yard, had a thick cobweb in one corner.

'Port Authority put in the roaming security guards a coupla years ago … was probably cheaper than repairing the CCTV,' Barkly said and shrugged.

Gallagher had seen the guards walking around appearing to be mostly bored. 'So ... the guards?' Gallagher asked. 'What about them?'

'Oh, I forgot ... they're in on it too,' Barkly said and hesitated for a moment. 'But they only get a standard payment regardless of how much we make.'

The workshop went quiet again as Barkly waited for Gallagher to say something. When he didn't, Barkly went on.

'Only potential problem we got is the cops who turn up every now and then.'

Gallagher nodded, then asked, 'How often do they get here?'

'Not sure ... just seems to be random to me.'

'How many of 'em?'

'Just two ... I think they're detectives,' Barkly said and finished off with another shrug.

Gallagher reckoned he'd seen them as well. On the odd occasion, he'd noticed two men dressed in suits who entered the yard. They mainly spoke with the security guards and the container management team and then left sometime later. He thought these two could be the detectives Barkly was talking about. One of them looked familiar. He believed he'd seen him as a kid when they were playing in the backstreets of Williamstown. His name was Colin Jacobs. As a boy, he'd heard from the other kids that Jacobs came from a broken family and that they didn't have much. According to them, Jacobs' father had simply not come home one day and nobody knew where he was. So that just left Jacobs and his mother at home. Gallagher wouldn't be surprised if Jacobs had become a cop. Jobs back in those days weren't easy to come by, but the police were always actively recruiting. A job with them would be good stable employment and provide a steady income. A number of other kids he knew had also joined the force. Perhaps Jacobs was looking after his mother in her old age.

Gallagher weighed things up in his mind. It was a gamble, but given Jacobs' background, he wouldn't be surprised if he was interested in making a little extra on the side.

'I think I know one of the coppers,' he told Barkly. 'I'll talk to him … see what he's got to say.'

Barkly was relieved. Maybe things would be okay. 'Thanks, Mick … that'd be great. So … you want in?'

Gallagher nodded and smiled. 'Yeah, but you boys will have to take a haircut if me and the cops are in on it.'

Barkly thought it over. 'No problems, Mick. We can work with that.'

Gallagher saw Jacobs the next time the detectives arrived on the docks. They hit it off straight away. Jacobs remembered Gallagher, and they exchanged old stories and reminisced. When the time seemed right, Gallagher asked him straight out if he wanted to be in on the pilfering activities. It didn't take Jacobs long to decide. He smiled and said he'd thought there was something going on, but he didn't know what. Now that he had the details, he said he'd be happy to turn a blind-eye and receive a brown paper bag every now and then but insisted his offsider, Detective Lucas, would also need to receive one.

'Okay, detective,' Gallagher said with a smile. 'You and your detective mate are in.'

* * *

Jacobs' partner, Detective Constable Tom Lucas, was the younger of the two detectives and a relative newcomer. He looked up to Jacobs and was unaware of the arrangement Jacobs and Gallagher had made. When Jacobs told Lucas the details, he was fearful the young man might spill the beans when it came time to receive his first payment.

But Lucas had a problem, a cash-flow problem. He was a

compulsive gambler, a nasty habit that constantly kept him cash-strapped. It was something he kept very private. He was currently being hounded by a stand-over man from a local SP bookmaker for an outstanding debt of two thousand dollars. A couple of days prior to the handing out of the 'brown paper bags', the man had called at Lucas' house, and his wife answered the knock on the door.

'Yes,' she said to the tall man standing on the top step.

'Your husband home?' he said in a deep, surly voice.

'Ahh … no … he … doesn't get home 'til late. Who should I say is calling?' Her heart started to beat a little faster. She didn't like the look of this man.

'What time does he get home?' he asked and moved a step closer.

She noticed the latch on the security door was in the open position. She must have left it that way when she'd gone outside to check the letterbox. She went to close it, but when he saw what she was about to do, he grabbed the handle and swung the door open.

'You … you can't come in here!' she said, trying desperately to pull the door out of his grasp.

'I can do anything I want,' he said and stepped inside. 'If he's home and you're lying to me …' He took a pistol out of his pocket and waved it in her face. 'It won't be good for you!'

She backed up and started to whimper, terrified of the gun.

'I asked … *when does he get home?*'

He grabbed her by the shoulder and squeezed hard.

'Ow,' she said and squirmed under his strong grip. 'A bit … a bit after seven.'

'Okay,' he said and let her go. 'Let's wait for him.' He put his hand on her back, and she stumbled forward as he shoved her inside the house.

In the lounge room, the man sat in a chair where he could see the driveway outside. He pointed to a chair opposite him and told her to sit. The house became deathly quiet as she stared at him and wondered what her husband had done to cause this man to come to their home in search of him. She rubbed her shoulder where he'd grabbed her and glanced around in the vain hope of finding an escape route.

'It could be a … a … a while,' she said. 'I could tell him you called and …'

'That's all right,' he said and glared at her with eyes so pale they seemed like passageways to the afterlife. 'We'll just sit here and wait.' He ran his fingers down the barrel of the pistol and continued to look out the window.

An antique clock on the mantelpiece ticked away, and the muffled burbling of talkback radio voices could be heard coming from the kitchen. It was close to an hour later when Lucas finally pulled up in the driveway. The man stood up and pointed the gun directly at her.

'Sit here. You move, and it won't be good for you … or him,' he said and waved the gun in Lucas' direction.

By now, Lucas had pressed the button on the remote control for the garage door. As he drove through, the man left the house by the front door and walked quickly to the garage. He ducked under the door as it rolled down and waited for Lucas to get out of the car. He pinned Lucas against the garage wall.

'Two grand … now!'

'Jesus!' Lucas said, startled. 'I … I haven't got it on me!'

The man glared at Lucas. 'You were told to have it last week … what happened?'

Lucas began to breathe heavily. 'I … I … had trouble with the bank. I just need a bit more time, and I'll have it!'

'You've got until tomorrow, or that pretty wife of yours gets it! Ya know what I mean?' His eyes raged like embers from a bonfire. 'No money … then after you, she gets it,' he said and pushed the pistol into Lucas' face.

Lucas nodded his head as the man left the garage by the side door. He was shaking when he walked up the steps to his house. His wife met him at the front door with tears in her eyes.

'Tom, who was that man?'

Lucas was breathing heavily and didn't answer.

'Tom, he hurt me!' she said and continued to rub her shoulder. 'He was waiting for you … He was really angry!' She wiped her eyes with the back of her hand. 'He forced his way in, Tom! I didn't know what he was going to do!' She started to sob. 'He could have done anything to me!'

Tears streamed down her face. 'Who was it? Why did he want you?' she yelled.

'Don't worry. Someone who's …'

'Tom! … He threatened me … with a gun!' she screamed and started to tremble.

'It's okay. Don't worry. I'll fix it … I'll fix it,' he said and put his arms around her.

The next day, in Gallagher's office, the brown paper bags were being distributed. Jacobs had insisted the bags for the police were to be handed out discreetly. He told Gallagher the men from the yard were not to know about it or be present when Jacobs and Lucas received their payment. Gallagher agreed. He pushed a bag across to Lucas.

'Detective Lucas, this one's for you.'

Lucas wrung his hands and stepped forward. His partner, Jacobs, grabbed the bag before Lucas took it.

'Tom. You don't ever discuss this with anyone!'

Lucas nodded. 'All right,' he said in a soft voice.

'This arrangement is between Mick and us,' Jacobs said and pointed to Gallagher. 'No one else needs to know … you comprehend? *No one!*'

'Yes … okay,' Lucas said and rubbed his brow.

Jacobs then handed him the bag of money and smiled.

'It'll be okay, Tom. You just shut up and do as I say around here and everything will be fine.'

* * *

So now, with Detective Lucas toeing the line, things moved along nicely for Gallagher. It improved even further once he was promoted to the job of managing the shipping containers for the entire Port of Melbourne. This prestigious new role gave him control of every container that reached the docks. It was now his responsibility, amongst a myriad of other things, to oversee the X-ray of each container and to confirm that every one of them had a seal that had not been tampered with. Gallagher made sure the paperwork for each container was in perfect order, and so the old arrangement of pilfering from them remained in very safe hands.

And the two detectives, Jacobs and Lucas, proved to be of further value to Gallagher. They recruited ex-cons recently released from prison to work for Gallagher in his shipping and loading area. These people made up Gallagher's 'general labour force' and were paid a pittance. But at least they had a job and a roof over their heads. They didn't have a lot of freedom, however, and their movements were restricted to the wharves. In a way, they weren't much better off than when they were in jail.

21

NOW THAT GALLAGHER had control of the shipping containers, it meant a wide variety of people from different backgrounds made it their business to meet with him. Most had good intentions, but a select few did not. It was shortly after 9:00am when he took a call from the main gate.

'Yeah.'

'Mick, two guys here want a face-to-face with you.'

'Who is it?'

'Dunno. Two blokes in suits.'

Gallagher frowned. 'Okay … show 'em through.'

Gallagher looked out the front door of his office and watched as two men in business suits walked down the wide path, dodging mud and diesel-stained puddles. The older one was grey-haired and strode towards Gallagher's office with a determined look on his face. The younger one was taller, and Gallagher could tell by the way he carried himself that he was not in charge.

Gallagher stood up when they arrived at the door and waved them in.

'Mick Gallagher. What can I do for ya?'

'Giuseppe D'Angelo,' the older man said and held out his hand. Gallagher shook it and was surprised by how much strength the old man had in his grip. 'This is my colleague, Bennetti Lucizano,' D'Angelo said and pointed to the other man.

'G'day,' Gallagher said and shook the hand of the second man. He pointed to D'Angelo and said, 'Take a seat.'

D'Angelo sat down and shifted uncomfortably in the dilapidated visitor's chair while Lucizano moved to a corner of Gallagher's tiny office.

There was a moment's silence before D'Angelo spoke. 'I understand you manage all the shipping containers that arrive here in the port.'

Gallagher nodded his head. 'That's right,' he said and sat down behind his desk.

D'Angelo stared at Gallagher with crystal grey eyes. 'I won't beat around the bush. I have arranged to receive a shipment of coffins every month or so.'

'Coffins?' Gallagher repeated.

'Yes. I'd like to know when the container arrives and for it not to be checked.'

There was a wary silence as the two men eyeballed each other. Outside, the noise of trucks and forklifts operating on the wharves drifted into Gallagher's office. The smell of seawater mixed unpleasantly with the stench of dozens of Gallagher's crushed-out cigarettes. In the distance, foghorns blowing out their lonely, mournful sound could be heard, together with the occasional piercing cry of seagulls. Gallagher's mind started ticking over.

What is this? An opportunity, a threat, or a test? Have the authorities, maybe an agency like the Essential Services Bureau, sent their people here to see if you will take the bait?

He leant forward. 'We check 'em all and don't call people each time a shipment arrives. They get notified by post … a bill of lading.'

There was another long pause. D'Angelo stared directly at Gallagher, his face the same slate-grey colour as the concrete his ancestors had poured for hundreds of years. Soon he broke into a smile and said, 'I would like to make you an offer.'

The office fell silent and time stood still as Gallagher sat there contemplating what might come next. He didn't reply. D'Angelo continued.

'It's cash … for you … each time a shipment arrives. I'll pay when my people collect it.'

Gallagher locked eyes with the middle-aged man dressed in a two-thousand-dollar business suit. He quickly came to the conclusion he'd not made his money by legitimate means and that he wasn't from some agency. His accent was European, maybe Italian, and he had a hard look about him. It was the appearance of a man who didn't take kindly to the word 'no'. But Gallagher wasn't fazed. He'd worked with tough buggers all his life, and perhaps this man was just another one of them. He wouldn't be pushed around and could easily tell him to leave, but there was a good chance that money could be made here, so he decided to test the waters.

'So … how much?'

D'Angelo's smile got wider.

'Ten thousand dollars cash, for each shipment!'

The dollar signs started to flash before Gallagher's eyes. He paused momentarily, then said, 'Twenty … upfront … *before* you pick up the consignment, and we can continue talking!'

D'Angelo leant back and peered over his shoulder to his companion. 'Ben, he wants twenty. What do you think?'

Lucizano didn't answer. He knew it was a rhetorical question. Only the head of the family, Mr D'Angelo, struck deals. The atmosphere became tense as D'Angelo mulled over Gallagher's demand. A deal might be done, but now suspicion would be one of its partners. D'Angelo shifted awkwardly in the broken-down chair and faced Gallagher.

'Okay,' he said. 'Twenty.'

Gallagher turned this over in his mind as he gazed at D'Angelo.

He rolled over way too easy. You should have asked for more!

'So give me some details. How do I recognise this container of coffins?'

'The addressee will be Dependable Funerals; it may also have a sticker on it … *from Colombia*.'

Gallagher nodded imperceptibly when he heard the word 'Colombia'.

Colombia. Probably cocaine.

'I guess you don't want me to call you … too many clever people can trace phone calls?' he said.

'Yes, that's right!' said D'Angelo. 'I have no number, but I have a man who works for me and lives in the Melbourne General Cemetery. You call him and give him the paperwork. He will contact me.'

'The cemetery?' Gallagher repeated and raised his eyebrows.

D'Angelo nodded again. 'So … what do you say?'

Gallagher leant back in his chair, thinking. He took his time before he spoke.

'All right. I can organise someone to deliver the shipping manifest, but no one ever comes here! No one contacts me here! Your man gives the paperwork to you. He never comes back here. Understood?'

D'Angelo smiled. 'Yes, but I want to collect the delivery the next night. I'll organise for a truck to pick up the coffins late … after hours. You make sure the gates are open!'

Gallagher didn't like being told what to do on his turf. 'Seems to me like I'm takin' all the risks!'

'That's what you get paid twenty for!' D'Angelo said and glared at Gallagher.

The tension rose as the conversation stopped. Gallagher pressed a button under his desk, and within a minute, two men from an adjoining office entered Gallagher's office. Lucizano reached inside his jacket. D'Angelo saw the danger and put his hands on the desk.

'Gentlemen! There's no need for bad blood. We come as friends … business colleagues.'

Gallagher turned and said to the tall man, 'It's okay, Frank!' Then he turned to D'Angelo. 'These are my associates, Frank Talbot and Grist. They take care of me!'

Gallagher stared at D'Angelo. Then without taking his eyes off him, he addressed the two men.

'Gentlemen, this is Mr D'Angelo and his associate …' Gallagher pointed at Lucizano.

'Bennetti Lucizano!' Lucizano said, a little pissed that Gallagher hadn't remembered his name.

Gallagher then added, 'We are finalising a business deal here, and I'd like you to witness it. There will be a little job I want you to do every so often.'

The situation settled. D'Angelo turned and nodded at Lucizano, who took his hand out of his jacket. Gallagher continued staring at D'Angelo and pointed to Talbot.

'*This* is how it will work!' Gallagher said and paused, wondering if D'Angelo would push back. 'Frank and Grist will take the manifest to your man in the cemetery. Your man will then meet with them later on, maybe the next day, when you have the payment ready!' Gallagher added, 'You collect your coffins … *after* I get the payment.'

D'Angelo paused. The arrangement wasn't exactly what he'd planned. He wanted to get his hands on the cocaine as soon as it arrived, but this would still work. Besides, he had negotiated a *bottom-of-the-barrel* deal with this dumb-arsed wharf worker.

'Okay, but the manifest, the bill of lading,' D'Angelo said. 'I'd like it to be delivered somewhere other than the cemetery itself. Somewhere close by, but not inside the cemetery.'

'All right. I'll leave it to Frank to work out the details,' Gallagher said and nodded to Talbot. 'Who do we deliver to? What's his number?'

'The man is Roy Eastern,' D'Angelo said. He took a pen off Gallagher's desk and scribbled Eastern's name and phone number on a scrap of paper.

D'Angelo nodded, got up, and put his hand out. Gallagher stood, and they shook hands. D'Angelo also took one of Gallagher's dust-covered cards off his desk. Gallagher watched but said nothing.

D'Angelo said, 'I expect the first shipment in about a week.'

'We'll be ready,' Gallagher replied.

D'Angelo walked out of Gallagher's office, followed by Lucizano. Gallagher turned to Talbot and Grist. 'Gentlemen, please show Mr D'Angelo and his friend out.'

'We know our way!' D'Angelo said.

Gallagher pointed at Talbot. 'They will escort you! You are in *my yard!*'

D'Angelo stared long and hard at Gallagher but waited for Talbot and Grist to lead the way out of the office. Then he and Lucizano followed.

* * *

Unbeknown to Giuseppe D'Angelo, Gallagher already had an arrangement in place whereby a bill of lading was delivered to someone else who also didn't want the authorities alerted when his shipment reached the docks. This consignment was made up of car and truck tyres and belonged to Gandolfo Biondi, the head of another Melbourne-based Italian family. Gallagher had no doubt the tyres were somehow filled with contraband, but he asked no questions.

When a shipment arrived at the docks, Gallagher organised for Talbot and Grist to hand-deliver the relevant paperwork to Biondi's business partner, Cain Trench, the president of the Victorian chapter of the Tarantulas motorcycle gang. Trench, in turn, handed the document to Biondi and received a payment for his trouble. Once Biondi received the paperwork, he organised the payment of twenty thousand dollars. A time to collect the delivery was determined, and after Gallagher received the 20K, he ensured the gates to his yard were open late at night, ready to receive Biondi's truck.

The only complication for Gallagher was the bikie gang. The noise they made when the truck was being loaded was deafening. Gallagher wanted to run a clandestine operation and didn't want them there at all. Biondi, however, wanted to make sure the pick-up and drive back to his premises went without a hitch, and so he'd organised, through Trench, for some of the Tarantulas to provide a secure escort. Gallagher was on edge every time Biondi's truck and the bikies turned up. He just wanted the truck packed and the bikies to be gone.

During the delivery, he spent most of his time in the yard ordering his men, the ex-cons, around, getting them to load the tyres without delay. He often wondered if the regular payment he received from Biondi was really worth it, but when it was over and the gates to his yard were finally closed and he was back in his office, his nerves seemed to settle. He would sink back in his chair and pour himself a whisky while he contemplated the organisation he'd put in place and the people who did his bidding. Biondi's delivery was always nerve-racking.

But in the end, he thought about the money – it was *always* about the money! It was twenty thousand dollars, 20K he didn't have yesterday!

22

HOME FOR DANNY was rudimentary. Gallagher put him up in a disused shipping container with three others, who were all foreigners. They spoke very poor English and kept to themselves. All three had tattoos. Not well-defined professional ones; these were ugly and poorly done, like someone had dipped a flick knife in blue ink and just cut the skin a bit. The men looked tough; he was sure they'd each done time in a prison at some stage in the past.

His bed was a thin mattress with a couple of equally thin blankets, but at least he felt safe. He figured the cops weren't likely to call here searching for him. And Gallagher was right about the pay. So far, after three weeks, he'd earned just sixty bucks. He couldn't leave, so there was nowhere to go and spend it, but there was a food truck where he could buy a pie and coffee. For a treat, every Friday, Gallagher ordered in pizzas.

As well as helping to load a couple of trucks late at night, Danny's other job was cleaning toilets. It was a bit after one in the afternoon, and Danny was in his third toilet block. The smell was horrendous, and the bleach and detergent in the bucket did little to counter it. He slopped the mop around on the gritty floors and stuffed it down the ancient toilet bowls, trying to remove what he thought may have been there for a decade or more.

Every now and then, he would step outside to get some fresh air and take a deep breath before plunging back in. Gallagher also wanted him to clean the portaloos, but he decided not to start them until the next morning, when it was still cold and the sun hadn't had the chance to ripen up the stench.

He heard someone outside.

'Strickland!'

It was Gallagher.

Danny walked outside and took a deep breath. 'Yeah?'

'Drop 'round my office when you finish up!'

Danny looked a bit worried. 'Everything okay?'

But Gallagher didn't answer. Instead, he took a call on his mobile phone and walked away. It was four in the afternoon when Danny arrived at Gallagher's office. He went to knock on the door.

'Just come in!' Gallagher said in his usual irritated manner. 'I've done a bit of digging 'round. Take a seat. We need to talk.'

Danny sat in the decrepit visitor's chair. Gallagher stared down at the pile of papers on his desk, then looked at him.

'You break out of a prison truck in Sydney a few months ago?'

Danny's heart sank; this could be the end.

'Yeah,' he said, resigning himself to his fate.

'You Wainwright?'

Danny nodded his head. Gallagher stared at Danny, his eyes steely hard like two ball bearings.

'So you know how to use a handgun?'

'Yes,' Danny sighed. 'I know how to use one.'

'You kill one of them Tarantula bikies in Sydney?'

'What is this, the court case again?' Danny said and straightened up in the chair.

'Whoa! Just want to confirm some facts!'

'You puttin' me in?'

'Nope!' Gallagher barked indignantly. 'I never said that, did I?'

Gallagher slowly shook his head, then pushed a huge mass of papers on his desk towards Danny.

'I'm givin' you a new job.'

Danny nodded his head slightly and squinted at the mountain of paperwork.

'I'm snowed under here, and I need an assistant. It pays a bit better, and I'll give the mop and bucket to one of the others.'

Gallagher paused, lit a cigarette, and shook out the match. 'So … what do ya think? You wanna help me?'

Danny didn't need long to decide. He'd do almost anything not to clean the toilets again. 'Yeah, sweet. What do you want done?'

* * *

The papers Gallagher gave Danny contained all sorts of documents including shipping manifests, bills of lading, invoices, and other assorted material. There was stuff going everywhere, lost documents that needed to be located, papers to be signed and sorted when a consignment was picked up, and a huge pending file waiting for Gallagher to attend to it. It was a hell of a mess; no wonder Gallagher was under pressure and so bad-tempered.

But Danny took to it like a 'duck to water'. Within a couple of months, he'd sorted out the chaos and had things running smoothly. And he worked the hours needed. As soon as a large shipment arrived on the docks, it came with a massive amount of paperwork. He worked hard and late into the night to clear it. Gallagher was impressed.

Things were going well until two consignments arrived and there was no one to contact. Danny waited for Gallagher to get back to his office to ask how to process them. He also found a crisp one-hundred-dollar note jammed between the pages of the ledger he was working on. He quickly grabbed it and tucked it away out of sight.

Gallagher walked into his office, sat down, leant back in his chair, and lit up a cigarette. He shook the match out and cursed silently as the dying flame caught his thumb.

'So, Danny, how's it goin'?'

'Yeah, good, but these two … I can't figure out who to contact. This one is coffins,' he said and pushed the document across the desk towards Gallagher. 'The other one is car and truck tyres.'

Gallagher took the paperwork from Danny.

'I also found this in the ledger.'

Danny took out the one-hundred-dollar note and passed it over.

Gallagher looked down at it. 'Where'd you find it?'

'Stuck between the pages,' Danny said and pointed to the huge ledger sitting on the desk.

Gallagher crossed his arms and stared at Danny long and hard. 'How come you didn't keep it?'

'It's not mine.'

'It's more than two weeks' pay. You could have doubled your money real easy, and no one would have known!'

'Like I said … it's not mine.'

Gallagher was satisfied. He'd put it there deliberately when Danny took a quick lunch break. He wanted to see what he'd do when he found it. He continued to stare at Danny.

'Okay. You've done a good job here … but can I trust you?' Gallagher said. He was not smiling.

'Sure. Why?'

Gallagher held up the one hundred, then pocketed it.

'Can I really trust you?' Gallagher said this as much to himself as to Danny. Danny was about to answer when Gallagher spoke again.

'You don't phone anyone for those two manifests. I organise that!' He sucked back on the cigarette, drew in a lungful of smoke, tilted his head back, and blew it out at the ceiling. 'There are … arrangements in place … things that we don't talk to people about.'

A quizzical look crossed Danny's face.

'Car tyres are going to Preston; you can see on the manifest it's for a mob called Quality Tyres & Repairs. They belong to Biondi.'

Danny pulled the document towards himself and reread it. He

could see the business name, Quality Tyres & Repairs, but couldn't find the name Biondi on it anywhere.

'Who's Biondi?' Danny asked, but Gallagher didn't answer. So he asked, 'Where's Preston?'

'It's a suburb just north of Melbourne. When Biondi finds out the tyres are here, he organises a truck to pick up the delivery late at night. That's one of the deliveries you guys help to load.'

Danny recalled lugging tyres with the three other men. Each tyre was sealed in a thick black plastic covering. They stacked them high in the back of a huge van.

'The other one, the coffins, are for Dependable Funerals.'

'Yeah, I remember packing them too.'

Gallagher ignored him again.

'They belong to D'Angelo; they end up in a funeral parlour in Carlton.'

Danny didn't bother to ask who D'Angelo was; he guessed Gallagher wasn't going to tell him.

'So do I contact somebody?'

'Nope!'

Gallagher gazed out past Danny at the vast canyons of shipping containers and sucked in another lungful of smoke.

'You tell me when that paperwork arrives ... *and you never talk to anyone about it!*'

23

Talbot and Grist walked through the front door of the King George V hotel, the agreed meeting place for the delivery of D'Angelo's bill of lading. They searched for Roy Eastern and didn't have to look far. As with every other time they made a delivery, they found him at the bar surrounded by a group of men. He was talking at the top of his voice and laughing; once again, he was very drunk.

Eastern staggered slightly as he poured half a pot of beer into his mouth. His face was red and bloated with the alcohol. His skin was tight and wrinkled, evidence of years of smoking and the taking of substances that most people would steer well clear of. He didn't see Talbot and Grist as they came through the door. Talbot walked over and grabbed him by the arm and led him to a spot out of earshot of the others.

'Roy, I need to see you.'

'Ahh, Frank, gooch to see ya!' Eastern said, slurring his words. He spilt some of his beer as he staggered alongside Talbot.

One of Eastern's cronies, in amongst a group of men, saw him moving away and yelled, 'Hey, Roy, where ya goin'? It's your shout … again!' The men all laughed.

'Hey, don't forget us!' a man from another group also yelled out.

'Don't worry. Be back priddy shoon,' Eastern said. 'Jush got some bush'ness to tend to!' Eastern leant against Talbot, who held him up.

'You shoutin' the bar?' Talbot asked, speaking softly so the others couldn't hear.

Eastern nodded his head up and down as he contemplated the question.

'Yesh, assh a matter of fact, I am!' Eastern said and belched. 'So what?' he added and swung unsteadily as he grabbed the counter.

Talbot glared at him with contempt. 'Where'd you get the money for that?'

'Ahh-ha!' Eastern said. He tapped the side of his nose and smiled, exposing a mouthful of crooked and decaying teeth. 'Wouldn't you like to know … huh? I got a li'l earner on the shide!'

Talbot was reluctant to hand Eastern the packet containing the bill of lading for the coffins. The man was so drunk he might lose it, but this was the arrangement Gallagher and D'Angelo had agreed on. Eastern snatched the package out of Talbot's hands.

'Thanks!' Eastern said and conjured up a sly smile. 'You wanna buy some exshitemet? Be the besht day of your life!' Eastern laughed, reached into his pocket, and brought out a small plastic bag containing a white powder.

'What's in it?' Talbot asked.

Talbot had a sneaking suspicion he knew what it was but wanted Eastern to confirm his hunch. Eastern tapped the side of his nose again and grinned. He staggered a little as he tried to focus on Talbot's face. He leant against Talbot, his breath reeking of alcohol.

'Cocaine!' he whispered and tried to hide a giggle that quickly became a phlegm-filled coughing fit. Just before he coughed up a lung, he stopped and took another mouthful of beer. 'Fifty buckshh and it's yours!' he said and held out his hand.

Talbot held Eastern by the arm and helped him stay upright. 'So, Roy … where'd you get it?'

Eastern staggered momentarily. 'Neversh you mind!' he said and swung unsteadily on the bar. He drank again. 'So … you want it?' he asked forcefully.

Talbot didn't reply. Instead, he asked, 'Is it pure?'

The smile left Eastern's face. 'Course it's fuckin' pure!' he blurted out. 'D'Angelo's stuff is … is alwaysh pure!' Eastern peered at Talbot with eyes that hadn't focused properly.

'D'Angelo's?' Talbot asked.

Eastern laughed to himself and glanced over at his group of friends. He kept his voice down.

'Yesh! … shh,' he said and crossed his lips with his index finger. 'I doesh the cut for D'Angelo … I cut it with the *shit* they give me!' He exhaled loudly. 'But … don't tell no one … okay?' He squinted hard at Talbot, who nodded his head. 'I keep a little for meself … replace it with baby powder … a little bit *more shit* goes in, and the good stuff comes out,' he explained with a laugh. 'But no one's ever gonna know!' A cunning look crossed his face, and he whispered, 'I sell some here in the pub and some on the shtreet … late at night … no one's ever gonna find out! Nife lill earner … real nife,' he said and rubbed his fingers together, imagining that he had money in them. 'That dumb Italian bastard … he'sh never gonna know … never!'

Eastern grabbed the counter again to steady himself and tipped more beer down his throat.

'Don't tell no one … okay?' Eastern repeated. The green irises in his bloodshot eyes stood out like a pair of weird traffic lights.

He looked like he was going to vomit, and Talbot stepped back. The grog had certainly taken hold.

'Hey, Roy!' one of the men yelled out. 'It's your shout!'

'Yeah, hang on,' Eastern said and pushed his way past Talbot to rejoin the men crowded around the bar.

Back in Gallagher's office, Talbot told him about his latest encounter with Eastern. 'Mick, the guy's a drunk. He's also a thief and got a very big mouth.'

Gallagher leant back and lit a cigarette as he listened to Talbot.

'A thief?' Gallagher asked. He flicked out the match and dropped it into the glass ashtray.

'Yeah, he's stealing D'Angelo's cocaine.'

Gallagher frowned but didn't speak.

'He says when it's time to cut D'Angelo's product, he also has a bottle of baby powder. He tips out the powder and fills the bottle with cocaine and keeps it for himself. The baby powder makes up for the amount of white powder he's taken out.'

Gallagher's frown deepened.

'He's selling the cocaine in the pub and on the streets,' Talbot added. 'He's a liability, Mick. I wasn't comfortable at all giving him the package. It could end up anywhere!'

Talbot stared at Gallagher, hoping he would at least acknowledge that Eastern could be a potential problem. Instead, Gallagher peered into the distance, nodded, and subconsciously tapped the ash from his cigarette into the ashtray.

'How much is he making?' Gallagher asked.

Talbot was stunned.

'I ... I don't know ... but he's shouting the bar! Do you think we should tell D'Angelo?'

Gallagher took a long drag on the cigarette and gazed out through one of the dirt-stained windows.

'No, Frank ... I don't think we should do that at all,' Gallagher said, almost to himself, as his mind ticked over.

Talbot wondered what the hell Gallagher was thinking.

Gallagher waited a moment and said, 'Frank, next time you see Eastern, make sure it's earlier in the evening ... get him well before he's shit-faced! See if he wants to make a deal and earn a little more on the side.'

'What you got in mind, Mick?'

Gallagher leant back in his chair.

'Frank, I want you to buy a bottle of baby powder and see if Eastern will fill it with some of D'Angelo's coke for us. Tell him we'll pay him cash for it. See if he'll take two hundred bucks. Get the coke off him next time you do a delivery. We could get a good little business goin'. We've got a ready-made client base here on the docks. I know a lot of the boys out there who already use it,' he said and jabbed his thumb towards the yard outside. 'We might make a little extra … right here at home!'

* * *

Talbot saw Eastern early one afternoon and put Gallagher's offer to him. Eastern was sober and took only a moment to consider the offer.

'Okay,' he said and smiled slightly. 'Make it two-fifty, and we got a deal.'

It was fifty bucks more than Gallagher had suggested, but Talbot figured he'd be okay with that. Talbot shook Eastern's hand and handed him the plastic container of baby powder.

This arrangement went well to begin with. D'Angelo's coffins rolled in, Talbot and Grist delivered the paperwork, and Eastern received his two-fifty and handed the container, now full of D'Angelo's product, to Talbot. Sales of the cocaine on the docks were brisk, and the profit Gallagher was making was significant.

However, things turned sour after a few months when Eastern told Talbot at one of the deliveries there was a problem and he wasn't able to fill the container this time, but to keep the arrangement in place, he insisted on receiving his two-fifty. He said he'd have it ready for them next time, but when that day arrived, once again, there was no cocaine. Gallagher became suspicious. He told Talbot to see Eastern late at night for the next delivery and see what he had to say.

A week later, Talbot and Grist rolled into the pub much later than normal. They found Eastern at the bar; he had his back to them. Once again, he was amongst his circle of friends and very drunk. He seemed to be handling money. Grist was about to walk over to him, but Talbot held him back.

'Wait … let's see what's goin' on.'

Eastern reached into his pocket and took out a small plastic bag that contained a white powder. One of the men drinking at the bar took it and handed Eastern a fifty-dollar note, which he pocketed. Eastern swayed on the bar and laughed.

'Youse gonna go to the moon with that!' he said out loud, and his laughter filled the bar.

Talbot walked over to Eastern.

'Roy, I need to see you.'

Talbot grabbed Eastern's arm and led him away from the group of men. Eastern was startled and squinted hard at Talbot and Grist.

'Oh … didn't think no one was comin',' he said. 'It's … it's late!'

Talbot took the delivery packet out of his jacket and gave it to Eastern. 'Here's the packet. Don't lose it!'

Eastern pocketed it.

'What did you sell that man?' Talbot asked.

Eastern stared at Talbot and struggled to focus. 'Nuttin!'

'I saw you give him a bag of something, and he gave you cash.'

'No … nuttin'!'

Eastern was about to walk away when Talbot motioned to Grist, who grabbed him by the arm and threatened to break it.

'Ahh,' Eastern yelled.

'I thought you said you couldn't get any cocaine,' Talbot said.

Eastern's bloodshot eyes struggled to focus as he stared at Talbot.

'It was jush … jush some I had leftover … you know, a little bit I had left …' He didn't finish the sentence. He leant on the bar and looked pleadingly at Talbot.

Talbot motioned to Grist to let him go. Eastern rubbed his arm where Grist had twisted it. He grabbed his beer and wandered back to his group of friends.

Back at the docks, Talbot walked into Gallagher's office and took a seat in the visitor's chair.

'Well,' Gallagher said, 'what's the go with Eastern?'

'I saw him selling it in the pub. He can still get it … he's probably still sellin' it on the streets as well. The man's a liar … a drunk and a liar!'

Gallagher stared out through one of the windows and scrunched his face into a tight ball. 'So he can still get his hands on the coke?' he said to himself.

'Yes, Mick,' Talbot said, trying to gain Gallagher's attention. 'What do you wanna do about it?'

But Gallagher didn't answer. He was still talking to himself. 'And we're paying him to sell *our* coke!' he muttered.

Talbot remained silent. It was clear Gallagher was getting angry.

Finally, Gallagher snapped out of it. 'Frank … we've gotta do something about this, and do it quick!'

Talbot waited for Gallagher to say what he wanted done, but Gallagher didn't speak. He just leant back in his chair and stared out into the pitch-black night.

24

TWO WEEKS LATER the phone rang in Gallagher's office.

'Gallagher.'

'I think I have a shipment arriving today.'

Gallagher recognised D'Angelo's voice.

'Yeah, just turned up. I'll get the paperwork to your man tonight.' He paused and then got angry. 'You don't ring me here. I told you no one ever calls me!'

'I know,' D'Angelo said, 'but I have a problem.'

Gallagher waited a moment, trying to guess which way the conversation would go. 'What?' he asked.

D'Angelo didn't answer straight away. Gallagher could hear his heavy breathing.

'There is a person dealing in my patch.'

Gallagher let the conversation hang, then said, 'Any idea who it is?'

There was hesitation, and then D'Angelo spoke. 'I think it's Eastern, the man you deliver to.'

Gallagher's heart skipped a beat. It looked like the anonymous note he had Talbot deliver to the mailbox at D'Angelo's warehouse had worked. It simply read:

'*Someone is selling in your neighbourhood*'

No doubt D'Angelo had arranged for some sort of surveillance and spotted who it was. Gallagher was anxiously anticipating what was coming next. There was silence on the line for a moment, and then D'Angelo went on.

'I want to sort the problem out before I take another delivery.'

Gallagher was sure that D'Angelo's 'sorting out' of Eastern meant he was to disappear – for good. He made his play.

'I may be able to help,' Gallagher offered.

'How?' D'Angelo asked. There was anger in his voice.

'I have a man who has … capabilities.'

'I have my own men!' D'Angelo spat the words out.

'This one is good,' Gallagher said, 'with a gun. You can trust him.'

There was silence once more as D'Angelo considered what Gallagher was saying. 'Who?'

'A man who works for me. Danny Strickland.'

'Never heard of him!'

Gallagher didn't speak; he waited for D'Angelo to calm down.

'Where did you get him from?' D'Angelo asked.

'It doesn't matter. But I'm sure he could sort your problem out for you.'

There was silence again.

'How do you know this man is good at the job that needs to be done?'

'He's got form.'

'What does he owe you?'

'Everything.'

Gallagher was pleased. He could tell D'Angelo was giving this serious thought.

'How do I know he won't talk?'

'You don't. But he can be trusted. He has no friends here. He won't talk to anyone.'

Once again, there was silence.

'This problem I have … it needs to be handled … *carefully*.'

Gallagher was unsure if D'Angelo was talking to him or out loud to himself. He waited a moment, then said, 'You have a cemetery.

You could …'

D'Angelo cut him off. 'I know how to handle my affairs!'

The silence returned.

'How much?'

The dollar signs lit up in Gallagher's head, and he thought he'd try a high figure. 'Fifty.'

There was a long pause.

'I never pay that much for such a job.'

'Like I said … this man is good.'

'I'll give you twenty.'

'No.'

Gallagher could hear D'Angelo's heavy breathing again as he considered the offer. He knew it presented a good deal for D'Angelo as he would be in the clear if it was an outsider who resolved the situation. It wouldn't be one of his people, so it would be unlikely the killing could ever be traced back to him should there be a police-type problem. Finally, D'Angelo spoke.

'You said fifty?'

'Yes … my rates are good.' Gallagher couldn't help smiling to himself as he said it.

'If I pay fifty, I want him permanently. I need someone to take Eastern's place in the cemetery.'

The adrenaline kicked in. Gallagher couldn't believe his luck; D'Angelo was going to pay *him* 50K to get rid of *his* problem. He hesitated, hoping D'Angelo would think he didn't want to lose Danny.

'Fifty is for my man to do the job … not for you to have him.'

D'Angelo became aggressive again. It was the final play for Gallagher, and if it went as he hoped, D'Angelo would take Danny.

'I normally pay much less for someone to remove a problem. If I pay fifty, he belongs to me!'

Gallagher nodded, satisfied; now he would have someone in the cemetery who he could control and someone he could rely on.

'How do I know he will be safe?'

'Why do you care?' D'Angelo snarled.

'He is my man. I protect my people.'

'He's in a cemetery! He'll be safe … I also look after my people!'

Gallagher paused and then finally conceded. 'All right,' he said and tried to sound as though he had been beaten into submission.

There was a long pause.

'When can I get him?'

'Give me a couple of days to organise things here.'

'Okay. Bring him to the Seven Veils as soon as you are ready. I want delivery of those coffins as fast as possible,' D'Angelo said and hung up before Gallagher could reply.

Gallagher placed the phone back in its cradle. He blew out his cheeks and sighed. It had all gone to plan – it was a good day, a very good day!

25

EARLY NEXT NIGHT Gallagher leant back in his chair and stared out at the long rows of shipping containers running as far as he could see. The door to his office was open, and the cold night air drifted in. He lit a cigarette and blew a lungful of smoke up at the ceiling. A smile of satisfaction crossed his face as he thought of the deal he'd done with D'Angelo, but he wondered what was in store for Danny once he left his yard – could he handle working for one of Melbourne's mafia families?

He knew he shouldn't worry about him, but he did. Danny wasn't like the other men Detectives Jacobs and Lucas organised for him every so often. As one ex-con left, escaped, or more likely was removed by Gallagher permanently, he simply mentioned it to them and a replacement was found. But Danny hadn't arrived that way. He'd just come out of the blue and asked Gallagher for a job. Gallagher could've said no and got security to get rid of him, yet he didn't. He kept Danny on. And it had been a smart move. Danny had turned out to be reliable and a good worker.

But the need to get rid of Eastern was paramount. The cocaine he'd provided to Gallagher had become another valuable source of income. Now, with Danny in place, he would have someone who could be trusted, someone who would continue to provide him with a regular supply of D'Angelo's product.

Gallagher got up from his desk, his mind racing as he walked into the crisp night. He peered out over the oily black bay and contemplated how he would tell Danny of his new job. He knocked on the steel wall of the shipping container that served as Danny's living quarters and flicked the burning cigarette butt away. Soon, the door swung open.

'Strickland … see me in my office,' Gallagher said and walked off.

Back in his office, Gallagher lit up his umpteenth cigarette for the day. He shook the match out and dropped it into the overflowing ashtray.

'Sit down,' he said and waited for Danny to take a seat. 'Danny, you've done a good job here.'

Gallagher let the comment stand for a moment.

'Thanks,' Danny said quizzically. The carnival music stirred faintly at the back of his head.

'But things have changed.'

Danny stared at Gallagher, trying to read what was going on. Gallagher sucked in a lungful of smoke and blew it out at the ceiling. He stared directly at the young man.

'I've got another job I want you to do. You're gonna finish up here with me.'

There was a long pause. Danny frowned but didn't speak. He watched Gallagher knock the growing length of ash from his cigarette into the ashtray before he went on.

'I want you to be a … a go-between … a deliverer of goods and services.'

Danny looked at Gallagher in bewilderment. He had no idea what Gallagher was talking about. The carnival music turned up a notch.

'So what do I do?'

Gallagher ignored him. Instead, he cleared his throat and fingered his cigarette.

'This is how it will go. You'll get new lodgings.'

'Where?'

'You'll find out soon enough. But don't worry. It's not too far from here.'

'Will the cops know?'

'Of course they won't fuckin' know!' Gallagher said and went red in the face. He paused for a moment as he composed himself and then went on.

'You'll get paperwork from my intermediaries, which you'll deliver to a designated place. At this place, you'll be given a package. A few days later, you will hand the package to my intermediaries, who will bring it back here. Once that has happened, the owner of the shipment will be advised of a pick-up time, and a truck will turn up at night and take delivery of whatever is described on the paperwork. You understand?'

Danny blinked twice, nodded, and said he did, but he really had no idea what Gallagher was on about, and after asking his dumb 'cop question', he was reluctant to ask any more.

Gallagher continued. 'You see, right now, there are two sets of documents that need to be delivered.'

Danny nodded, thinking back to the time Gallagher told him about the shipments for D'Angelo and Biondi.

'But there is a problem with one, an issue that needs to be resolved.'

Gallagher let the comment hang in the air. The bellow of a ship's foghorn reverberated in the tiny office, and the night air turned just a little bit colder.

'Danny, this new home you're gonna get will be a lot better than what you've got here. And you'll make good money. I think you'll be happy.' Gallagher paused. 'But I want you to be careful, Danny … *really* careful.'

Gallagher smiled a doubtful smile. He pressed the button under his desk, and soon two men entered his office.

'Here are my good friends, my intermediaries. Frank Talbot, meet Danny Strickland.'

Danny stood up, and Talbot, the taller of the two, stepped forward and shook his hand. He stared at Danny with eyes so black it wasn't possible to see where the iris finished and the pupil started. It wasn't a friendly gaze.

'And this is Grist.'

Danny was shocked by the power in this man's grip. He was built like a wrestler, and Danny was sure that Grist, if he chose to, could kill someone with just his bare hands.

'Gentlemen, Danny here is going to be our new contact. He'll be helping us with the deliveries. I trust him.'

Talbot turned to Gallagher. 'So do we have a solution for the Eastern problem?'

Gallagher smiled. He glanced at Talbot and then across to Danny.

'Oh, we do. *Oh yes, we do!*'

Danny's breathing got a little heavier as he looked from one man to the next and wondered what the hell they were on about. Gallagher continued.

'Danny, I will ask Frank here to contact you and tell you when to be ready for a delivery. You'll get a bill of lading for each consignment from him and deliver it personally.'

'Where?' Danny asked with a frown.

'Frank will let you know. You'll also be given a parcel to bring back. You're not to open it. I'm the only one who opens that parcel. But don't worry … it's all nice and legal.'

Only half of what Gallagher was saying to him was making any sense, and the damn carnival music surely wasn't helping.

'There will also be a small package for you personally,' Gallagher said and smiled. He leant back in his chair and lit a fresh cigarette from the embers of the dying one. 'As you know, there are two families.'

Danny nodded and was about to speak, but Gallagher waved his arm in the air and cut him off.

'Each one gets a separate consignment. I handle both, and I organise when their shipments get picked up. It's never at the same time; I don't want them here together. As far as they're concerned, I handle only their consignment for them. They don't know I manage both. They don't need to know everything. That's the way I like it. I organise it all, Danny. It runs just like clockwork!'

Gallagher sucked on the cigarette and blew out another layer of rancid, grey smoke.

'You're leaving tonight, and you won't be coming back. It's been good. You've done well, but remember to keep your mouth shut. You don't know us, Danny. You don't know *any of us* … understand?'

'Yeah … okay,' Danny half whispered.

Gallagher stared at him. 'I trust you, Danny, but if you let me down …'

'I … I won't let you down,' Danny said, not knowing what else to say.

Gallagher smiled and said, 'Don't worry. The job's easy. Just deliver some paperwork and bring back packages … there's nothin' to it. But there is something we want you to see to first. Something that's right up your alley!'

A knot tightened in Danny's stomach. Someone hit the button for the carnival rides, and in his head, they started to slowly spin into life.

'There is a man who has done the wrong thing. We'd like you to fix it for us.'

Gallagher looked across at Talbot. 'Danny knows how to use a gun.'

With that, Gallagher bent forward and opened a drawer of his desk. He took out a small wooden box and slid it across the desk towards Danny.

'Take this. You're gonna need it. Keep it. It's yours. There are no markings on it … it can't be traced.'

Danny opened up the box and saw a pocket-sized handgun, a

Colt Mustang, together with a number of packages of ammunition.

'Take this as well.' Gallagher pushed a mobile phone plus a phone charger across the desk. 'It's a burner. There are no names attached to it. Make sure you keep it charged. You use it to take calls from Frank or me only. You don't make any calls, Danny! You never call us … okay?'

Ashen-faced, Danny nodded and stared at Gallagher. Gallagher smiled one last time, got up from behind his desk, and patted Danny on the back.

'Don't sweat it. You'll do well. There's nothin' to worry about!'

Danny peered down at the handgun and the phone, both potent reminders of his recent past. His ears filled with cotton wool and his head started to spin as the carnival came to life and roared into full swing.

26

DANNY RODE IN the back of Talbot's black Lexus SUV. It was the first time he'd been out of Gallagher's shipping container yard since he walked across the narrow bridge that crossed over the Yarra River nearly a year ago. Talbot told him he was meeting a Mr D'Angelo at the Seven Veils Casino and Nightclub. Before he left, he was given new clothes and told to shave. Gallagher told him D'Angelo liked his people to look smart.

His people! Are you gonna be one of D'Angelo's people?

Talbot drove through the city streets of Melbourne with Grist riding shotgun. Bright lights from theatres, shopfronts, and office towers bounced off the car's highly polished Duco. Trams and cars fought their way along the streets. Crowds of people waited to cross with the traffic lights, some, however, ducked out of side streets and weaved their way across the roads taking their lives in their hands. Danny sat in the back, mesmerised by the sights of a city that, like Sydney, was alive at night.

They soon turned onto King Street and pulled up under the portico in front of the Seven Veils. Expensive chandeliers hung in the main entrance. Taxi cabs lined up outside, and there was a concierge directing traffic. Men in suits and women in their finery were in the foyer laughing and milling about. Talbot got out and handed the keys to a valet who appeared out of nowhere. Talbot stuck his head back in the car and glared at Danny.

'We're here, Strickland. Get out!'

Grist remained in the passenger seat while the valet drove the car into the underground car park. Danny followed Talbot through the gleaming metal and glass doors of the nightclub. Once inside, he couldn't believe the size of the place. More chandeliers hung from the ceiling. A sleek wooden bar, crowded with patrons, ran the entire length of one wall while rows of poker machines, roulette wheels, and card tables lined the other. A four-piece band played 'swing music' on a softly lit stage. In the restaurant area, wait staff busied themselves serving tables. At the bar, scantily clad girls with tall ostrich feathers in their hair talked casually to the drinkers. Danny couldn't take his eyes off the incredible scene; it was like he'd entered another world.

Talbot turned to Danny.

'Strickland, I'm going to introduce you to Mr D'Angelo. He owns this joint! You only ever address him as Mr D'Angelo. It's "Yes, Mr D'Angelo," "No, Mr D'Angelo," and "Thank you, Mr D'Angelo." Don't ever forget it!'

'Yeah, right,' Danny said just a little too casually.

Talbot eye-fucked him. But Danny wasn't fazed. He knew he was never going to get along with Talbot. He wasn't about to be told what to do by someone like him. He'd play along for a while, however now he was out of Gallagher's immediate control, he could start to work things out for himself. He'd do what they wanted until things settled down, but soon he would start to make some plans, and he had a gun; if all else failed – he had a gun!

He trailed Talbot as he made his way through the crowd. They headed towards the back of the venue, where it was quieter. Talbot stopped in front of three men who were sitting in leather-clad chairs. The seating area was slightly elevated, giving each man a clear view of the nightclub and its patrons. Two men stood on either side, undoubtedly some sort of security. Empty cocktail glasses sat on a beautifully carved wooden table in front of them. The older man in the middle was Giuseppe D'Angelo. To his right sat Bennetti Lucizano, D'Angelo's enforcer, and to his left was Lorenzo Jnr D'Angelo, Giuseppe D'Angelo's grandson and heir apparent.

Talbot walked up to the table and stood there waiting for a pause in their conversation. The old man looked directly at him, then turned away, put his hand in the air, and caught the eye of a passing waitress.

'Ebony, freshen up these drinks and take the empties, thank you!'

'Yes, Mr D'Angelo,' the young girl said.

She immediately stopped what she was doing and started to clear up the table. D'Angelo then turned back to Talbot.

'Frank, good to see you,' he said, finally acknowledging Talbot. 'You're looking well.' D'Angelo smiled and held out his hand, which Talbot shook.

'Thank you, Mr D'Angelo,' Talbot said and bowed his head ever so slightly.

While D'Angelo and Talbot were talking, Danny watched as Ebony started wiping down the table; he couldn't take his eyes off her. She was young, about his age, and very, very pretty. She glanced up at him momentarily, and he chanced a smile. She quickly looked down and kept wiping, but just before he lost all hope, she briefly glanced up at him again. He wasn't sure if she smiled, but he thought she did. He got a feeling he hadn't experienced before. His heart began to beat at almost twice its normal rate. Talbot brought him back down to earth.

'Mr D'Angelo, I'd like to introduce you to Danny Strickland.'

D'Angelo stared down at Danny, paused, and then held out his hand. He bared his teeth as he smiled, but his eyes were set like rock.

'Danny, I've heard a lot about you. I'm pleased to meet you.'

Danny took D'Angelo's hand and shook it. There was power in the old man's grip, and it put Danny on edge.

'Thank you … Mr D'Angelo.'

'Danny, I hear from Gallagher that you are a good worker and have talents we can use.'

The carnival music in Danny's head spun into life.

'There's a certain problem we have which we think you can help us with.' D'Angelo paused and stared at Danny. 'In return, I can offer you a job. It pays very well. Isn't that right, Frank?'

'Yes, Mr D'Angelo,' Talbot said and stared hard at Danny.

The old man's smile got wider. He peered across, in turn, at the men sitting either side of him, and they both nodded in agreement.

'Did Frank tell you that the accommodation I can offer you is much better than what you had during your time with Gallagher?' D'Angelo laughed, and the others joined in.

Talbot was going to speak, but D'Angelo held up his hand.

'That's okay. Frank is a very busy man, so maybe there was no time.' He smiled at Talbot, then went on. 'Yes, I can offer you a much better place than a rundown shipping container, and the job's interesting. I think you'll like it. What do you say? Would you like to work for me?'

Say yes! SAY YES!

Danny knew he was trapped. Saying no was not an option. He watched while Ebony took away the empty glasses, but she didn't look back.

'Yes, Mr D'Angelo. Thank you. How can I help?'

D'Angelo ignored him.

'Excellent. This is Ben Lucizano, my trusted colleague.'

Lucizano didn't smile as he held out his hand. His shock of black hair was perfectly cut, and his day-old beard had been immaculately trimmed. His blood-red tie stood out like a beacon against his white shirt and dark, pinstriped suit. To Danny, this guy had an air of arrogance about him, just like Talbot. Lucizano grabbed Danny's hand and squeezed, and a look of superiority crossed his face as he tightened his grip even further and threatened to crush Danny's hand. Danny squeezed back hard, and after a moment, he felt one of Lucizano's finger bones shift. It was a tiny but important victory. Lucizano whipped his hand away and glared at Danny. It was a moment that wasn't lost on either man.

D'Angelo spoke. 'Go with Ben. He'll explain what needs to be done. Do you still have the *present* Gallagher gave you?'

Danny was sure D'Angelo was referring to the handgun, not the mobile phone. 'Yes, Mr D'Angelo.'

'Good.'

D'Angelo turned to Lucizano.

'Ben, you better take Danny now. I'll talk to you later on this evening.'

'Yes, Giuseppe,' Lucizano said and got up.

While this conversation was taking place, Danny watched as Frank Talbot made a tactical withdrawal. He walked quickly through the crowded nightclub and pushed his way towards the door. Within a minute, he was gone.

Now Danny was on his own with these strangers. He had no doubt they were very dangerous people. It was the first time in such a long, long time that he'd felt so scared and alone.

PART FOUR

IN HIS FATHER'S FOOTSTEPS

Giuseppe D'Angelo …

27

GIUSEPPE D'ANGELO WAS the son of Lorenzo and Ysabella D'Angelo, both immigrants from Sicily. When they first came to Australia the family settled down in Carlton, an inner suburb of Melbourne occupied by many other Italian migrant families. Giuseppe's time growing up was hard. But he learnt early on how to fit in with the neighbourhood kids and soon ran with the pack. He learnt how to steal, and he learnt how to fight.

He would often come home from school with a black eye or bloodied knuckles. His father, Lorenzo, was pleased when he saw young Giuseppe like that; it meant that he was toughening up.

Lorenzo came from a particularly harsh background. As a young man, he had joined a violent gang active in and around Messina, Sicily. From an early age, he learnt many of the brutal and vicious ways of the gang and became immune to the handing out of bashings, or worse. As long as it pleased the boss and brought in the highly sought-after cash, or rid the gang of a rival, Lorenzo was always at the forefront. It was a dangerous lifestyle, and for a long time it looked like this would be how he would spend the rest of his days. However, it all changed when he met Ysabella. She was a beauty, and he knew from the moment he met her that he didn't want to lose her. He wanted to be with her and protect her. He hoped to settle down with her and perhaps raise a family. And he knew he could never do these things if he remained part of the gang.

He often told his son, Giuseppe, stories about the old days. He told him that he loved Sicily but said he loved Giuseppe's mother even more and decided that if they were to have a better life, they would need to find another place and leave Sicily behind. He said he'd heard many rumours in the town that Australia, a place they called the 'lucky country', wanted both skilled and unskilled people from overseas and that there was plenty of work. The cost to get to Australia was within Lorenzo's reach, and so that is where he and Ysabella decided to go.

In Australia, however, Lorenzo found it wasn't as easy to find work as he thought it would be. He had no real skills and spoke very poor English. His only hope for making any money was to fall back on the ways he'd learnt in the gang. And so he would wait for drunks to leave hotels late at night, and when they were on their own, he would bash and rob them. He was also a master pickpocket, another skill he'd perfected while in the gang. He would hang around the Queen Victoria Market in Melbourne and wait for a purse to be sitting in an open basket or a wallet to be sticking out of a hip pocket. However, these methods of making money were rudimentary and unreliable and brought in very little cash; at times there was not enough to put food on the table. But in the market, he found a silver lining. He met a stallholder, Angelo Accardi, who also came from Messina. They struck up a friendship, and during a casual conversation, Accardi mentioned that he needed someone to drive his van and deliver fruit and vegetables.

Lorenzo's eyes lit up. 'I can do it,' he said, and then added, 'but … I have no driver's licence.'

Accardi just shrugged his shoulders. 'So what?' he said and felt around in his pocket.

He took out the keys to his tired and rusted-out delivery van and handed them to Lorenzo.

'The money isn't great, but I will pay you every week,' Accardi added.

'Thankyou … thankyou, so very much Angelo,' Lorenzo said.

Finally, after such a long time, Lorenzo had the opportunity to make a legitimate living.

28

THE CHANCE MEETING between Lorenzo and Angelo Accardi went well. Accardi was pleased to have someone working for him that he could trust and gave Lorenzo unrestricted use of the delivery van.

Lorenzo's deliveries took him throughout Carlton and Brunswick, where he learnt the ways of hard-working Melburnians and befriended many in the businesses he delivered to. Part of his clientele included the local hotels, and it was at one of these that he met Jack Harrison, the publican of the Great Western Arms, a hotel situated not far away from the market. They got to know each other well and would often have a chinwag when Lorenzo delivered vegetables for the hotel's counter meals. It was during one of these casual conversations that Harrison mentioned to him that he had a plan, an idea that could make them both some extra cash.

Lorenzo leant on the bar and sipped on a beer.

'Okay ... so, your plan ... what is it?' he asked with a smile.

Lorenzo was only mildly interested, but the thought of making some extra cash had appeal.

'Have you heard of sly grog?' Harrison said.

Lorenzo shook his head.

'You know I have to close here at six o'clock at night?'

'Yes.'

'Well, a lot of my customers have told me they'd like to have a drink after six. If I could find another place to sell grog later on in the night, I could improve profits significantly!'

Lorenzo looked at him quizzically and shrugged. 'So, why don't you?'

'The set-up is expensive. I need someone to help me, someone who can add a bit of their money. I also need a place, somewhere away from the prying eyes of the police, where I can get things organised.'

Harrison leant on the bar while Lorenzo sipped at his beer. 'You interested?'

Lorenzo thought for a moment, then said, 'Maybe. But if I add my cash, we would have to split any profits fifty-fifty!'

Harrison considered this for a moment, then nodded. 'Yes, of course. That sounds okay.'

Lorenzo gazed out the hotel window and across to the market as a tram rattled past. 'I know a place we could use. I've driven past it many times before … it looks deserted.'

Harrison's ears pricked up. 'Where? What sort of place?'

'It's an old warehouse that backs onto a lane in Carlton. I don't think anyone's been in there for years.'

Harrison was interested.

'Okay, Lorenzo,' he said softly, his mind ticking over. 'Show me tonight. We might have a deal!'

Lorenzo picked Harrison up later that night, and they ventured into the lonely backstreets of Carlton. They pulled up out the front of a rundown warehouse. The wooden walls were slowly giving way to the years and were pock-marked and rotten in places. Two grimy windows high up in the building looked out onto the deserted street below. There was no lock on the door and no sign saying it was for sale or lease. Lorenzo twisted the ancient door handle, and, with hesitant steps, both men walked through into the cavernous insides.

Their footsteps echoed eerily on the smooth concrete floor. Cobwebs hung from ancient wooden beams. A small amount of light, from a waxing moon, found its way through a cracked and broken skylight and helped to relieve the gloom. They walked over to a wide roll-up door. Lorenzo worked chains that hung down the walls, and the door slowly opened up to an empty lane outside.

Harrison turned to Lorenzo. 'You're right, Lorenzo. It looks abandoned. This will be perfect.'

Business at first was sluggish until word of mouth took hold. One or two patrons slowly became a small crowd and sales picked up as the venue became a favourite after-hours watering hole. Soon, it became Lorenzo's main source of income, and he decided to give away his daytime delivery job. He went back to the market and saw Accardi to give him the news.

'Angelo, how are you?' Lorenzo said. He extended his hand, and Accardi shook it.

'Good, Lorenzo, good ... how are you?'

'I'm well, my friend, but I have some bad news.'

Accardi looked worried.

'Angelo, I have to give the delivery job away. I have found something else.'

For a moment, Accardi was dumbstruck.

'What is it you will do?'

'It's a business I've started up in Carlton. It's taking up all my time.'

'What sort of business, Lorenzo?'

The smile left Lorenzo's face.

'Angelo, it's best that you do not ask.'

There was a long pause, and then Accardi spoke. 'Lorenzo, my delivery van. I ...'

'Don't worry, Angelo. Wait here.'

Lorenzo walked away, and within minutes, he drove a brand-new delivery van down the tight lane behind Accardi's stall.

'For you, Angelo. It's a gift, for you ... for helping me when I was down on my knees.'

Tears started in Accardi's eyes.

'Thank you, Lorenzo. Thank you so very much!'

29

TWELVE MONTHS DOWN the track, and the business became too much for Lorenzo and Harrison to handle by themselves. The money was good, but the workload was crazy. They agreed there was a need to bring in others to help. Lorenzo, who had a knack for organisation and management, said he could fix the problem. He would hire some of his family and migrant friends. He soon organised the labour required, which also included his teenage son, Giuseppe. But it was not long after these new people had started that Harrison became disgruntled. He asked to see Lorenzo one evening.

'Lorenzo, I'm worried.'

Lorenzo looked at him and frowned. 'What is the problem?'

'The people you have brought in ...' He paused and stared at Lorenzo. 'You now outnumber me. I am concerned you will take over the business.'

Lorenzo waited a moment before he spoke. 'We agreed we needed more help; all I have done is provide that help.'

Harrison considered what was said, but he was still unhappy. 'Lorenzo, we are business partners. I want to bring in my people and replace some of yours. I want to even up the numbers. You have too many!'

Lorenzo was taken aback; he was becoming wary of Harrison and his motivation. 'Yes, we are partners, but I have already given my people work. Some are very poor. They need the money.'

'That's not my problem,' Harrison said and shrugged.

Lorenzo didn't know how to respond. 'I will not sack them!' he said.

The warehouse seemed to grow colder as the conversation became tense.

Harrison continued. 'Their money worries are their problem. If you don't agree to reduce your numbers, I'll tell the cops about this place and deny I had anything to do with it. I'll put you out of business just like that!' he said and snapped his fingers.

The threat surprised Lorenzo. He could see this newly forged business could be in trouble, and his friends would be in the same predicament he had been in only a year or so beforehand. His mind was racing. He stared at Harrison and could see in his eyes that he was no longer a man he could trust. Something had to be done. He hesitated for a moment.

'Okay, Harrison … *my friend*,' he said and paused before he went on. 'Give me a day or two to sort things out.'

Harrison smiled to himself and walked off. He was pleased that his threat had worked, and now he would bring in his people and get control. But he had no intention of evening up the numbers. His objective was to replace Lorenzo and his people altogether. And it would be timely too as there was a rumour going around that the government was relaxing some of the hotel trading hours, and it sounded like this would happen soon. With the supply lines already set up for this business, Harrison knew he could easily redirect them to his hotel, increase the intake at the Great Western Arms, and really make a killing. The only roadblock now was D'Angelo; once he had him out of the way, there would be no more sharing of profits. He would have it all to himself. He was a businessman, and *business was business.*

It was two days later, a Thursday night, always a profitable time as it was payday and people had more money in their pockets, when

Lorenzo saw Harrison and said he'd thought things over and would agree to meet his demands. Lorenzo suggested that they meet inside the warehouse after closing up and discuss the arrangement. Lorenzo said he would make sure the staff had been sent home for the night.

Shortly after 11:00pm, Harrison rolled the corrugated-steel door down on the now deserted lane. He turned off the outside light and walked deep into the interior of the warehouse. With the door in place, the ever-present gloom of the warehouse returned in full force. Tiny globes strung high in the rafters of the open ceiling did little to illuminate the huge expanse, and in many spots, there was no light at all. Dark shadows followed Harrison as he walked over to where D'Angelo was sitting at an old wooden table lit by a desk lamp. A chair was placed on the opposite side. He slid it out and sat down.

'So, Lorenzo, what have you decided?'

Harrison smirked and waited for D'Angelo to roll over and reduce his numbers there and then. He fidgeted in his seat and sat side-on.

'Well, Harrison, the business is running well, and I do not want to rock the boat.' D'Angelo was looking down at the table as he said this, with his hands resting on the edge.

Harrison fidgeted again. 'So … you agree that some of your people must go?' he said, becoming a little irritated.

'Yes, I do … here is my offer,' D'Angelo said and pushed a single-page document over the desk.

'Offer?' Harrison said, surprised.

Lorenzo watched while Harrison swivelled around in his chair and faced him directly. He waited until Harrison began to read the paper, then slid his hands along the table and gently tapped it three times.

This was the sign that young Giuseppe was waiting for. Three taps on the table meant Harrison had his back directly to him. He stepped out of the shadows and raised the baseball bat high in the air. He took careful aim, then slammed it down on Harrison's head as hard as he could. There was a sickening crack as wood split bone. He waited for Harrison to fall to the floor, then hit him again hard across the temple.

'Don't bring blood! Don't bring blood!' his father shouted and held up his hand.

Harrison was semi-conscious and groaning loudly. Lorenzo pushed his chair away from the table and walked around to the man lying on the floor. Giuseppe watched as his father knelt down and slid one arm under Harrison's chin, bringing it tight up against his throat. He used the other arm to push Harrison's head forward. It was a classic chokehold that cut off Harrison's airway. Giuseppe could hardly believe what he was seeing as Harrison, who only moments ago was in a stupor, burst back to life.

Harrison kicked and struggled as the air to his lungs was being denied. His arms and legs flailed around in a desperate bid to break the stranglehold, but Lorenzo never let go. He held him from behind in the death grip and followed Harrison around on the floor wherever he scrambled. Harrison kicked the chair over and smacked his heels hard against the concrete floor as he struggled. He reached behind, trying to grab Lorenzo's head and eyes, but Lorenzo held his head back and away.

Harrison started to make horrible grunting and gurgling sounds as he fought for air. He tore at Lorenzo's arms, but Lorenzo's hold was strong.

With every move, Lorenzo tightened his grip even further, and finally, Harrison's thrashings became less and less. Giuseppe watched as Harrison's arms flopped down to one side and then listened as a horrible guttural noise escaped his tortured throat. Harrison became very still. It was another full minute before his father eventually let go, and then he gently placed the dead man's battered head on the cold concrete floor.

Lorenzo stood up, breathing heavily. They both stared at Harrison to see if there were any signs of life. Lorenzo knelt down and checked the body for a pulse, then turned to Giuseppe.

'Help me carry him!'

Giuseppe grabbed Harrison by the feet while his father took his arms. They carted him to the roll-up door. Lorenzo put him down, worked the chains, and lifted the door. He checked the lane outside. When he was sure it was clear, they picked Harrison back up. Together, they lugged the body out into the night and loaded it into the boot of the family car. Lorenzo slammed the lid closed.

'I'll take it from here,' he said to his son. 'You can go home now, Giuseppe.'

'Papa?' Giuseppe said.

'Yes?'

'Papa, I need to see this through. You said someday I would inherit the business. I need to see how things like this should be done, right up until the end.'

D'Angelo gazed at his son, and his face broke into a broad smile. He grabbed Giuseppe around the shoulders and hugged him. He was very proud of his boy; it was clear that one day he would make a very good businessman.

'Okay, get in the car. We are taking him to a friend.'

Lorenzo drove his car out of the lane and into the quiet streets of Carlton. They passed through the city and kept driving. After another half an hour, Lorenzo pulled off the bitumen and found a dirt road that led to a set of market gardens in Moorabbin, a suburb young Giuseppe had never heard of.

He turned off the headlights, not wanting to attract any unnecessary attention. It was slow going, with the moon providing the only light. Eventually, he saw a familiar turnoff and pulled through an open gate. The car pitched and heaved on the potholed driveway, and soon they pulled up in front of a farmhouse. It was surrounded by a massive garden with row after row of freshly dug earth.

Lorenzo turned off the engine, and both he and Giuseppe sat in the car in the dark.

'Papa, who lives here?'

'My friend. I rang him early this week.'

A porch light blinked on, and the front door opened. A man dressed in working overalls and a loose-fitting jumper walked over to them. Lorenzo rolled down his window.

'Lorenzo!' Vincenzo Bortoloni said and pushed his body halfway through the open window.

The two men embraced, and then Bortoloni glanced over at Giuseppe.

'Ahh! I see you have brought an apprentice. Young Giuseppe! You helpin' the old man, hey?'

Giuseppe smiled back but didn't speak. Bortoloni laughed and turned back to Lorenzo.

'So, you have some fertiliser for me, yes?'

Lorenzo smiled and nodded as he and Giuseppe got out of the car. All three men struggled as they lifted Harrison's body out of the boot. They carried it a little way and put it on a small wooden trailer attached to a tractor. Bortoloni started the tractor up and turned to both Lorenzo and Giuseppe.

'He's a good size ... plenty of good nourishment for my vegetables!' He laughed again. 'I need to get started. Cut him into nice small parts, then dig them in. It won't take long!'

Lorenzo shook hands with Bortoloni and handed him a thick envelope. 'For you, Vincenzo. Thank you very much.'

'Anytime, Lorenzo, my friend. You give me a call anytime. We should catch up! You bring your family here for dinner sometime, okay? My wife, she makes the best lasagna!'

'Yes, Vincenzo, I will. Thank you once again.'

Bortoloni smiled. He put the envelope on the tractor seat and sat down on it. He drove off with Harrison's body to an open shed covered by a weather-beaten corrugated-iron roof. By the time the bandsaw had started up, both Lorenzo and Giuseppe were back in the car and bouncing down the driveway towards the gate, on their way back to Carlton.

During the trip, Lorenzo turned to his son.

'Giuseppe, in business, it's very important to find people you can trust and then pay them well for their loyalty. It's important to make good contacts. If you help them when they are in need, they will then help you should you be in need.'

Giuseppe considered this for a minute, then asked, 'Papa, how do you know this man?'

Lorenzo stared out at the dark bitumen road ahead before glancing across at his son.

'When you were very young, I worked for a man who wanted someone to deliver fruit and vegetables. During my deliveries, I met many people who lived and worked around Carlton and the Queen Victoria Market. I made strong contacts; this man was one of them. We said we would help each other when the need arrived, that we would look out for each other.'

Giuseppe turned to his father.

'Papa, what will he do with the body?'

'You ask many questions, Giuseppe, but they are good ones! He will burn the clothes and cut the body up and mince it. Everything will be buried in his huge garden. It will help his plants to grow!' Lorenzo smiled, then added, 'Giuseppe, it's very hard to find a body when you bury it deep.'

There was no more talking as they drove back home, but his father's words stayed with the young man. It was guidance Giuseppe would heed and find to come in very handy many years down the track.

30

AND SO IT came to pass that when Lorenzo D'Angelo passed away some twenty years later, his son, Giuseppe, gained control of the business. He took to it enthusiastically and within a very short time could see that profits from the sale of sly grog were drying up. The government had eased the restrictive laws for selling alcohol, and the appeal of the speakeasy was beginning to wane. But Giuseppe recalled his father mentioning to him that a man who frequented the Queen Victoria Market, Adami Schiavo, was selling a drug to some of his clientele who drank at the warehouse in Carlton. He told Giuseppe the drug was called heroin and was catching on fast; apparently, it gave a bigger hit than alcohol, and once people had tried it, they were desperate to get more. Lorenzo said he thought Schiavo was doing well. Giuseppe had never heard of such a drug but decided to investigate and see what was involved. It was clear that something had to change, and so he arranged to meet with Schiavo.

It was a Saturday lunchtime in the Queen Victoria Market and the food court was buzzing. Giuseppe D'Angelo was seated with a younger man, Bennetti Lucizano. Lucizano had grown up in the same neighbourhood as D'Angelo and had gone to the same school. He looked on D'Angelo as an older brother and was always trying to please him.

They sat quietly at one of the outdoor tables and watched as the lunchtime crowd milled about either shopping or eating, or both.

Lucizano said to his friend, 'Giuseppe, your old man was into grog. I don't think he ever sold drugs.'

Giuseppe slowly nodded his head. 'Yes, I know,' he said and stared into the distance. He seemed lost in thought for a moment as he remembered his father, then he snapped back to reality.

'Ben, my father ran a tight ship and made a good living from grog, but things have changed. In business, you have to diversify. You have to be prepared to do something different. Move with the times. Do something your competitors are not doing, or not doing well. You have to be brave!'

Lucizano glanced across to his friend and said nothing. He knew when not to speak. Giuseppe went on.

'This could be a game changer for us, Ben. People these days want a bigger and better hit all the time.' D'Angelo raised his arms in the air. 'They want to fly!' He laughed and reached across and clapped his friend on the shoulder.

Lucizano winced as Giuseppe's hand hit him but said nothing. He reached for his pack of cigarettes, lit up, and blew out a cloud of blue-grey smoke.

'Put that out!' Giuseppe snapped.

'What?'

'Put it out now! We are surrounded by people eating their lunch … put it out!'

'Yes, Giuseppe. I'm … I'm sorry,' Lucizano said. He looked crestfallen as he stubbed out the cigarette.

Giuseppe looked around at the crowd.

'Ben, we need to meet with this man and make a good impression. We have to appear to be businessmen. My father said Schiavo was making good money selling the drug. I want to see if we can do something similar.'

'Yes, Giuseppe,' Lucizano said quietly.

Lucizano waited until he was sure it was okay to speak. 'Giuseppe, this guy Schiavo, can we trust him?'

'Good question, Ben. We will soon see.'

Lucizano was pleased with himself. He'd asked a sensible question and given his friend something to think about.

'My old man said he was trustworthy, but let's move slowly and see what he has to say.'

'Yes, Giuseppe.'

A short time later, a man approached them. He had shopping bags with him and appeared to be in the market to pick up supplies for the week. He checked out the people sitting nearby before he pulled out a chair and sat at the table directly across from Giuseppe. Schiavo was middle-aged and had a hard look about him. He surveyed the two men opposite, then placed one of the shopping bags on the table. Giuseppe noted Schiavo had come by himself – he didn't bring security.

He must still be a one-man band!

'So, you are Giuseppe D'Angelo ... Lorenzo's son?' Schiavo said.

'Yes,' Giuseppe said and held out his hand.

Schiavo shook his hand; his grip was strong. 'I thought so. You look a lot like him. I am Adami Schiavo.'

Schiavo fossicked around in the shopping bag. 'So, you are interested in buying?' Schiavo asked and smiled.

Giuseppe shook his head slightly.

'No. I'm interested in knowing how you sell your product.'

The smile left Schiavo's face. 'Why do you want to know that?'

'I would like to learn where you get your supply and understand how you sell.'

'You want to be a dealer?' Schiavo asked. 'I thought you would sell grog just like your father!'

'Well ... I think it's time to expand the business.' Giuseppe eyed Schiavo, not wanting to give too much away.

Schiavo's attitude turned aggressive. 'Do you intend to sell in my territory?'

'No! No! No!' Giuseppe said. 'I believe if I can get a supply, I can build a network of buyers. I can then share the new network with you!'

Giuseppe stared the man straight in the eye and didn't blink, just like his father had taught him to do – particularly when he was lying. Schiavo was wary but also interested. New clients in a new neighbourhood would be good for business.

The buzz of the afternoon crowd filled the air as the two men studied one another.

'Where were you thinking of selling?'

'Anywhere that is not in your territory,' Giuseppe said and laughed. 'But I have a good idea of the streets in Carlton and Brunswick … maybe also in the city.'

Schiavo ran his thumb and forefinger down the sides of his mouth as he stared at D'Angelo. 'I sell in the city.'

'Okay, Adami. I will not sell there. The city is all yours!' Giuseppe said and waved his arm around in the direction of the CBD as a huge smile lit up his face.

Schiavo stared at him and nodded. 'But you will sell in Carlton and Brunswick … yes?'

'Yes. I know those streets well. I can start there.'

Schiavo waited a moment, then peered down at the shopping bag and opened it.

'Okay. I knew your father well. I drank in his establishment, and he also let me sell in there, but I never sold outside in the streets.' He gazed out across the marketplace. 'It could be good,' he muttered to himself.

Giuseppe and Lucizano remained silent as they watched Schiavo turning over the offer in his mind. He slowly nodded his head.

'He was a good man, your father. If I could trust him, then I believe I can also trust his son.'

Giuseppe's heart started racing. It seemed like this meeting could be successful. Schiavo reached into the shopping bag and took out a small packet of white powder. With his palm downturned, he handed it over to Giuseppe.

'This is what it looks like.'

Giuseppe took the packet and slowly turned it over just enough to see.

'What you have in your hand, Giuseppe D'Angelo, is the new type of gold, *white gold!*' Schiavo said and laughed quietly. 'There is enough there for maybe half a dozen hits, depending on how much a punter wants to use. Each one will send him to heaven. Then he will come back to you craving more!'

Giuseppe went to hand it back to Schiavo.

'No, no … you keep it! Give it to someone to try, and watch, they will soon be back to see you again. Of course, you can name your price. But let me advise you. Don't make it so high that they cannot afford it and will look for another source, but make sure it is high enough so you have a good profit!'

'Thank you,' Giuseppe said. 'So, do we have a deal?'

'Yes, with these terms.' Schiavo paused and stared at Giuseppe. 'I will introduce you to my contact, but you must give me a cut of your turf, plus fifty percent of your earnings.'

The men stared at each other again. Schiavo was waiting for Giuseppe to baulk and try to negotiate better terms for himself, but was surprised when the young man agreed straight away.

'Okay, Adami … this agreement we have will be lucrative for both of us. I will see to it personally that you get a significant increase in your profits,' Giuseppe said and held out his hand. 'You can trust me.'

And so the deal was done. Schiavo introduced D'Angelo to his distributor and was given a modest quantity of heroin to sell to see how he would go.

31

SIX MONTHS LATER, and Giuseppe's drug business became his main source of income. Sales were high and starting to skyrocket. He made contacts all over Carlton and Brunswick, but running the business from his father's warehouse in Carlton was becoming difficult. It was too far away from the real action, which was in the city, where he sold most of his product. He knew this would soon be a problem as he'd agreed with Schiavo not to sell there, and it wasn't long before Schiavo called him and left a voicemail demanding a meeting.

It was raining heavily when D'Angelo called him back.

'Adami, it's Giuseppe ... Giuseppe D'Angelo, returning your call.'

'I have been waiting for you to ring,' Schiavo snarled.

There was a long silence on the line as the rain outside continued to pelt down.

'Adami, you said we should meet.'

Schiavo ignored him and got straight to the point.

'You are selling in my turf!' Schiavo's voice turned to anger. 'You said you would not!'

Giuseppe could hear Schiavo breathing heavily.

'I know, but things have taken off better than I could have imagined. We are busier than ever. Profits are good!'

Schiavo waited a moment before he spoke. 'I want to meet with you and discuss this! I want a greater share of your area *and* your profits. You also need to get out of my neighbourhood!' he shouted.

'Yes, yes, I know, Adami. I'm sorry. I have been meaning to contact you,' D'Angelo lied, 'but I haven't had the time. We will sort this out, and everything will be fine.'

There was another long pause. Only the continual noise of the rain came through the phone.

Giuseppe continued. 'Do you have a place in mind where we can meet?'

'No. Somewhere … maybe somewhere here in the city.'

Giuseppe could hear there was doubt in Schiavo's voice. It gave him an idea; his mind started racing.

'Adami, there are too many cops in the city. If you like, we could do this over the phone?' D'Angelo prompted.

'No. Too much of a risk,' Schiavo replied.

D'Angelo knew Schiavo would never agree to a meeting on the phone and made his play.

'Look, Adami, why don't we meet here at my place in Carlton? My father's old warehouse?'

There was silence again.

'We can meet here and straighten this right out,' Giuseppe pressed. 'No one will bother us here. We can draw up the new areas to make sure we don't step on each other's toes and discuss the sharing of profits.'

Giuseppe could hear Schiavo breathing heavily again, thinking it over.

'All right,' he said. 'I'll get a cab. I'll be there in fifteen minutes.'

'Okay, Adami. It will be good to see you again.' D'Angelo hung up and immediately called Ben Lucizano.

Adami Schiavo arrived at the warehouse in the driving rain a little after 7:00pm. By 7:15pm, he was dead. Giuseppe's father would not have approved. There was far too much blood from the three bullets Lucizano had pumped into Schiavo's back. Both Giuseppe and Lucizano spent the best part of an hour mopping up the mess.

They wrapped the body in a large tarpaulin and loaded it into the boot of Lucizano's car.

The arrangement for disposal was always the same, and one which Giuseppe's father, Lorenzo, had put in place many years ago. Back then, during a casual conversation Lorenzo had with Evan Blackwood, one of his regular drinkers at the warehouse, Blackwood told him that the cemetery where he worked had fallen on hard times. He said the cemetery trust people could no longer afford to retain gravediggers and other general maintenance people. Lorenzo listened closely to what Blackwood had to say and recognised an opportunity, one that could perhaps serve him well. He told Blackwood he may be able to help. He said he would fund the cemetery's trust account provided he could supply the gravediggers. Blackwood put this to those who ran the cemetery and returned to D'Angelo's establishment the next night to tell Lorenzo they were happy to go ahead with his offer. Blackwood also added that there was accommodation for the gravediggers onsite and that they would be comfortable there.

And so now Lorenzo D'Angelo had a more permanent place where he could dispose of his problems. The market garden where his friend Bortoloni worked was one such location, but he didn't want to put too much pressure on him. This new arrangement would make it easy to dispose of any new problems that might come his way. Back then his sly grog business was growing fast, and he'd taken many customers from his competitors. His rivals were not happy, and confrontations with them were frequent. And now this old arrangement, which Lorenzo had successfully organised, would also benefit his son. It would serve him well also.

Giuseppe saw Lucizano the next day.

'So, Ben, did you deal with Schiavo?'

'Yes, Giuseppe. He is buried, but without much of a send-off,' Lucizano said and laughed. 'The ceremony was brief!'

Giuseppe smirked and ran his hands through the massive

number of plastic bags, all containing the white powder that would make him very wealthy.

'Ben, we need to get to work.'

Now with Schiavo's distribution chain in his hands, Giuseppe D'Angelo had control of the whole network, and the cash began rolling in. Within twelve months he had enough to build an empire, and his ideas were big. He bought a rundown building in King Street, the seedier part of Melbourne's CBD, and set up a casino. He met with an influential, but corrupt, official of the gaming licensing authority and paid him a significant amount to secure a licence to run the casino, together with a liquor licence that would allow him to serve alcohol into the early hours of the morning. A regular payment was made to this man to ensure the licences remained current and were easily renewable.

D'Angelo also decided to add a restaurant to the casino and organised for a kitchen to be built. He hired a five-star chef who brought with him his team of cooks. Dining tables were introduced, along with waiters and waitresses. Girls were also brought in for those patrons who wanted something extra. They worked the bar area and frequented the rooms on the second floor that had been specifically renovated to cater for those activities.

D'Angelo made a number of contacts from his heroin business. He also tried other sources of income such as cannabis and illegal tobacco. He tinkered with methamphetamine, or ice, as it's known on the streets, but found that the junkies who used it were unreliable. They commonly ended up dead or sitting in a jail cell or rehabilitation house for years on end. The income from that drug was what D'Angelo called lumpy, and for the time being, he has decided to stay clear of it.

D'Angelo did his research and found out cocaine was the drug of choice. He put feelers out and made a useful contact overseas. The man D'Angelo deals with has a direct link with a Columbian drug cartel where the product is high quality and readily available.

D'Angelo pays his supplier a premium to ensure the shipments, which arrive in coffins, are delivered regularly and on time.

He knows his father would be very proud of him. As he had predicted, Giuseppe has proven himself to be a very good businessman. Not only has he ensured that his main source of income is secure, but he has also made a deal with another man who runs the movement of shipping containers at the docks in Melbourne. He pays him well and, in turn, is contacted when a delivery of the white powder arrives. The gates to the wharves are always open when his truck arrives late at night, and he is provided with safe and easy access.

D'Angelo's product has become well-known for its purity. The cocaine is sought after by most of Melbourne, from nightclub-goers to professional footballers and other celebrities. Its reputation has risen to the point where D'Angelo has been able to expand his borders from the CBD, Carlton, and Brunswick and has started to sell in places like Preston, Coburg, and Pascoe Vale. He has taken customers from another well-established Italian family who normally sell their product there. It's a push into a competitor's territory that is being vigorously defended by them and can bring nothing but trouble.

PART FIVE

THE CEMETERY

old ground … new rules …

32

IT WAS CLOSE to midnight, and Roy Eastern stood in the park just across the road from the Melbourne General Cemetery. He'd taken a call during the night from Gallagher saying a delivery was on its way. It was unusual getting such short notice and strange to be meeting here at the cemetery. Talbot always handed over the paperwork in the pub.

A freezing wind knifed its way through the dark trees lining the street and chilled him to the bone. He held his hands up to his face, blew on his fingers, and wished he'd thought to wear gloves. He was bone dry; it had been hours since he'd had a drink, and his body was craving alcohol. He peered down the long shadowy road bordering the cemetery and waited impatiently for Talbot's black Lexus to appear. He shook his fingers, then stuffed his hands in his pockets. After what seemed like an eternity, car headlights appeared, and a solitary dark vehicle made its way in his direction.

About time too. He's half an hour late – Talbot's never late!

Danny sat in the back of the limousine with Lucizano next to him. The interior was luxurious, and the smell of the expensive leather seats permeated the cabin. The ride was so smooth he could hardly tell he was moving at all as the car sped through the dark streets. He closed his eyes for a moment and wondered where he was going to end up.

'Strickland,' Lucizano said. 'You know what needs to be done. It has to be done quickly!'

Danny opened his eyes and glanced across at Lucizano. He nodded but didn't speak. He stared out at the black night and questioned if this, *the killing*, would ever end. It was like he'd chosen a path years ago that had nothing but killing as its goal. Thoughts flooded his brain. It all seemed to stem from Brennan and the stabbing of the bully.

Maybe, back then, he should have let himself be humiliated and beaten up – *again*.

Maybe he should have walked away – *again*.

Maybe he should have run back to his mother and let her tend to his wounds – *again*.

But he hadn't. He'd stood up for himself. He decided he wasn't going to be pushed around anymore. The only trouble with that stand was the bully ended up dead at his feet with a knife in his heart. As far as he could tell, the mould had been set from there.

And so, the killings had continued. There was the time in the gang when he'd disposed of Whelan to prove himself worthy of Ainsworth and Assad, then the victims from his vocation as a professional hitman and, finally, the hit on Draken and his subsequent betrayal by Gagliano. And after all that, where had it got him?

It got you here! Sittin' in the backseat of a limousine with a mafia strongman who will, no doubt, make sure that you do the killing – again!

Danny shook his head as the thoughts turned over and over in his mind. And still the killing wasn't going to stop. Somewhere out there, in the dark, was someone who didn't suspect his time was up, didn't know this would be his last day on Earth, had no idea he would be on the wrong end of a bullet, and it would be him, Danny Wainwright, or Strickland, as he was now known, that would be the one pulling the trigger – *again!*

Look, it's no good worrying about it – there's no turning back now!

Maybe there is! I tried with Whelan, but perhaps I can save this one – start to set things right!

How? It's too late for that! You fail this job, and Lucizano will kill you!

Lucizano raised his voice when Danny didn't answer him.

'I said … this job is to be done quickly, Strickland. *No fuck-ups!*'

Danny stared at the Italian in the expensive business suit and wondered if he ever had to do anything like what he was expected to do.

'Yeah, okay … just make sure *you* stay well out of the way!'

The comment stung Lucizano.

'You don't tell me what to do, Strickland! You are just a piece of shit that we use to fix problems for us!' Lucizano started to breathe heavily. He fidgeted in the seat, put his hand inside his jacket, and took out a pistol. 'People like you come and go. When you're no longer useful to us, *then* you'll find out who does the killing!'

Danny slowly ran his hand into his pocket and held the Colt Mustang. He quietly flicked the safety off.

Lucizano glared at Danny.

'You just do what we want, Strickland. You run errands when we want you to run errands. You kill when we want you to kill.'

Danny gently fingered the gun. 'Who's the target?'

Luciano hesitated, considering if he should tell him. 'Eastern … Roy Eastern.'

'What did he do?'

'None of your business!' Lucizano snapped and laid the pistol on his lap.

Danny watched as Lucizano flicked the safety off.

'Just do the job!'

Danny turned and peered out of the window at the pitch-black night. 'Where's it to be done?'

'You'll see soon enough,' Lucizano said and motioned ahead at the dark road.

Danny followed Lucizano's gaze and could see they were pulling up outside a cemetery.

By now, Eastern had a better view. He could see it was not a Lexus; it was a limousine coming towards him. This wasn't Talbot; it was D'Angelo's right-hand man, Bennetti Lucizano. He started to feel uneasy. He was always on edge when Lucizano came to the cemetery. A visit from a high-ranking member of one of Melbourne's mafia families was enough to make anyone nervous. He reached inside his jacket and stroked the pistol he always carried with him.

So, where's the hearse? Lucizano only turns up when there's a coffin full of cocaine to cut! What's going on?

The limo pulled up to the side of the road opposite the cemetery gates. Eastern stayed partially hidden as two men climbed out. Sure enough, the first one was Lucizano, but he didn't recognise the other one. Lucizano stopped on the footpath while the second man walked past him.

The wind howled high up in the trees. Black rain clouds scudded across a pale-yellow moon. The night seemed to get deeper and darker. Eastern gripped the handgun a little tighter and pulled his jacket around himself as he watched the man approach.

'G'day,' he said.

Danny walked up to him without responding. 'Run,' he whispered.

'What?' Eastern said, confused by what this man had said to him.

Danny peered over his shoulder at Lucizano, then back to Eastern. He whispered again, 'For God's sake … *run!*'

But Eastern stayed rock-still. His heart started beating double time. He glanced down at Danny's hand and saw a dull light bouncing off the barrel of a handgun. He panicked, pulled the gun out of his jacket, and fired. The bullet sizzled past Danny's shoulder.

The carnival music started pumping hard in Danny's head. The Wipeout spun crazily. Girls screamed. The cars on the Big Dipper rushed downwards, surely sending everyone to their doom. The Ghost Train ghouls shrieked louder than ever.

Danny returned fire. Eastern lurched back crazily like a puppet that had lost its strings as three bullets struck home. He crumpled to the ground and lay motionless on the wet grass. Danny walked over to the body. Eastern groaned for a moment, then became silent.

'Finish him off, Strickland!' Lucizano yelled and pointed his gun in Eastern's direction.

But Danny didn't move. His mind was racing.

Why the hell didn't you run?

'I said, *finish him off!*' Lucizano yelled.

'No need … *he's done!*' Danny spat the words out and sneered at Lucizano.

'Bullshit!' Lucizano said.

Lucizano strode over to Eastern and shot him twice in the head, then turned on Danny, taking deep breaths.

'Eastern fired a shot, Strickland! How did that happen?'

Danny hesitated. 'I guess he was wary. Maybe he knew something was wrong!'

'How?'

'Probably didn't trust someone. Someone like *you!*'

Lucizano bristled at the comment.

'You fucked up, Strickland. He could have shot either one of us!'

'He's dead, isn't he?' Danny said and picked up the spent cartridges. 'He was dead before you shot him!'

Lucizano started breathing heavily again.

'You spoke to him … what did you say?'

Danny didn't answer at first. He made sure Lucizano had already pocketed his pistol.

'I said … *goodnight, sweetheart!*'

The wind roared through the dark trees. Lucizano's eyes narrowed.

'You're a smartarse, Strickland! Don't fuck with *me*!'

He gave Danny a further look of contempt, then walked over to the limousine and grabbed a large calico blanket and threw it to him.

'Wrap him up!'

Danny pocketed the gun. The carnival music began to recede; the rides began to slow, and eventually, everything faded into the background. Danny spread the blanket out and struggled to roll Eastern's body onto it.

'Come on!' Lucizano said, exasperated, as he watched Danny wrestling with the body. Then he said, 'Wait here!'

Lucizano strode across the road to the main cemetery entrance, where a tall black man was standing. He pointed towards Danny and snarled aggressively, 'Get over there! Give him a hand! Get him in here quick!'

The man ran across the road and helped Danny lift Eastern. They lowered the body into the middle of the blanket and lugged it back into the entrance to the cemetery. As they passed through the gates, Lucizano walked over to them.

'Strickland, that's your new accommodation,' he said and pointed to a small building bordering the side of the cemetery. In the distance Danny could also see a church and what looked like some reception rooms. 'You'll be rooming there with your new partner,' Lucizano added and pointed at the black man.

He walked back to the limousine, got in, and rolled down the back window. He didn't speak but eyeballed Danny one last time before ordering the driver to go, and the limo slipped away into the night.

The black man said, 'I'll lock the gates. Then we better get him into the accommodation unit. We can get something in there to soak up the blood.'

Once the gates were locked, they grabbed opposite ends of the blanket and started to heave Eastern's body along a winding brick path towards a small building in the cemetery.

'By the way, my name is Chips.'

'I'm Danny,' Danny grunted as he struggled with the weight. 'Danny ... Strickland.'

'That's where we stay.' Chips motioned with his head. 'It's got two separate bedrooms.' Chips stared down at the body in the blanket and sighed. 'It's not that bad here. Real quiet. Well, most of the time!' He gave a half-hearted chuckle and gazed down at Eastern's body with a sad look. 'But, you know, it's comfortable. You'll get used to it.'

At the unit, Chips pushed open the door. They dragged the blanket with Eastern's body on it through the doorway and laid it out on the floor in the small kitchen area. Eastern's mutilated head lolled out and blood began to pool on the cold tiles. Chips quickly closed the door, then found a large plastic bag and put it under Eastern's bloodied skull. He grabbed a scrubbing brush and filled a bucket with water.

'I'll give you a hand,' Danny said. He took the brush and began scrubbing at the fresh blood.

'Your room's there ... it *was* his!' Chips said a little distantly and pointed towards a closed door. 'Give me the brush. I'll finish this off. You go bring his stuff out; we'll bury the lot with him tomorrow morning ... real early! Make sure you get all of it!'

33

DANNY WALKED INTO the bedroom and retrieved Eastern's effects. The room was sparse. There was a bed, a cheap wooden chest of drawers with a mirror on a stand, a small table with a chair, and hanging space for a coat or two. A door separated the bedroom from the shower and small vanity cabinet. Danny went through the drawers and grabbed Eastern's clothes and bundled them up. He grabbed a thin waterproof jacket and a photo in a frame off the table. In it was a picture of a young girl standing in what looked like a backyard and smiling awkwardly at the camera. He went into the shower area and collected a toothbrush and a couple of other toiletries. He checked around, but there was nothing else. He walked back into the kitchen and laid Eastern's belongings out on the table.

'Thanks,' Chips said as he grabbed it all and stuffed it in a hessian bag. He tied the ends and said, 'Help me wrap him up.'

Danny held either side of the calico blanket while Chips drew a couple of long pieces of thin rope around it. He folded the blanket over Eastern's body and, lastly, over his bloodied face, then tied the rope tight.

'Good enough,' Chips said to himself. 'Take a seat, Danny. I'll make us some coffee.'

Danny sat at the small table in the middle of the tiny kitchen. He scanned the rest of the unit. It was basic with plain kitchen cupboards and benches. There was a small oven with a stovetop and a kettle. The clock on the wall was the major feature, but its stark white face with gold numerals and spiked black hands did little to cheer the place up. Two windows looked out on different aspects of the cemetery.

Chips brought over two cups of steaming coffee.

'So that's Roy Eastern?' Danny asked as he took a sip of coffee and pointed down to where the body was neatly wrapped.

'Yep,' Chips said. 'How'd you know his name?'

'The other guy in the limo, Lucizano, he told me he was the target.'

Chips became pensive. 'Lucizano … he's a dangerous man, Danny. You be real careful when he's around.' Chips fiddled with his coffee cup and, after a moment, said, 'You sure know how to use a handgun!'

Danny smiled. 'Uh-huh. I've done it more than once.'

Somewhere in the back of his mind, the carnival music started to jingle-jangle.

'So how come Roy was marked for a hit?' Danny asked.

Chips sighed and took a mouthful of coffee.

'Roy was dumb! Smart at first, but finished up dumb … real dumb! He took stuff that wasn't his and made the mistake of double-crossing the wrong man.'

Danny hesitated a moment. 'Who?' he asked.

Chips stared outside before he answered.

'Man called Gallagher,' Chips said. 'He runs the docks down on the waterfront.'

Danny was surprised. 'I know him … that's where I come from!'

'What?' said Chips.

'Yeah, I worked for him for a while.'

Chips put his coffee cup down. 'Did some detectives get you a job there?'

'No,' Danny said.

Chips shook his head. 'Oh, well … small world, hey, Danny? I used to work for Gallagher too.'

'Wow!' Danny said. 'Did Roy work for him also?'

'Don't know. Roy was already here when I arrived. He said he did all sorts of jobs for Mr D'Angelo. Roy, he showed me around, told me what needed to be done, but I don't know where he come from. He never did say.'

Danny took a sip, then asked, 'You been here long, Chips?'

'Well, not that long. Only about six months, or thereabouts. But I tell you what, Danny. It's long enough to know to shut my mouth and just do as I'm told!'

Danny nodded. 'So how'd you get a job with Gallagher?'

Chips stared at Danny. 'Two detectives got me the job. I was there for a while until I was sent here to work for Mr D'Angelo.'

There was a long silence before Chips spoke again.

'You see, Danny, I did time here in Melbourne … coupla years!'

Chips let out a long sigh and drank more coffee. He gazed out the window and then back at Danny. 'How come you ended up with Gallagher?'

For a moment, Danny thought about keeping his past a secret, but decided against it.

'I'll come clean with ya, Chips. I'm what you might call escaped and at large … you know, on the run!'

Chip's eyes widened as he looked at Danny. 'Oh! Which jail?'

'Not a jail, a prison van in New South Wales.'

'Wow!' Chips said as he picked up his coffee cup and took a long sip. 'How'd you get down here?'

'Train.'

Chips shook his head slightly, and his eyes narrowed. 'So how'd you get a job with Gallagher?'

'I just walked in and asked him!'

Chips was dumbfounded for a moment.

'What about the cops? They never followed you?'

'Don't think so … well, not those from New South Wales anyway!'

'Oh well, I guess it don't matter much,' Chips said. 'You're here now. I don't expect Gallagher or Mr D'Angelo gonna tell the cops 'bout you. You're pretty safe here, Danny!'

For a short time the room fell into silence as both men drank their coffee.

Danny finally spoke. 'So, what did Roy actually do to get on the wrong side of Gallagher?'

Chips took a deep breath before he answered. 'Roy started sellin'!'

'Sellin'?' Danny asked.

'Uh-huh,' Chips said and stared at Danny. 'Cocaine, Danny!' Chips said forcefully. 'Gallagher's cocaine or, more correctly, Mr D'Angelo's cocaine!'

Danny looked at Chips quizzically. Chips continued.

'Roy, he was out there at night sellin' it. He wasn't s'posed to be outside at all, but he was! You see, the only time he was meant to be out of the unit here at night was when he was doin' a 'livery. He'd get the paperwork from Talbot and deliver it to Mr D'Ange-lo's warehouse when a load of them coffins turned up. Then he was s'posed to come straight back here. But sometimes he didn't. Sometimes he stayed out there makin' a little extra on the side.'

Chips eyed Danny, who stared out the window at the cold, black night. Danny remembered the meeting with Gallagher when he was told of his move to the cemetery. He recalled Talbot and Gallagher discussing something, but they never explained what it was.

Danny was snapped back to attention when Chips said, 'Gallagher is a dangerous man. Don't ever cross him!'

Danny nodded but was distracted.

'You got me fascinated, Chips. What do ya mean when you say D'Angelo's cocaine?'

Chips sighed and sipped the coffee.

'Well, it's a long story, but I guess you got time to hear it,' Chips said and grinned. 'You see, them coffins that Mr D'Angelo gets, well, some of them ain't empty. They got cocaine in 'em. They're from Colombia. Every so often, Mr D'Angelo would get me and Roy to cut the cocaine.'

Danny was about to ask Chips about cutting the cocaine, but Chips held his hand up.

'Don't worry, Danny. I'll explain that a bit later. Anyhow, to make a long story short, Gallagher, or more correctly, Talbot, would give Roy a container of baby powder and get him to use it when we did the cut.'

Chips drank more coffee.

'It works like this. Roy would tip the baby powder out and fill the empty container with pure cocaine. To make sure Mr D'Angelo had the same quantity of the white powder that he started off with, Roy would replace the cocaine he stole with the baby powder. Get it?' Chips said, and a knowing look crossed his face.

Danny nodded, mostly grasping what Chips was saying to him but desperate to ask more questions. Chips continued.

'Then, when there was the next 'livery of D'Angelo's coffins, Roy was s'pose to hand over the container full of cocaine to Talbot, who'd give him an envelope with cash in it. Pretty sure that coke ended up with Gallagher. Anyways, this went on for a coupla months or more, and then Roy told me he could make more money if he sold the cocaine himself, so that's what he started doin'. Trouble was, he was still taking the cash off Gallagher.'

Chips smiled and played with his coffee mug.

'Reckon Gallagher was mightily pissed off when he found out what Roy was doin'! Word got back to Mr D'Angelo somehow that Roy was sellin', and … that was the end of Roy.'

Chips fell silent for a moment while he took a mouthful of coffee. The only sound was the clock ticking away in the background.

'Lucizano, he gives me the third degree!' Chips said. 'Wanted to know if I was sellin'. I said no! Then he wanted to know if Roy was leavin' here when he shouldna been. So, you know, Danny, I wanted to stay livin', so I told him Roy was leavin' late at night, a lot, and probably had a coke dealer on the side. I didn't want to tell him Roy was stealin' Mr D'Angelo's cocaine. Thank God Lucizano believed that much of it. Saved myself but … you know … helped get Roy killed.'

Danny sat quietly, lost in his own thoughts, wondering what he'd got himself involved in. Chips continued.

'Roy told me once he thought he saw someone watchin' the cemetery. Mr D'Angelo, he got lots of people who work for him; probably it was one of them that saw Roy. I tried to tell him to slow up a bit, to play it cool, but it didn't stop Roy. When he got the drink into him, which was often, he wasn't gonna take no notice of me. He said he was makin' money, a stack of it. So he just kept on goin'. I think Mr D'Angelo trusted Roy to begin with, but when he found out what Roy was doin', well, you know the rest. Mr D'Angelo just needed someone to pull the trigger, and guess who that was, Danny?' Chips made a gun out of his fingers, pointed them at Danny, and mouthed the word – 'bang'.

His voice faded away for a moment as he took another sip of coffee.

'It must have been oppo'tune for Mr D'Angelo that you arrived when you did. You, the shooter Danny! You see, nothin' ever gonna be traced back to him, not the body, nothin'. If anyone gets done for the killing of Roy, it's gonna be you! I reckon they gonna be usin' your talents in the future! Long as you got that gun, you're gonna be useful to Mr D'Angelo.'

Danny fingered the Colt in his pocket, and the carnival music stopped, but Chips hadn't finished.

'Did that rat Lucizano get involved in killing Roy?'

'Yeah … well, sort of,' Danny said. 'He put the last two bullets in Roy's head, but he was already dead by then.'

'Oh!' Chips said, surprised. 'So did you …?'

Danny took a deep breath. 'Yeah … I did it. It was a matter

of survival,' Danny half whispered. 'I tried to get him to run,' he muttered, 'but he didn't.'

Chips nodded knowingly.

'They usin' you, Danny. You need to be careful, *real* careful!'

Danny nodded as Gallagher's words came floating back to him. He stood up and stared out of one of the windows. In the pale moonlight, he could see row upon row of tall headstones. Some were topped off with angels crying or pointing towards the dark heavens while others simply showed the cross of Christ. Smaller ones, for children, were fenced off with low metal barriers. In the distance, Danny could see graves that had caved in, their headstones perched precariously over the sunken ground. Perhaps these ones, Danny mused, realised they were never going to rise and were slowly giving themselves up to a destiny that lay for them deep down below.

Is one of those for you?

Danny turned to Chips.

'Did Gallagher treat you well, Chips?'

'Yeah! Well, you know, he says he gives us ex-cons a second chance, but we gotta do what he says. If you don't, then people just disappear. When I was there, only first couple o' months, two men just vanished. No explanation. One, I think, tried to leave, and the other one took some of Gallagher's money he had hid. Word was they both ended up weighed down in that cold watery bay. Gallagher saw me next morning and said I had a new job cleaning out them shipping containers. I asked where the other two were and he said best I don't ask no questions. So, you know, I just kept my mouth shut.' Chips took another sip. 'I also did things like helpin' to pack trucks at night! You do that too?'

'Yeah,' Danny said and nodded.

Chips paused before he spoke again.

'I found out where them coffins and car tyres were goin', but I kept quiet 'bout that; you blab too much, you end up in trouble. Then one day, Gallagher told me I was meeting a Mr D'Angelo. Apparently, he needed someone to work here in the cemetery. Anyway, for me that was okay. Got better pay and better housing!'

'So you said yes?'

'Yeah, don't think I had much choice really. You don't say *no* to Mr D'Angelo. Anyways, pretty hard for a black man with a crim'nal record to get work 'round here. I was happy to have a job! I just do what they want, you know, dig graves, cut the product, and bury coffins. No idea who's in them coffins when they arrive, and I don't care neither!'

Danny contemplated what Chips had told him and then asked, 'So D'Angelo's product … it's pure?'

'Uh-huh,' Chips said and smiled. 'Well … starts off that way!' He laughed.

'How does the cocaine get here?'

Chips reached out across the table and held up a mobile phone.

'Lucizano calls and tells me when to be ready; it's always in the dead of night. The product comes in a coffin, in the back of a hearse. All that coke is packed in big plastic bags. Lucizano follows the hearse here. He doesn't let it out of his sight!' He took another sip and eyeballed Danny.

'Roy took calls from Gallagher when there was a 'livery to do, but not me. Don't think they trust black guys leavin' the cemetery at night to do a 'livery. I reckon they think I might go on the run!'

A large smile crossed Chips' face before he went on.

'Only time I do get out is during the daytime, once a week, to get supplies.' Chips pursed his lips and blew out a sharp puff of air. 'Gallagher give you a phone?' he asked.

'Yeah.' Danny took the mobile out of his pocket, a bit embarrassed.

'You white. They trust you!'

Chips didn't look happy, so Danny changed the topic.

'So, Chips, what's the deal with the cut? How do you do it?'

Chips stared out one of the windows.

'Well, Danny,' he said and laughed. 'It's easy. You just take the big bags and make 'em into little ones!'

'That's it?'

'No, just kiddin'. We have to cut it with other stuff Lucizano gives us to make it go further. As long as it's a white powder, I guess Mr D'Angelo don't care much what it is. Takes a few hours to do. Then it all goes back in the coffin. Lucizano picks it up next night, at 11:00pm sharp. We just gotta make sure it's ready. You don't wanna be runnin' behind schedule, Danny. Lucizano and his men done beat me and Roy one time, and we only 'bout ten minutes late!'

'You ever keep some for yourself?'

Chips slowly shook his head and didn't answer straight away. A sly expression crossed his face.

'Danny, you keep any of that stuff, and you'll end up dead, just like Roy. It'll kill you, whichever way you go. You steal it; you'll end up dead! You snort it up your nose; you'll end up dead that way too!'

Chips laughed out loud again, but that sly look never left his face.

34

NEXT MORNING CHIPS knocked on the door of Danny's room at 6:00am.

'Yeah!'

'Come on, Danny. We got burials to do today.'

'Okay, give me a minute!'

Danny was exhausted from the night before. He hadn't slept well; a hit always took it out of him, and the dreams he had were vivid. He dressed and greeted Chips, who retied the bag of Eastern's belongings and placed it next to his corpse.

'We don't have no coffin, Danny. We just have to put him on this trolley and get as far as we can … then we carry him!'

'Okay,' Danny said.

He helped Chips lift Eastern's body and belongings onto the trolley. 'Where we takin' him?' Danny grunted.

'Already dug a double plot. They buryin' Esme Fitzgerald this afternoon. Hope she likes comp'ny!' Chips said and laughed.

Danny opened the door, and Chips manoeuvred the trolley outside. 'How do you know when to dig a hole?'

'A *plot*, Danny. It's called a *plot!*' Chips said and frowned at Danny. 'I'll show you the burial roster later on. It's in the office of the chapel; the mausoleum placements are there too.'

A frozen wind sliced its way across the cemetery and howled in the tops of giant trees. Chips pushed the trolley along a brickwork path lined with beautiful shrubs and flowers. Soon they came to a narrow road that wound its way around row after row of head-stones. Danny walked behind him carrying two shovels. He gazed around, amazed at how big the cemetery was and how many graves were jam-packed in.

'Chips, this place is enormous. How the hell do you know which way to go?'

'You'll get used to it, Danny,' Chips said and laughed. 'It gets easy after a couple of months.'

Eventually, they arrived at a bend in the road.

'Okay, Danny. We have to carry him the rest of the way.'

They heaved Eastern's body off the trolley and lugged it over to a pile of freshly turned earth.

'Get his belongings, Danny.'

Danny grabbed the hessian sack containing Eastern's belongings and placed it next to the body. Chips took it, leant over the grave, and dropped it in. He glanced down and, satisfied with the result, gave Danny the thumbs-up.

'Righto, Danny. Give me a hand.'

Chips and Danny grabbed either end of the calico blanket and lifted it up. Eastern's body sagged towards the middle.

'On three, we let it go, okay?'

'Okay,' Danny said, straining under the weight.

They swung the body back and forth, and Chips counted it out. On three, they dropped it into the grave. Eastern's body landed with a dull thump. The blanket burst open, and his arms flayed out. One landed across his bloodied chest, and the other went up to his head as though feeling for the two large red holes in the side of his skull. Chips peered in.

'Good and flat … he won't take up too much room. Plenty of space for Miss Esme!' he said and chuckled. 'Okay, Danny … start shovellin.'

Both men dug into the loose dirt on the side of the grave. Chips peered over the edge and checked it again.

'That's enough. He's well covered!'

Danny leant on the shovel and sucked in the cold morning air.

'Hey, Chips. How'd you know there were two people gotta be buried in that hol ... ahh, plot?'

'Always dig 'em double deep, Danny. You never know when Lucizano gonna turn up with another body! Sometimes, they in a coffin. Sometimes, they not!'

On the way back to the unit, Chips showed Danny the chapel. He unlocked the doors and entered. Danny followed him into what was a small but beautiful church. A number of highly polished wooden pews stood on either side of a central aisle with a golden pulpit at its end. The ceiling rose in an impressive vaulted shape. Numerous brightly coloured stained-glass windows showed the life and times of Jesus, with the large central window showing Him dying on the cross.

'Pretty impressive, hey?' Chips said, proud of the display.

Danny didn't answer. He just stood in one spot and took in the incredible scene in front of him. He'd never been in a church before. He thought this place was magnificent. His mind wandered.

In a place like this, you could believe everything that was written in the Bible.

At home, in some of the books his mother brought him from the library, he'd read stories about Jesus being persecuted and dying on the cross. The book had pictures of Him being beaten and close to death. But the pictures were nothing compared to the stained-glass windows that towered overhead. The light from outside shone through the glass panes and filtered down into the body of the church, bringing it to life.

Is Jesus around now? Does He know of this place?

Danny was lost in his own thoughts. He reflected on the irony of it all. Of him, Danny Wainwright, being here in a cemetery, standing in the middle of a church, surrounded by thousands of dead people. He wondered if he'd dealt with any of the poor souls that were lying here. Was he the reason this was their final resting place? And just how long would it be before he joined them? What would be the circumstances that caused him to meet them once again? He slowly shook his head, and his mind wandered back to his younger days. He remembered asking his mother if she believed in the stories in the Bible.

'Mum, do you believe in Jesus?'

'Maybe,' she said. 'It's a difficult question, Danny. It's a faith, something you either believe in or you don't.'

Danny looked at her, perplexed. 'So, Mum, do you believe in it?'

Her tired face seemed to get heavier. The lines around her eyes became darker as though the question was an extra burden she didn't need to carry.

'I don't know, Danny. I just … I haven't got the time to ponder … I … I just don't know.'

Danny stood in the chapel contemplating his sins. Would his also be forgiven if he believed in Jesus, or was there some sort of sliding scale? Were some sins simply too big to ever be forgiven?

He snapped back to reality when Chips called him over to a large noticeboard.

'Okay, Danny, here is the roster, the burials for the next few days. Cemetery trust people post the weekly roster on a Monday and update it every morning. We gotta check this daily. See here, Esme Fitzgerald gonna be buried at 2:00pm today. We gotta be there, Danny. We're the official gravediggers for the cemetery.'

Chips walked up to the pulpit and into a small room that ran off to the side. 'This is where they keep the keys.'

He opened a cabinet on the wall, and there were a number of keys inside, each suitably labelled.

'There's one here for each gate in the cemetery.'

* * *

Later that afternoon, a church bell tolled mournfully. Both Danny and Chips stood well in the background as Esme Fitzgerald was laid to rest. They removed their caps and bowed their heads while the priest led the burial service.

'*... and so, we are gathered here today to say farewell to Esme Fitzgerald, who has gone to the hands of God ... from dust we came, and to dust we shall return ...*'

The priest finished the eulogy, then glanced over to the funeral parlour officials who activated the lowering device. Slowly, the coffin began to disappear from view. A few of the women attendees began to quietly sob. The priest waited a respectful minute, then grabbed a handful of dirt and threw it into the grave. There was a crackling sound as small bits of fresh earth hit the top of the highly polished wood. The mourners followed suit, each one throwing in a tiny flower. Danny and Chips waited until they had all left, then stepped forward and started to shovel.

'So, Chips,' Danny said, panting between shovel loads. 'How come D'Angelo don't just get the bodies cremated?'

'No crematorium in this cemetery, Danny,' Chips grunted. 'Closest one is miles away.'

'Oh,' Danny said and went on shovelling. 'So, what did you call them, the cemetery trust people, are they happy to have us as grave-diggers?'

Chips looked up from the pile of dirt and wiped the sweat from his forehead onto his shirt sleeve.

'Mr D'Angelo donates generously to the trust; they believe he must be a very religious man. But he told 'em he wants to pick the gravediggers. Word has it that he showed 'em each a picture of their family and said he hoped nothin' bad would ever happen to 'em. I think that sort of helped 'em make up their minds!' Chips said and chuckled a little, then continued shovelling.

35

TWO MONTHS LATER Danny took a phone call from Gallagher late in the afternoon.

'Strickland.'

'Yeah,' Danny replied.

'Gallagher. There's a delivery to do tonight. Biondi's car tyres have turned up. I want you to meet Frank and Grist at the George. Be there a bit before 8:45pm. They'll tell you where to deliver the paperwork.'

'Okay.'

Danny was wary. The Biondi delivery would be new.

'By the way, have you done a cut for D'Angelo yet?'

'No,' Danny said as a worried expression crossed his face.

'Good. As well as the papers, Frank will also give you two small containers. I want you to use them.'

'What are they for?'

'Don't worry. Frank will tell you what to do.'

There was silence on the line. Danny swallowed hard.

'You still there, Strickland?'

'Yeah.'

'Make sure you're at the George tonight … don't be late!'

The line went dead. Danny was anxious. So far, he'd only done the D'Angelo deliveries to the warehouse in Carlton. This would be the first delivery for Biondi, and he didn't know where it would take him. As it turned out, it would be bad timing as Chips had also taken a call – from Lucizano.

* * *

Danny closed the main gates to the cemetery at 6:00pm sharp, finished tending to some of the older graves in the rose garden, and then called it a day. Chips looked like being in late, so Danny had a quick shower, dressed in some fresh clothes, and made two coffees. He sat at the small kitchen table and waited. It was 6:20pm when Chips finally rolled in and had a quick shower. Ten minutes later he came out of his bedroom towelling his hair dry. He sat down and picked up the coffee mug.

'Thanks, Danny,' he said and took a sip of the lukewarm beverage. 'Big day, hey!' Danny didn't answer. Chips could see he was on edge. 'You okay, Danny?'

'Yeah,' Danny said and shifted uneasily in his chair.

'You got somethin' on?'

'Yeah, there's a delivery to do tonight.'

'That a problem?' Chips asked.

'Not sure. It's a delivery for Biondi. I've only ever done the D'Angelo deliveries. I dunno where the Biondi one goes.'

Danny frowned and sipped at the coffee.

'Oh,' Chips said and put his coffee mug down. 'Not good!'

'Why?'

'Lucizano called me today and said we gotta meet him at the main gate at eleven tonight. He's gonna deliver one of Mr D'Angelo's special coffins.'

Chips looked at Danny with a worried expression. 'What time you leavin', Danny?'

'Leavin' here about eight,' Danny said.

'You goin' to the George?'

'Yeah, Chips. Funny doin' it at a pub, but I guess it's out of the way, and, you know, still not too far from here. Maybe they think there's no pryin' eyes there,' Danny said and shrugged.

Danny took a sip of his coffee. 'You been there?' he asked.

'No, Danny,' Chips replied. 'They don't let me out of here to go to no upmarket hotel.'

'Ain't upmarket, Chips. Far from it!' Danny blew out his cheeks and shook his head. 'Fancy name, but that's about it!'

The conversation stopped briefly as the two men drank their coffee. Danny sighed and stood up. His mind wandered as he thought about the series of events that had led to him being here in a cemetery. It was as though he had no control over his life. Things just happened, and he was simply dragged along by some irresistible force that landed him at the next place. He slowly shook his head and stared out a window at the row upon row of concrete headstones marking thousands of graves and wrung his hands. Two hundred years and more of the dearly departed lay in the ground. At times it was a bit quiet and eerie, but at least he felt safe and secure here. It was a sanctuary from both the cops and the bikies. He figured no one would ever think of checking a cemetery for someone on the run. It was when he left the cemetery that he was uneasy – out there, it wasn't safe!

Chips broke the silence.

'Biondi, hey! Danny, you could get in big trouble one day. If D'Angelo finds out what you're doin', I'll be burying you in one of those graves!' Chips sniggered and pointed outside.

'Yeah, I know!' Danny said. 'I guess I gotta trust Gallagher; just hope he doesn't get D'Angelo's delivery mixed up with Biondi's and vice versa.'

The thought of what lay ahead that night caused the adrenaline to kick in. Danny clenched his fists to try to stop the tingling sensation in his fingertips.

'At least I'm makin' some money here. Each time I do a delivery, Gallagher slings me some cash.'

'That's good, Danny. A bit of icin' on the cake for what D'Angelo pays us,' Chips said casually. 'Maybe you might end up rich if you do enough 'liveries,' he added and laughed.

'Huh,' Danny grunted. 'I really just wanna go back home one day, you know, go and check things out.'

Chips frowned. 'No good you goin' home, Danny. Ain't nothin' for you but jail time back home. You much better stayin' here.'

Danny stared down at the floor.

'I know, but I wanna see if I can find my mother. See if she's okay … see if she's still alive!'

Chips shook his head.

'You a crim'nal on the run, Danny. Cops catch you, they won't let you see your mother. You just be lookin' at four walls and waiting for the one hour a day they let you out to see the sunshine!'

Chips took a long sip of coffee and stared hard at Danny.

'We gotta be at that front gate by eleven tonight. You can't be late! You better make sure those 'livery times don't cross over. If we're late for Lucizano, it won't be good. In fact, it'll be real bad! Lucizano don't wait for nobody!'

'Yeah, okay. I don't s'pose you can take the delivery solo this time, can ya, Chips?'

'No way!' Chips said in a stern voice. 'Lucizano wants to know we both here in the cemetery when he's delivering the product. When that coffin gets dropped off, he wants to see me, *and you*, at the gate. If only one of us is around, he'll want to know where the other one is and what they're up to! He don't trust no one, 'specially, I reckon, since Roy done stuffed things up!'

Chips went quiet for a moment, then said, 'Lucizano does the same thing every time, so be ready, Danny. Once we finish the cut and get the coffin back to the front gate, he'll frisk us. Then his men will check the unit to see if we kept any of D'Angelo's product. It's dangerous, Danny, so when he says *we* take the delivery, he means both of us!'

Chips stared at Danny long and hard, then said in a softer voice, 'I like my job here, Danny. I don't want nuthin' to go wrong! But Lucizano … I don't trust him! If we ain't ready …!'

'Yeah, okay, Chips, okay. I understand!' Danny said, a bit exasperated.

Chips grabbed the remote control and flicked on the TV, then added, 'Danny, you be careful. You be *real* careful … *and … don't be late!*'

Danny tipped the rest of his coffee down the kitchen sink and rinsed the mug under the cold-water tap.

'See ya, Chips.'

But Chips, now glued to the TV, just waved his hand in the air and didn't respond.

36

DANNY GRABBED HIS jacket off the coatrack, opened the door to the unit, stepped outside, and gently closed it behind him. He walked down through the cemetery grounds to the east gate and left using the key he'd taken from the chapel. Out on Lygon Street he zipped up his jacket and hunched down against the scudding rain. He checked to see if anyone was around, but the street was empty.

Not surprising in this weather!

He strode out on the wet footpath and within ten minutes arrived at the George. He pushed open the door, and the pub's warm atmosphere immediately wrapped its arms around him. His preferred seat at the end of the bar was free. He walked over and sat down.

It was Thursday night. There were maybe a dozen people in the pub. Half a dozen suits were gathered in a tight circle, clutching their drinks and talking at the tops of their voices. Clearly, the end of a very long workday. Two younger men were playing pool. The others were loners sitting silently at the bar by themselves, leaning on their elbows and occasionally pushing their faces into a pot of their favourite brew.

Dave Crease, 'Creasey' to everybody, the owner and only barman on tonight, spotted Danny and wiped down the bar as he walked over to him. He was a gentle giant of a man. He slapped his huge hand down on the counter and smiled his big, friendly smile.

'Danny, my man, your usual poison?'

'Thanks, Creasey. Make it a pint.' Danny took a twenty out of his wallet and put it on the bar.

'You busy today?' Creasey asked as he pulled the beer.

'Yeah, people dyin' all over the place!' Danny said with a laugh.

Creasey put the pint down in front of Danny, who waited for the head to settle. He then took a long hard swig and sighed as the ice-cold beer raced down his throat.

Just one. Only have one.

Creasey put Danny's change on the bar and walked off to serve one of the half-dead who'd finally finished their drink. Danny checked the time on his mobile phone. It was 8:33pm. The delivery would be here in twelve minutes, just like clockwork. He took another long sip, then reached into his pocket and touched the cool metal of the Colt Mustang. He checked the safety was on, flicked it off, then flicked it back on again.

He gazed around at the pub walls decked out in all sorts of football memorabilia. Ancient photos of Carlton premiership teams from the thirties and forties hung in loose order. There were a couple of yellowing footy cards signed by players now long gone, together with a dozen or so moth-eaten football scarves covered in dust. The TV on the wall, in the middle of all of this, was permanently tuned to the sports channel. Danny could see it but not hear it; the volume switch had died years ago. A couple of sports commentators were in muted conversation, no doubt discussing the weekend's upcoming matches.

At 8:45pm the door to the main bar swung open. Frank Talbot burst through dressed in a long overcoat. As always, his attitude was all business. He caught Creasey's eye and didn't smile.

'Usual,' he said.

He walked up to Danny with Grist in tow. Without Gallagher around, Talbot seemed pushier than normal. He held open his jacket as he stood over Danny, making sure his handgun was visible. Danny felt like it was a challenge – one shooter to another.

He stared at Grist, who seemed meaner than ever in this light. His face looked like he'd gone ten rounds with the champ. He was forever clenching and releasing his fists. Danny knew neither man was to be messed with. Talbot had been known to use his artillery. Gallagher had told him of a time when there had been a problem on the docks. Five men had broken in at night and were rifling the shipping containers. Word quickly made it to Gallagher, who sent Talbot and Grist in to deal with the situation. Talbot shot all five of them. Four were killed outright; Grist finished the fifth one off with a baseball bat. Their burial at sea was unceremonious. The tugboat Gallagher had inherited from his father had come in handy once again.

Creasey poured a generous snifter of Johnnie Walker Green, the pub's best, and opened a stubby of VB. He placed both drinks on the counter and watched the men from behind the bar but didn't speak. Talbot and Grist stood around Danny and made sure no one could see what was happening.

'Strickland,' Talbot said in a softer voice, 'you got your walkin' shoes on?'

Danny nodded and gave the thumbs-up sign. Talbot handed him a slim parcel and smiled to himself. At last, he had someone else to do the Biondi delivery.

'Get this to 7 Main Road, tonight … by ten,' Talbot added.

The number 7 caught Danny off guard. It reminded him of the room number he had back in the juvenile centre; memories of Ainsworth and the troubles he'd had in there flooded back.

'You okay with that, Strickland?' Talbot demanded when Danny didn't answer straight away.

'Yeah, sure,' Danny said as he was jolted back to reality.

He took the package off Talbot and slid it into his jacket pocket. 'So, 7 Main Road ... is that a warehouse as well?'

'No, it's their clubhouse.'

'Whose?'

'Tarantulas! Didn't Gallagher tell you Biondi does business with them?'

Danny's heart froze.

'Ahh yeah ... that's right. I forgot,' he lied.

Talbot eyed him suspiciously, then took an envelope out of his coat. 'This one is for you,' he said.

Danny took the envelope and pushed it into his hip pocket.

'Take these as well.'

Talbot gave Danny two plastic containers of baby powder. Danny's heart skipped a beat as he took them.

In a softer voice, Talbot asked, 'Did Gallagher tell you what he wanted done with them?'

'No,' Danny said. His stomach started to tighten as memories of Chips telling him about Roy and the container of baby powder came rushing in.

'You use them when you do the cut.' Talbot leant closer to Danny. 'Show them to Chips. He'll explain what needs to be done.'

Talbot stared long and hard at Danny, then said, 'The bikies will give you a satchel. Bring it back here this time on Saturday night.'

'Okay, but what about these?' Danny asked as he slid the containers into the pockets of his jacket.

'Wait 'til you've done the cut, then bring them here on the next delivery.'

'Okay,' Danny said.

With that, Talbot motioned to Grist, and they walked back to the bar. Talbot winked at Creasey, lifted the whisky, and drank it in one swallow. Grist picked up the stubby of beer, and both men left using the same door they'd come in by. Creasey waited for it to swing shut.

'Great friends you keep, Danny. Gonna send me broke this way!'

But Creasey knew not to ask too many questions. The streets around here were dangerous. Men like Talbot and his offsider, Grist, were best left alone.

'Just businessmen,' Danny said and drained his pint. 'Thanks, Creasey. See you Saturday night. Big game. Swannies gonna kick the blue baggers' arses!'

'Yeah, right!' Creasey replied.

Danny checked the time – 9:05pm. He didn't waste any more time and left by a side door.

Outside, it started to spit. He wished he'd worn his cap. The trip to Main Road would be a bit of a hike, but he knew if he hightailed it, he could do it by ten. Danny didn't own a car, didn't need one where he lived. Besides, the cops were constantly checking vehicles. So Danny did everything by Shanks's pony. He was like a walking GPS. Chips had an old Melways in the unit, and Danny had studied it night after night. He memorised every street, lane, road, and avenue in these parts – you name it, he knew it. And he was always on the lookout for cops. He thought he could slip them easily if need be.

Time ticked to 9:35pm, and he reached Alabaster Way. The footpath here wound around and followed the streets, but there was also a park that was a shortcut and would save him a good ten minutes, and he was already running late. Trouble was, the park had a bad reputation. Just recently a man had been found in there shot dead. Cops still didn't have a suspect, and late last year a woman had been bashed and raped at knifepoint. He hesitated momentarily at the entrance as a cold wind sliced through the air. It came in bursts and moaned high up in the dark trees that ran along the park's perimeter. He could still go around and take the footpath – at least it received some light from the occasional streetlamp – but time wasn't on his side and it would be quicker this way. He scanned the darkness one last time, then gingerly stepped in.

The carnival music in his head started up as the Tornado Hell ride flashed briefly in front of him. He fingered the Colt, and it eased back a little. His heart was thumping as he strode along the lonely footpath. The place wasn't lit at all; ten metres in and it was almost pitch-black. Above, the sky was a brooding mass with clouds scudding across the moon. His footsteps echoed on the cold, wet concrete. Every twenty steps or so, he did a full 360 to see if anyone was following him. Menacing shadows moved everywhere. Every bush seemed like a man. Every sound like someone cocking a gun.

Five minutes later, and in the distance, he could see a light on the other side. Finally, he made it through and directly onto Main Road. This was the poorer part of town. Houses here were rundown. Some had fences, and some did not. Weeds lined the cracked footpaths. He walked along, checking for street numbers until he found 281. At least he was on the right side of the road. He checked the time on his mobile – 9:49pm. Eleven minutes left, and he started to jog. The Laughing Clowns game slipped past his mind's eye, smiling heads rolling from side to side.

At 9:57pm, and breathing heavily, he found number 7. Massive steel double gates stood in the centre of huge walls made from railway sleepers. A CCTV camera was mounted high up on either side of the entrance. He checked for a bell. The butterflies started in his stomach as the time ticked over to 9:59pm. Finally, he found an intercom switch. He pressed it and waited.

'Yeah?' a tinny voice blared out from the speaker.

'I've got Gallagher's package,' Danny said, gasping for breath.

'Anyone follow you?'

'No, don't think so.'

'See any cops on your way here?'

'No. None.'

'Wait there!'

Danny stood in the dark as a freezing wind scythed its way down the road. Soon there was an audible click. One of the gates swung open, and a bikie appeared.

'Package!' the bikie said, holding out his hand.

Danny dug into his jacket and handed him the thin, plastic-wrapped parcel. He followed the bikie into the dingy courtyard as the gate slammed shut behind him.

'This way.'

Danny's heart was in his mouth as he entered the Tarantulas' clubrooms. The walls were covered in posters of motorbikes, various beer ads, and naked women. In the background, an old jukebox was playing 'Gimme Some Shelter' by the Rolling Stones. A rough-hewn bar dominated the décor, and a couple of billiard tables were tucked away in the corners of the spacious room. A group of bikies stood at the bar drinking while two others were playing pool. Everyone stopped what they were doing and stared when Danny and the bikie walked in.

'Who's this?' asked a bikie who was playing the role of barman.

The first bikie held up the parcel. 'Gallagher's man.'

The barman nodded and brought out a satchel from behind the bar. 'What's your name?' he asked as he handed it to Danny.

'Danny.'

'Where you from?'

Danny started to sweat in the warm clubhouse. He just wanted to get out of there. 'Carlton,' Danny said and left it at that. He didn't want to be too specific.

Just then, a bikie who'd been playing pool walked over still holding a pool cue.

'You look familiar,' the bikie said and stared hard at Danny and squinted.

Danny froze, then forced a laugh. 'Just one of those faces, I guess.'

The bikie kept staring at him.

'You ever been in New South Wales?' the bikie asked.

Danny shook his head. 'No,' he muttered.

But the more Danny looked at him, the more he knew there

was something familiar about this man. His heart started pumping twice as hard.

'Balmain, New South Wales … you ever been there?'

'No … no, ain't never been there!' Danny said but sounded unconvincing. His mouth became as dry as second-hand carpet left out in the hot sun.

Another bikie yelled out, 'Hey, Eddie, how come you reckon everyone's come from New South Wales?'

A couple of the bikies laughed.

'Just 'cause you spent you're entire fuckin' life there doesn't mean everyone comes from New South fuckin' Wales!'

More bikies laughed, and the atmosphere settled a little.

A bikie clapped Danny on the shoulder. 'Don't worry, mate. He's just moved down from there. He don't have no friends and is always tryin' to make a new one!'

The bikies laughed again. But the man they called Eddie wasn't convinced. 'I reckon I've seen you before!' He stared hard at Danny, then walked off.

Danny watched him as he leant over the pool table and played a shot. Danny noticed a red spider tattoo on the back of his hand, and his heart almost stopped.

The first bikie glanced at Danny. 'Okay, you better piss off!'

Danny couldn't get out of there quick enough. The bikie led him out of the clubhouse, unlocked the gate, and watched him walk outside.

'You make sure you look after that!' the bikie said, pointing at the satchel.

'Yeah, I will,' Danny said. He put the satchel inside his jacket and zipped it up.

The bikie slammed the gate closed. Danny stood outside and breathed a sigh of relief. He checked both ends of Main Road but could only see the occasional parked car; no one was out in the cold this time of night. The wind picked up and blew through the dark trees lining the road, showering him with freezing rainwater.

He checked the time – 10:15pm; he had exactly forty-five minutes to get back to the cemetery. He could do it, but it would be tight.

37

DANNY STARTED TO run. He clutched the satchel tight to his chest and made sure the containers of baby powder stayed in his pockets as he raced along the dark, deserted streets. The rain had stopped, but now the wind was howling. The path in front of him was glistening wet. He stuck to the dark patches and prayed there were no police driving around doing routine checks. Eventually, the cemetery came into view. He was almost out of breath as he reached the east gate. He checked the time. It was 10:53pm. He had exactly seven minutes to get to the main entrance on the other side but knew the trip took about ten. He squinted hard as he sucked in the cold night air and started out on one of the walking paths. He checked the time again and knew the only chance he had of making it was to run. He pulled the satchel even tighter against his chest and started to sprint. He bolted off the path and straight across the flattened graves. Headstones like ghosts loomed towards him, then flashed past. He arrived at the main gates completely spent. Chips already had them unlocked and open when Danny arrived.

'Oh! About time, Danny!' Chips hissed. 'I didn't think you were gonna make it!'

Danny couldn't reply. He bent over, put his hands on his knees, and sucked in the cold night air. Just then, a black hearse pulled up to the kerb, followed by a similar-coloured limousine. The hearse made a three-point turn and reversed through the entrance into the cemetery grounds. Tony, the driver, and Alfonso, his passenger, climbed out. They moved to the back of the vehicle and pushed up the rear door.

'You got the trolley?' Tony asked.

'Yeah,' Chips said.

Chips took a collapsible trolley from the shrubs where he'd put it earlier that afternoon. The legs sprung out automatically as he lifted it up. He positioned it behind the hearse, and Tony and Alfonso rolled the coffin onto it.

'All yours!' Tony said without humour and pulled down the rear door of the hearse.

Danny grabbed the trolley as the hearse left. Chips was walking over to close the gates when a window rolled down at the back of the limousine.

'Chips, Strickland!'

Both men walked over to the limo.

'Take this!' Lucizano said and thrust a full shopping bag at Chips. 'I'll be back at eleven tomorrow night; you make sure everything's ready on time!' Lucizano stared long and hard at them, then added, 'Chips, you better not be late!'

Chips looked at him, and his stomach churned as he remembered the vicious beating Lucizano had handed out the one time when he and Roy had missed the deadline by only a few minutes.

'Yeah … okay,' he murmured.

But Lucizano didn't hear him. The window of the limousine was already closed, and the luxurious car disappeared into the jet-black night.

Finally, Chips regained his composure. 'Good night to you as well,' he said. 'And pleasant dreams!' he added.

Chips locked the gates as light rain started to fall. Danny grabbed the trolley and pushed it towards the unit. Once inside, they left it in the kitchen area and locked the door.

'See you in the morning, Danny,' Chips said and he went to his bedroom.

'Yeah, goodnight, Chips!'

Danny walked into his room and quietly closed the bedroom door. He put the Colt and the satchel on the bedside table. He started to undress, but curiosity got the better of him. He undid the leather straps on the satchel, opened it up, and reached inside. He pulled out a wad of fifty-dollar notes that were neatly stacked and secured with rubber bands. He found another three wads of a similar size, also made up of fifties. He pulled out a scrap of paper from the bottom of the satchel. It had a spider insignia on it plus the number 20 written inside a circle.

Whoa! Must be twenty grand!

He put the cash back in the satchel, closed it up, and decided to hide it and the containers of powder. Then he remembered Chips saying Lucizano's men would check the unit to see if they'd kept any of the product after they'd done the cut. If they found the satchel, it would be a problem. It was payment to Gallagher from Biondi, not from D'Angelo, and Gallagher had told him he didn't want either family to know he handled separate shipments for them. He decided the safest place to hide this stuff was inside the mattress. He walked out to the kitchen and took a sharp knife out of a drawer. In the bedroom, he sliced the side of the mattress. He pushed the satchel and the containers of baby powder in, then he pulled the sheets and blankets over it. He didn't notice when the scrap of paper from the satchel drifted underneath the bed.

As he finished getting undressed, the second envelope from Talbot dropped from the pocket of his jeans and into his lap. He opened it and counted the notes – 250 in fifties. Gallagher had been generous.

He closed his eyes and waited for sleep to take hold, but it didn't come straight away. The night had been too intense. His mind wandered, recounting everything that happened, one situation after another. Then he pictured her, the pretty girl Mr D'Angelo had called Ebony. He remembered her smile, or what he thought was a smile, and the way she had looked up at him as she cleaned the table. She was a beauty, and he wondered if he would ever see her again. It was the last thought he had before sleep finally claimed him.

38

NEXT NIGHT CHIPS locked the main gates at around 6:00pm. It had been a big day with four burials. He met Danny in the unit. This would be Danny's first time cutting the product.

'Okay, Danny. Let's check it out!'

Chips opened up the coffin; it was packed full of large plastic bags of white powder. Danny peered in, then stared at Chips.

'Wow. Pure cocaine, hey?'

'Yes, Danny, it's pure all right! Comes from overseas ... Colombia,' Chips reminded him. 'Mr D'Angelo has plenty of contacts. If that cocaine was already cut, there'd be hell to pay!' Chips closed the coffin lid, then said, 'Wait here.'

He walked into his bedroom and came out with bathroom scales. He put the scales on the floor and weighed the bag Lucizano had given him.

'Five kilos,' he said to Danny.

Chips put the scales and the bag on the trolley with the coffin. 'All right, Danny. Let's get goin'!'

'Aren't we gonna do it here?'

'No, we ain't doin' it here. We're goin' to the old Goldstein mausoleum!'

'Where's that?'

Chips grabbed a cup down from a cupboard over the sink and tipped out a key. 'Follow me!'

'Just a minute,' Danny said.

He walked back into his bedroom, felt around inside the mattress, and grabbed the two containers of baby powder. He stuffed them in his pocket and walked back into the kitchen.

'Okay,' he said to Chips.

Outside, Chips switched on a torch and strode out along one of the walking paths. Danny followed behind, pushing the trolley weighed down by the heavy coffin. The wheels ground down and spun noisily on the uneven bricks as night started to close in. Not too far along, they stopped at a stretch of small concrete buildings. Some looked like tiny churches, whereas others were more simple rectangular shapes. There were angels here as well. Some stood on the rooftops reaching for the heavens, while others lined the entrance to the mausoleum doors as though preventing an unholy evil from entering their inner sanctum.

Chips stopped at one that appeared to be very old. The headstone read 'Goldstein'. He took the key from his pocket and unlocked a chain holding together the crypt's two ancient wrought-iron doors. A high-pitched sound of grating metal pierced the air as Chips pushed them open.

Danny stood back and took in the sight. Dust-covered coffins were stacked high against the walls, one on top of the other. In the middle of the mausoleum, on a concrete ledge, was a large black-and-white photo of an old couple staring out from a glass frame covered with years of grime. The photo looked like it had been taken early last century. The caption underneath read:

'Meir and Batya Goldstein'

Danny guessed it was a photo of the original occupants.

'So why we doin' it here, Chips?'

Chips switched on two more field torches, and the dull beams lit up the eerie surroundings.

'Danny, this is a good place. I ain't never seen no one come here to grieve or place flowers. I guess the Goldsteins used to be a wealthy

Jewish family, but maybe they all dead now!'

Chips pushed the trolley beside one of the stone burial vaults, then lifted the coffin lid.

'Yeah, but how come we don't do it in the unit?'

Chips smiled, took a bag out of the coffin, and eventually spoke.

'Because that's where Lucizano thinks we do the cut … in the unit. He'll check there when he picks up the coffin tonight!' Chips paused, then went on. 'You see, Danny, when we hand over the coffin to Lucizano, they gonna pat us down and see if we kept any of it! They'll also check the unit to see if we've hidden some there. That's why we doin' it here … okay?'

'Okay,' Danny said and watched as Chips spread a layer of thin plastic sheet on the burial-vault lid. Then he took a bag of cocaine from the coffin and slit it open with a knife. White powder spilled out.

'Danny, there's somethin' else I need to know before we go any further.' Chips grabbed a handful of the smaller plastic bags. 'You've been here a while now. We good friends, aren't we, Danny?'

'Yeah, I guess so, Chips.'

Danny was worried about where this conversation was headed.

'So, Danny … can I trust ya?'

The mausoleum fell silent. Danny thought back to his time with Gallagher. After a moment, he said, 'Yes, Chips, you can trust me!'

Chips considered what Danny said and nodded his head.

'Well, you see, it works like this. The coffin gets weighed by D'Angelo's people in the hearse before it gets to us. They have some kinda weighin' scales in the vehicle underneath where the coffin goes.'

'Okay,' Danny said softly.

'Then Lucizano tells us to mix in this stuff here.' Chips held up the shopping bag Lucizano had given him. 'This time, it's baking soda and laundry powder. You cut the pure product with some of this to make it go further. Each of them little bags got mostly cocaine and a bit of this. Lucizano gave us five kilos this time, so when he picks up the coffin tonight, it should weigh five kilos heavier, give or take, dependin' on how many plastic bags we use. And we gotta be careful we don't add too much to each bag. Mr D'Angelo has a reputation that his product is clean.'

Danny became a little bit wary.

'Yeah, but so long as we use it all, it should be close enough!'

'That's right, Danny, but there's somethin' else! You gotta promise me you won't say a word to no one.'

The carnival came to life in Danny's head. The merry-go-round started up and painted wooden horses began bobbing up and down as they circled, endlessly chasing each other.

'There's another reason I brought them scales.'

Chips paused, and now the sounds of the night filled the concrete mausoleum. The air turned a little colder. Chips took a package of white powder out of his jacket and held it up so Danny could see.

'You see, Roy and me, we got to addin' another half kilo in and takin' out a quarter kilo each. This is just powdered milk, won't hurt no one. I measured it. Half a kilo of this goes in, and a half kilo pure product comes out.'

Danny shook his head. 'I thought you said stealin' that stuff would get you killed!'

Chips raised his eyebrows and smirked. 'Well, it will. It got Roy killed!'

Both men chuckled, and then Danny looked at Chips.

'Chips,' Danny said and took the two containers of baby powder out of his pocket. 'Talbot gave me these. He said you'd show me what to do with them.'

'Oh,' Chips said, 'looks like Gallagher's still up to his old tricks!' Chips sighed long and hard. 'There used to be only one container of baby powder, but now there's two! Whoa! D'Angelo's product gonna be just that little bit dirtier.'

Chips put his hands on his hips.

'Gallagher, he trusts you, Danny … you won't go sellin' that stuff, will ya?'

'No way!' Danny said and stared at Chips.

The mausoleum fell to silence once more. Chips took the containers of baby powder off Danny and stood them on the burial vault.

'Okay. That's good to hear. Let's get started.'

But Danny didn't move. He put his hand up and said, 'Chips, before we start … I want Roy's quarter!'

The smile left Chips' face. He could sense that things had changed. It was clear to him that Danny was no longer the new boy; Danny had found his place here in the cemetery and was going to exploit it.

After a brief pause, Chips nodded his head and said, 'Okay, Danny. No sweat. You can have Roy's quarter. So, you get your slice, I get mine, and Gallagher gets his. Everybody's happy … now, *let's get started!*'

It was well after ten thirty when they finished. The product had been cut, and the coffin was full of small sealed plastic bags. Chips closed the lid and turned to Danny.

'Okay, Danny, here's our hidin' spot.'

Chips took a large porcelain cremation urn from the back of the mausoleum and stood it on the floor. He lifted out a piece of cardboard and put his stash of drugs in it. He then put the cardboard back in and placed Danny's quarter on top of it. He winked at Danny and smiled, then lifted the urn and carefully pushed it back into position.

'You better hide those containers of Gallagher's somewhere in here. Like I told ya, they'll pat us down when we hand over the coffin.'

Danny found a spot and made sure the containers were out of sight.

'And, Danny, if you got any excess cash in the unit, I suggest you hide it in here too. Tony and Alfonso ain't exactly good, moral citizens. One time, they found all of mine and Roy's cash when they checked the unit … they left us with nuthin'. They knew we wasn't gonna complain to Lucizano, and I bet there was no way they were gonna tell him either. I reckon they just kept it all for themselves,' Chips said and shook his head.

'Okay, Chips,' Danny said and nodded.

There was silence for a moment.

'So the urn?' Danny asked, trying to take the conversation down a different path. 'What happened to whoever was in there to start off with?'

'Well, a long time ago, me and Roy decided the roses needed some fertilisin', so one night, they got some!' Chips laughed loudly.

Danny smiled and said, 'Bet them roses are doin' just fine now!'

Chips smiled and nodded. 'Okay, we better get that to the main gate, Danny,' he said, pointing to the coffin. 'Lucizano will be there soon. Don't wanna be late!'

Chips rolled up the plastic sheet and wiped off any excess from the lid of the burial vault. Danny rolled the coffin out into the night while Chips used the chain to lock the mausoleum doors. They made it to the main gates with a couple of minutes to spare. Chips unlocked and opened them and peered down the road. It was just on 11:00pm.

'Here they come,' he whispered to Danny.

Ominous dark clouds swept across the starless black sky. A cold wind picked up and sighed through the trees at the side of the road. Butterflies stirred in Danny's stomach as he watched Lucizano's black limousine pull up and park by the side of the road. The hearse then arrived and reversed in. Lucizano climbed out of the limo while Tony and Alfonso exited the hearse. Tony took the trolley from Danny and lifted the rear door of the hearse.

'Roll it in!' Lucizano said to the men.

Tony began to push the trolley towards the hearse.

'Wait!' Lucizano said and held up his hand. He opened the coffin lid, peered in, and ran his hands deep underneath the layers of plastic bags. 'Okay!' he said and pointed to the two men.

Tony and Alfonso lifted the coffin off the trolley and slid it into the back of the hearse. 'Weigh it,' Lucizano ordered.

Tony walked to the front of the vehicle and checked the instrument panel. 'Bit over eighty-five!' he called out.

'Okay. Sounds right,' Lucizano said, happy with the weight. 'Search 'em!'

Lucizano waited while both Danny and Chips were patted down. Then Lucizano pointed to the unit. 'Check it out! Chips, give 'em your keys!'

'Ain't locked,' Chips said.

He was about to add there was no reason to lock it in a cemetery but thought better of it. Lucizano eyeballed him, then motioned to Tony and Alfonso with his head, and the two men started off.

Danny and Chips stood at the cemetery gates and watched and waited. Danny's mind was racing as the carnival music started up.

The satchel – what if they find the satchel?

Danny saw the lights go on in the unit. He could see the two men moving around checking the kitchen and then watched as they went from one bedroom to the other. Ten minutes passed, and they returned.

'Found this, boss.' Tony handed something to Lucizano.

Danny's heart froze. Chips looked across at Danny and scowled.

'Where'd you find it?'

'In Strickland's room!'

The carnival music in Danny's head started screaming. Lucizano turned to Danny.

'What's this?'

Lucizano held out the scrap of paper from the satchel. A vein in Danny's neck started to pulse rapidly.

'It's ... not mine.'

'You found it in Strickland's room?' Lucizano asked and turned to Tony for confirmation.

'Yes, boss ... under his bed,' Tony said and nodded his head up and down.

'It must have belonged to Eastern,' Danny said in desperation.

Lucizano held the paper out and frowned. Then he pocketed it and locked eyes with Danny. Tony and Alfonso stopped in their tracks. Chips didn't move. The wind wailed high up in the trees again as the two men faced each other. All eyes were on Lucizano – everyone wondering what he was going to do next.

'You better not be lying to me, Strickland,' Lucizano said with venom.

Still, no one moved or spoke. Eventually, Lucizano turned towards Tony and Alfonso. 'Did you boys check that place thoroughly?'

'Yes, boss!' they said in unison.

Danny was praying that Lucizano didn't ask them to go back and look around again.

Lucizano stared back at Danny one last time, then said, 'Okay, let's go!'

Danny's heart finally started to beat again as Lucizano walked over to the limousine and climbed into the back seat. Tony waited for Alfonso to pull down the rear door of the hearse and get in the passenger's side. He then started it up and slowly pulled away, with the limousine following close behind.

'Danny, that's why we don't do any cuttin' in the unit. Those dumb bastards never gonna find nothin' in there ... except that piece of paper! I thought you said you picked up all of Roy's stuff.'

'I'm sorry. I guess I missed it!'

Chips shook his head, but his mood quickly lightened.

Well, tomorrow we'll visit the Goldsteins again and see just what we have. Thank you, Mr D'Angelo!'

He locked the gates, and Danny and Chips stood in the cold and watched the vehicles disappear into the inky blackness of the night.

39

IT WAS 7:45pm on Saturday, and the George was jumping. There was no room at the bar. Everyone had pushed forward and taken up a front-row position to watch the football match on the television. As per usual, Creasey had strung a transistor radio by its strap underneath the set and had it tuned to the game. He turned the volume up as far as it would go, but it had little effect, and the game was almost impossible to hear over the noise of the crowded pub. But that wasn't the only problem. The radio broadcast was ahead of the TV transmission by a couple of seconds, and everyone was complaining.

'Jesus, Creasey, when you gonna buy a bloody decent TV?'

But Creasey didn't answer. He was flat out pulling beers down the other end of the bar. He was happy; the pub was full. The footy on Friday and Saturday nights always drew a good crowd.

And to ensure they arrived early and left late, Creasey introduced some special help. A year ago, he'd organised a roster at the local university for those who wanted to earn a bit of extra cash. But the students knew he only wanted females to apply, and then, only the good-looking ones. After a while he had a select group of young women who were his favourites. And it was working well. The one on tonight was a stunner and a good worker. She'd done the weekend shift a number of times now and had developed a tough skin. She mostly ignored the bawdy remarks that came her way;

nothing seemed to faze her much. And with so many in the pub, it was hot, and she'd taken off her cardigan and was working in a thin tee shirt. If the patrons weren't watching the footy, they were certainly watching her.

A group of six had set up camp next to the taps and weren't about to lose their prime spot. They'd arrived well before the game started and were all getting a little messy. The biggest one, who was drinking pints to the others' pots, piped up and said at the top of his voice, 'Hey, darlin', you're good at pullin' beers … how 'bout pullin' this!'

He burst out laughing, and his friends all joined in as he grabbed his crotch and jiggled it. She glanced his way, shook her head slightly, and walked off to serve another drinker who'd managed to muscle his way to the bar.

'Hey, that's enough of that!' shouted Creasey. 'Keep it down!'

'Oh, okay, Creasey. Sorry, mate!' the man yelled back and smiled broadly, but his friends didn't stop laughing.

Danny sat in his usual spot, away from the main crowd but still close enough to see the game. Sydney was up by ten points, but it was still early on in the match and only a fragile lead. He'd seen them fritter away starts like that before.

He had the satchel safely zipped up inside his jacket and the containers in his pockets. He sipped on his pint and kept watching the front door, waiting for Talbot and Grist to arrive. A patron walked past on the way to the men's room, and he hugged the satchel just a little bit closer. Sydney kicked a goal, and the pub moaned in unison, complaining about the 'crap umpiring'.

'That was definitely in the back!'

Danny was happy but didn't dare voice support for the Swans in this crowd. Besides, he wasn't really concentrating on the game. He had something else much more interesting on his mind tonight.

The game became intense as the scores tightened up; everybody was glued to the television. But Danny kept a watch out on the front doors. Sure enough, at 8:45pm, precisely on time, Talbot and Grist shouldered their way in. Talbot eyeballed the crowd, then pushed his way through the mass of people when he saw Danny. Grist followed, his eyes moving from side to side. They stood around Danny, making sure no one could see what was going on.

A tall man standing in the crowd by the rear wall recognised them. He watched what they were doing but stayed in the background and remained inconspicuous.

'Strickland, you got the merchandise?' Talbot asked. He had to raise his voice to be heard above the noise in the bar.

Danny unzipped his jacket and handed the satchel over. Talbot immediately jammed it inside his coat. Danny grabbed the baby powder containers, now full of D'Angelo's cocaine.

'Got these as well,' he said and handed them over.

Talbot took both containers and pushed them into the inside pocket of his coat, then turned and headed for the door with Grist in his wake. Danny watched them leave.

No free drinks tonight, hey, boys?

On the way out, Talbot was jostled by a drinker who staggered and clutched at his coat. He turned to Grist, who grabbed the unfortunate man.

'Move!' yelled Grist and shoved him hard to one side.

The man's beer spilled as he crashed backwards against the pub wall. He stared down at his near-empty glass and then back at Grist. His eyes were on fire.

'Fuck you!' he yelled.

The drunk came at Grist and threw a wild punch, which Grist easily ducked. Patrons on either side forced themselves back, trying to avoid the action. Grist punched the man in the face, and the guy went down. But Grist hadn't finished. He leant down, grabbed him by the hair, and pushed his head against the wall. He smashed him twice more in the face. Blood splattered across the pub wall and ran down in tiny rivers, adding fresh red stains to the pub's already ancient and beer-soaked carpet.

'That's enough!' Talbot shouted.

But Grist still wasn't finished. He grabbed the semi-conscious man in a vicious headlock and dragged him outside. Talbot took a quick look around and followed.

With the fight over, it didn't take long for the crowd to move back into the empty space, the violent half-time entertainment soon forgotten. They squeezed together, shoulder to shoulder, and resumed talking as loud as they could in an effort to make themselves heard.

Danny waited for the next quarter to start, then forced his way through the crowd and left. There was no opportunity to say goodbye to Creasey, who was still eagerly pouring drinks. Outside, it was bitterly cold. Rain scudded in intermittently. He stepped over the unconscious body of the drinker Grist had beaten up and hunched his jacket around himself. Then he headed off down the rain-soaked footpath – towards the city.

40

DANNY REACHED THE top of Spring and Bourke Streets just as a tram rattled past. He jogged to the tram stop and jumped on. He rode it down Bourke and got off at William. He decided to walk the rest of the way and keep an eye out. His stomach was doing cartwheels as he strode along. He wasn't supposed to be out this late, and he certainly wasn't supposed to be in the city. By now, he was meant to be back in his room – in the cemetery!

He was surprised by the number of people who were around at this time of night. Down this end of the CBD, it was mainly business houses, but there were those who were still out and about. He arrived at King Street and turned left. He walked past a busy late-night diner on the corner and a group of young men milling about in front of a couple of strip clubs. He skirted around them and further on he could see the venue he was looking for. The bright lights of the Seven Veils stood out vividly under the portico of the massive casino and nightclub. His heart started pumping hard, and the carnival came back to life as he walked towards the entrance. Hoping to turn the volume down, he reached inside his pocket and touched the Colt.

He hesitated near the front door and waited for a group of people to enter, then followed them in. Memories came flooding back when he saw the chandeliers and dazzling lights. The place was filled with the hubbub of people talking and the constant ring and clatter of slot machines, together with a band that was trying desperately hard to be heard over the top of it all.

He walked to the bar and moved as close to the front door as possible, just in case there was a need to make a quick exit. He ordered a beer, casually leant on the counter, and looked around. There were more tables in the restaurant area than he'd remembered, and most were full. He glanced up to the other end of the nightclub and, in the distance, saw D'Angelo sitting in his usual spot with a few of his lieutenants. Lucizano was there, chatting casually to his boss.

A tall, half-naked girl with huge feathers in her hair walked over and stood next to him. She smiled sweetly, and when it was clear he hadn't noticed her, she gently pushed her body up against his.

'Hi, honey ... you here alone?'

Danny swung his head around, surprised. For a moment, he was lost for words.

'I ... ahh ... I'm just waiting for someone!' he said and desperately hoped she'd go away.

'That be a girl or a boy?' She sighed, and her smile grew a little wider. She put her hand on his.

Danny didn't answer. The last thing he wanted was to bring attention his way. Just then, one of D'Angelo's henchmen walked up to her.

'Darleen ... front door!'

She peered over to the entrance and made a beeline for a well-dressed older gentleman who had just arrived.

'Sorry, mate,' the man said to Danny. 'There'll be another one along soon!'

Danny held up his glass in acknowledgement and quickly turned away, hoping he wasn't recognised. He started checking the tables and looking at the waitresses – then he saw her. His heart jumped, and the adrenaline kicked in. The waitress called Ebony was attending to a couple not far from where he was standing. He waited for a table to be free and then walked over and sat down. It took five minutes before she finally arrived.

'Hi. What can I get you?' she asked and stared down at her order pad as she finished scribbling some notes.

'Anything you like!' he answered with a chuckle.

'I'm sorry, sir?' she said, but still didn't look up.

He tried again. 'You know, whatever you think!'

She became a bit peeved.

'Sir, I need an order!' she snapped as she turned her head and checked the nearby tables to see who else was waiting to be served.

'Yes, I'm sorry … I mean … what time do you get off?'

His comment caught her off guard, and she finally looked directly at him. Her cheeks flushed red as she remembered his face. She stopped fiddling with the pad, and there was an awkward pause.

Finally, she said in a soft voice, 'You work for Mr D'Angelo … don't you?'

Danny nodded.

'You probably shouldn't be here!'

'Yeah, I know … but I thought maybe I could buy you a drink or something, you know, when you finish up tonight.'

'You could get in big trouble!' she whispered, checking to see if anyone was taking any notice of them.

'So … what do you say?'

A patron from the next table piped up. 'Miss, can we order some drinks, please?'

'Yes, certainly. I'll be right there!' she said.

She turned back to Danny and whispered forcefully, 'You should go!'

But Danny took no notice. She was easily the prettiest girl he had ever seen and worth taking a risk for. He decided to try a different tack.

'I'm not leaving until you say yes!' he said and smiled up at her.

She glanced around, flustered, hoping no one was taking any

notice of them. 'I ... I shouldn't. I could get in trouble too, you know!'

'So, take a chance ... I'm harmless.' He held up his hands in a playful display, and she giggled slightly.

'Miss!' the person on the other table said impatiently.

'Be right there!'

She looked down at Danny and whispered, 'Oh ... okay!'

Danny's heart threatened to jump out of his chest; he could hardly believe she'd agreed to see him.

She turned back to him, bent forward, and whispered, 'Meet me at Theo's in Little Collins Street, near Southern Cross Station. I leave here at eleven.'

Danny was sure he saw that tiny smile appear on her face, just like the first time he'd seen her.

'Now, what can I get you?'

41

DANNY ORDERED A whisky and Coke, drank it quickly, and left. He didn't want to hang around in there too long and run the risk of someone remembering his face. Outside the Seven Veils he asked for directions to Little Collins Street and after a couple of minutes walked down the narrow road towards Southern Cross railway station; the sight of it brought back old memories.

Halfway along he found Theo's Bar tucked away next to an Indian restaurant. He took a table at the back and ordered coffee. *No more alcohol*, he told himself. A little bit of 'Dutch courage' was fine, but he wanted to impress her and not come across as some drunken sleaze.

He sat there watching the time and waited. It got to 11:15pm. He hoped she wasn't going to stand him up. His heart began to sink, and just when the doubts were really kicking in, she walked through the door. She had changed out of her waitress uniform and was dressed in a skirt and high heels. She had a thick camel-coloured coat draped casually over her shoulders and wore a small maroon beret pushed casually to one side of her lovely head. Her gorgeous dark eyes and ruby-red lips shone out against her pale skin. Danny couldn't believe how beautiful she looked. She walked up to the table, and her smile, which was normally ever so slight, became a little larger.

'Anyone sitting here?' she said and pointed to the spare chair.

'Yeah, the prettiest girl in Melbourne!' he said.

'Oh! If that's your best line!' she said as she pulled the chair out and sat down.

He was stopped in his tracks momentarily and went red in the face. She smiled at him and put her handbag on the table. Before he could speak, a waiter walked over to them.

'Usual, Miss Ebony? Pink gin and tonic?'

'Yes, thank you, Wilfred.'

'And you, sir?'

'Ahh ... a light beer, thanks.'

'Light beer!' she said. 'You driving?'

'No, no. I just want to stay alert.' He smiled, and she smiled back at him.

'So here I am with a strange man, and I don't even know his name!'

'I'm Danny.' He held out his hand, and she took it.

Her hand was so soft, and her grip so tender. He hoped she didn't ask him for his last name. It wouldn't be good to have to lie to her so soon in a hopefully blossoming relationship.

'I'm Ebony,' she said, and her tiny half-smile remained.

The drinks arrived. She took a sip of hers and asked, 'So ... how come you work for Mr D'Angelo? What do you do?'

His forehead prickled as his mind raced for an answer.

'I ... ahh ... I pick up and deliver packages for him.'

'Oh,' she said and smiled again. 'So you live nearby?'

'Yeah ... Carlton. I've got a place there. I room with another guy. Separate bedrooms!' he added and laughed, and she joined in.

'Have you always lived around here?' she asked.

Butterflies started in Danny's stomach. 'No, I'm originally from New South Wales.'

'Oh. Where? Somewhere in Sydney?'

'Yeah, near there, for a little while anyway, and then ... it was becoming a bit crowded, so I thought I'd come here and have a look around.'

'Uh-huh,' she said and smiled.

Danny was desperate to change the subject.

'What about yourself? Have you always lived here in Melbourne?'

'No,' she said and paused. 'I come from Adelaide.'

'Wow! Long way away from home!' he said and smiled back at her.

'Yes, I wasn't enjoying it, so I left.'

'Oh,' he said. 'So you came here ... for all the sunshine!' he added, hoping she'd see his poor attempt at humour.

She laughed.

'I was rooming with some people ... another set of ... *friends*,' she said and briefly glanced down at her drink.

Danny nodded. He sensed she was telling him something difficult. She hesitated before she went on.

'They started off nice, but in the end, were just like all the others ...' She didn't finish the sentence.

'What was wrong?' Danny asked, not sure what else to say.

Ebony paused for a moment. 'Well ... I found out some of them were wanted. The police knocked on the door late one night, looking for them. It frightened me. So the next day, I just left! I guess you could say ... *I escaped!*' she said and chuckled.

Escaped, hey? You already have something in common!

'Good for you!' he said and decided, at this stage, it wouldn't be a good idea to tell her of his past.

Another couple walked in and sat at the table next to them. Danny sipped his beer and kept his voice down. 'So now it's my turn ... how come *you* work for Mr D'Angelo?'

'Oh, I met a friend when I got down here. She put in a good word for me. But guess what? I've heard Mr D'Angelo has also had his run-ins with the law.' She paused and looked into her drink briefly. 'Seems I'm destined to always be in the company of those sorts of people,' she said and shook her head ever so slightly.

Danny smiled and nodded; the irony of the situation wasn't lost on him. They kept talking for another half hour or so until she finally glanced down at her watch.

'Oh! I'd better go. The trams that go my way to St Kilda finish up soon.'

'Okay,' Danny said.

They finished their drinks, and he walked her to the tram stop on Spencer Street. Soon there came the screeching sound of metal wheels on metal tracks as the 96 inched its way around the corner. It stopped in front of them, and the doors flung open. They stood together for a moment, and his heart started beating faster as he worked up the nerve to speak. Finally, he blurted out the words.

'Is it okay if I see you again?'

She smiled at him. 'Well … you know my favourite café, *and* you know where I work, but you might have to be careful!' she said and gently bit her bottom lip.

The doors started to close, but Danny reached out and held them open. He knew this was going to be a bit forward, but he thought he'd try anyway.

'Do you have a phone number I could call?'

She raised her eyebrows, and a half-smile crossed her lips. 'Not yet, but maybe later on,' she replied.

She saw the perplexed look on his face, then stood on her tiptoes and gently kissed him on the cheek. It caught him off guard; his heart now threatened to explode out of his chest. He watched as she boarded the tram.

She turned around and said, 'You better let go of those doors or you'll get into trouble.' And that beautiful smile of hers got even wider.

Danny released the doors, and the tram moved off with an electric hum. He watched it glide along Spencer Street until, eventually, it disappeared from view. He checked the time; it was well past midnight. A cold rain scudded through the city. He turned around and touched his cheek where she'd kissed it, then stuffed his hands in his jacket pockets. He started the long trek back to the cemetery and could have sworn his feet never once touched the ground.

It was well past midnight when he quietly opened the door of the unit and made sure he didn't wake Chips. He went to his bedroom and closed the door behind him. He lay on the bed and soon fell into a deep sleep. Once again, his dreams were vivid, but this time, the theme centred around someone very new in his life.

PART SIX

TIPPING POINT

the net closes ...

42

THE TALL GLASS and metal building of the NSW Police Head-quarters sparkled in the brilliant morning sunshine. In a conference room on the fifth floor, two men sat at one end of a highly polished conference-room table and cooled their heels. One was Detective Senior Sergeant Presley Cooper, and the other was his subordinate from Victoria, Detective Constable Tom Lucas. They were waiting for Assistant Commissioner Aubrey Warner-Smith to join them. Cooper had been told to be there at 10:30am sharp for a very important meeting. It was already 10:38.

'So much for punctuality!' Cooper snapped and glared at Lucas.

Cooper was in a perpetual bad mood and had been for the last twelve months, ever since Danny Wainwright had escaped and, along with him, his chance of promotion. Lucas kept his thoughts to himself and didn't comment.

Jesus, he wants it so bad!

At 10:42, Warner-Smith opened the sliding glass door of the conference room. He was dressed impeccably. The creases in the rich blue of his police uniform were pressed to perfection. His jacket provided a magnificent backdrop to the gleaming silver buttons and epaulettes that adorned his uniform. His shirt was a brilliant white and was offset by the deep-blue tie, knotted in a half-Windsor and

pinned to the shirt by the gleaming police tie-pin. His black pat-
ent-leather shoes shone brightly, and his shock of blond-grey hair
was precision cut to set off his razor-sharp features. His name badge
proudly stated: '*Warner-Smith Assistant Commissioner*'.

'Sorry, gentlemen. So many administrative things to attend to,'
Warner-Smith said and smiled at the two men.

He flicked a speck of dust off the chair at the head of the table
before he took a seat. He stared down the other end of the table at
Cooper, frowned, and said in a condescending manner, 'So, Pres, I
understand things haven't gone so well for you … searching for this
fugitive!'

Cooper started to sweat. He wriggled in his chair, trying to find
a comfortable position. 'Ahh … no, sir … but we're continuing to
search!'

Warner-Smith nodded his head ever so slightly.

'Been looking for him here in New South Wales for the last
year, I understand!' Warner-Smith said. He stared long and hard at
Cooper, then turned his head and gazed out the window.

Cooper's sweating got worse.

'He has many hideouts and a gang who can help him. We've
questioned them all, and we think there's a good chance he's still
here somewhere!'

'Hmm,' Warner-Smith murmured as he continued to peer
outside, his thoughts seemingly consumed by another matter.

The room fell silent. A worried expression crossed Cooper's face
as he continued to stare at Warner-Smith, waiting for him to say
something. Outside, clouds spread across the city for a moment and
the conference room became darker, matching Cooper's increasing
dread. Soon the sun broke through and the building creaked as it
expanded under the strong rays. It snapped Warner-Smith back to
the moment at hand. He leant back in his chair and turned and
faced Cooper.

'Well, Senior Sergeant … after we did some digging here,

actually *a lot of digging,* Warner-Smith emphasised, 'we unearthed an interesting fact. If it turns out to be correct, we'll set up a task force and find our man in another state!'

Cooper interjected straight away.

'Sir, we asked our interstate colleagues to keep an eye out for him, but nothing has come back!'

Warner-Smith nodded, his face expressionless.

And this man wants to be an Inspector!

Cooper was worried when Warner-Smith didn't reply. He'd also mentioned a task force; he wondered if he would still head it up.

'So, sir, what have you been told?' Cooper asked and sat forward.

Warner-Smith paused dramatically, enjoying watching Cooper dangle on the hook. 'It's not so much what we've been told. It's what we've found!' Warner-Smith said and crossed his arms as he stared at Cooper. 'Recently, a dedicated group has gone back over hundreds of pieces of information … things like witness statements, snippets of CCTV, etcetera.'

Warner-Smith wondered if Cooper had done anything like that, or had even thought of doing it.

'Two separate sources reported seeing a man jump from the XPT near Melbourne the day after Wainwright escaped. Originally, this appeared to be a simple case of fare evasion, but we have contacted both witnesses. One was a passenger, and the other, a ticket inspector. We've had sketches done of the person in question and also obtained grainy CCTV images of all those passengers who caught the train in Sydney the day before. We then gathered up all of this information and matched it with the images *we* have of Wainwright.'

Warner-Smith kept Cooper in his direct line of sight.

'You'd understand, Pres, that this course of action is something good policing calls for!'

Warner-Smith waited for the barb to sink in.

'Yes, sir,' Cooper said and rubbed his brow with the back of his hand.

'The drawings and CCTV somewhat match our fugitive. We believe there's a good chance he's down in Melbourne somewhere.'

Warner-Smith leant back in his chair and tugged on a sleeve of his blazer to straighten out a non-existent crease. He waited to see if Cooper had anything to say, and after a brief moment of silence, he continued.

'The commissioner called yesterday and asked me to chase this down. He suggested that I set up a two-pronged approach; that is, two lines of inquiry. So, I'm putting together two separate arms of the task force.'

Warner-Smith let his comment hang in the air.

'Therefore, I will need two lead detectives. Of course … I get to select them!'

Cooper swallowed hard; he could see his chance slipping away.

'I'm going to ask Detective Sergeant Nickels from Penrith to lead the first arm.'

Cooper frowned and took a deep breath. 'Jeremy Nickels?' he said. 'Sir, no disrespect, but he's junior to me in both experience and rank. I think …'

'Nickels is a bright up-and-comer!' Warner-Smith shouted, cutting Cooper off. 'He headed up the team that found the matching fare-evader instances. He's young and hungry, very ambitious, and has done a lot of things *right*!'

The emphasis on Warner-Smith's last comment wasn't lost on Cooper.

'Don't worry, Pres, you will be the other lead detective,' Warner-Smith said and smiled like a cat that had cornered a mouse.

Cooper's relief was instantaneous.

'The commissioner and I like a bit of competition amongst the men.'

Warner-Smith took out his mobile phone and spoke into it

briefly. Soon, a young policeman entered the room. Like Warner-Smith, this man's uniform was also pristine. His shoes shone brightly; he even had the same haircut as Warner-Smith.

'Morning, Pres!' Detective Sergeant Jeremy Nickels said as he took a seat next to Warner-Smith at the head of the table.

'Morning, Nickels,' Cooper replied in an unfriendly manner.

'Gentlemen, I'll introduce you to your teams at lunchtime today. We'll discuss tactics and the way forward. Also, you'll both be given an experienced detective from Victoria to work with you. Pres, I see you've already met Detective Constable Tom Lucas.' Warner-Smith pointed to Lucas. 'Tom comes to us with first-rate references from his superiors in Melbourne.

Tom, I understand you have considerable experience and good knowledge of the docks and CBD area of Melbourne.'

'Yes, sir,' Lucas said and went red in the face.

'Good. I'm sure you'll be able to show Detective Senior Sergeant Cooper and his team around when they arrive down there.'

Lucas nodded. Warner-Smith then turned to Nickels.

'Jeremy, Detective Senior Constable Bradley Adams will report to you. He has an excellent understanding of the workings in the suburbs of Melbourne.'

'Thank you very much, sir,' Nickels said and beamed brightly at his superior.

Warner-Smith continued.

'Gentlemen, the Victorian commissioner has promised us complete cooperation. You will be supported in every way possible. Are there any questions?'

The room went silent. Warner-Smith stood up, straightened the pleats of his trousers, and brushed a tiny speck of dust from his cuff.

'Jeremy, perhaps you'd like to bring Detective Senior Sergeant Cooper and Detective Constable Lucas up to date with what we've learnt so far.'

'Yes, sir,' Nickels said.

Warner-Smith began to walk out of the room but then stopped and turned around.

'Oh ... by the way, Jeremy, Pres ... the inspector role is still vacant. Whoever brings Wainwright in will be in line for that promotion.' He let the comment sink in, then added, 'Good morning, gentlemen!'

With that, Warner-Smith turned, opened the glass sliding door, and walked out into the corridor.

43

DANNY AND CHIPS were finishing breakfast when Chips chuckled quietly and put his coffee cup down.

'Okay, Danny,' he said. 'Let's go see what the Goldsteins have got in store for us!'

He retrieved the key from the cup, and both men walked to the Goldstein mausoleum. Chips unlocked the chain and opened the doors. Inside, he reached behind the coffins and gently pulled out the large cremation urn. He placed it on the floor and took off the lid. He lifted out a small plastic bag filled with white powder.

'Okay, Danny, here is yours!' he said and handed the bag to him. 'Mine are under this.' Chips lifted out a slither of cardboard from the urn and pulled out four large bags of white powder.

'Whoa, Chips! You gotta lot of product there. What you gonna do with all that?'

'This is my retirement fund, Danny.'

Danny's eyes opened wide, and a smile crossed his face. 'You got a stack of buyers for it?'

Chips shook his head.

'No, when I get a good quota, I'm gonna sell it all in one hit.'

'Who's gonna buy that much?'

'Don't worry, Danny. I know of at least one person who'll buy it!'

Chips put his bags back in the urn and the cardboard on top. 'Maybe three or four keys there,' he muttered to himself.

Danny gave his bag back to Chips, who put it back in the urn and returned the urn to its hiding spot.

Danny laughed. 'What are you gonna do in retirement, Chips?'

'Well, Danny, I'm goin' somewhere warm; this state is ninety percent cold most of the time. I'd like to go back home to Mississippi, but that'll never happen, so I was thinkin' of somewhere way north of here. Someplace where the sun shines most of the time, you know, like Far North Queensland. As long as you stay away from them saltwater crocs, you be pretty safe and warm up there, I reckon!' he said and laughed.

Danny paused as he took this in, then asked, 'So, Chips … what happened in Mississippi?'

Chips gazed out into the cemetery and sighed.

'Well, I was working on those big river ships and got to know a man who worked on international cargo ships. He said they was looking for a crew to go from the States to Australia and back again. He told me the pay was good, and I'd be away no more than two months. Sounded fine, so I signed up. Thought once I was there, I'd take in the sights. Anyways, it never turned out like that … the captain, he was carryin' somethin'… somethin' he shouldna been.'

'Like what?' Danny asked.

'Like weapons, Danny, all sorts of automatic weapons!'

'Why was he carryin' weapons?'

'Don't ask me! I didn't know he had 'em until we got boarded. I just thought we was loaded with general merchandise. Anyways, the authorities came aboard as we made it into Port Phillip Bay, and that was that.'

Chips shook his head.

'I got three years for being an accessory. Did two and got parole.'

'It's a wonder they didn't deport you when you got out.'

'Friendly judge, Danny! I told him I had no one back there Stateside and asked, no *begged*, to stay here! Couple of detectives put in a good word for me, and with the help of the court, I got a visa. Them detectives, they also helped me find a job on the docks, with Gallagher. You know the rest.'

Danny nodded. 'Yeah, yeah … I know the rest,' he muttered.

They walked out of the mausoleum, and Chips locked the doors. 'You ever been to Queensland, Danny?'

'Nope, but I've seen it on TV plenty of times.'

'Me too,' said Chips. 'I saw a doco 'bout the far north. They always seem to buying and selling land up there. Must be a heap of it; someone's makin' a killin'! Reckon that's what I'm gonna do when I get there. Be good, Danny. You know, you could visit. We could watch the sunset while drinkin' cocktails in some swanky bar!'

'Yeah, sure, Chips!' Danny said sarcastically as they walked through the door of the unit. 'Sure!'

Chips smiled at the thought of drinking cocktails.

'All right, Danny. We better grab those shovels and get to it. Got more plots to get ready for tomorrow.'

Danny nodded his head. 'Okay, Chips … okay.'

44

CHIPS AND DANNY were in different parts of the cemetery digging plots for the next day's burials.

Danny was preparing a double grave. There'd been a murder-suicide recently. The husband was ex-army. He'd done two tours of Afghanistan and was discharged with full military honours. But things hadn't worked out well for him. He couldn't handle the humdrum of civilian life and was continually in and out of work. As hard as he tried, he just couldn't hold down a job. He saw a shrink who diagnosed him with PTSD, but never did attend any of the sessions the psychologist organised for him. He began to drink heavily, and as his life slowly spiralled out of control, he became more and more aggressive.

It came to a head one day when he and his wife argued. She told him his drinking was the reason he'd been sacked again and that he should give it up. He burst into a rage and strangled her to death on the kitchen floor. The teenage kids found her first and then found their father in the lounge room surrounded by photos of his army buddies. He'd shot himself in the head. It was a dreadful tragedy. However, the kids decided that despite the terrible circumstances surrounding their parents' deaths, they wanted them to be together, and so they paid for a suitable-sized grave where they could visit knowing they were still with one another.

Chips was working near the cemetery's front gates when he

heard the roar of a motorbike. He looked over as the bike appeared in the main entrance. The tall bikie switched off the chopper, stood it up, removed his helmet, and walked in.

'Can I help ya?' Chips called out.

The bikie walked over to him.

'I'm looking for a friend. I think he works here.'

Chips eyed him suspiciously.

'You got someone who works here with you, haven't ya?' the bikie pressed.

'Yeah … Danny works here.'

The bikie's pulse quickened when he heard the name Danny. He knew he was on the right path.

'So where can I find Danny?'

'He's down the other side of the cemetery.' Chips pointed in the general direction. 'Bit of a walk, though!'

'Don't worry,' the bikie said and spat on the ground. 'I won't be walkin'.'

With that the bikie strode back to his chopper, climbed on, kicked it into life, and began to ride down the path.

'Hey, you can't ride that in here!' Chips shouted.

'Get out of the way!' the bikie yelled and roared off along the winding path.

Danny was inside the plot, finishing it off and getting the corners nice and square. It was deep, and he didn't hear the motorbike until it was almost on top of him. He used the small aluminium stepladder to climb out and stood frozen to the spot. A bikie in Tarantula leathers stood in front of him.

'You're Wainwright, aren't ya?' the bikie snarled.

Now in the bright daylight, Danny recognised him. He was the one at the Tarantulas' clubhouse who thought he knew him, the pool player, the one they called Eddie. Now Danny remembered him clearly. He'd seen him at the Halifax pub when making his getaway after shooting Draken. This was not going to be a friendly meeting.

He kept staring at the bikie but also tried to take in his surroundings. The shovel, the only thing he could use as a weapon, lay just beside the grave but well out of reach.

'What makes you think I'm him?'

'I saw you in the car park after you killed Lex, you bastard! You shot him in the back of the head!'

The bikie reached behind and unclipped the pack rack. As he did, Danny noticed the red spider tattoo on the back of his hand. He pulled out a snub-nosed pistol. Danny took a step towards the shovel.

'I thought it was you in the clubhouse. All fuckin' sweet and innocent in there, weren't ya?'

The bikie levelled the handgun and pointed it at Danny.

'Well, we have a code of honour in the Tarantulas … it's an eye-for-an-eye, a-kill-for-a-kill!'

'You've got the wrong man!' Danny said, hoping like hell he could talk his way out of this.

'Bullshit! It was you, all right!'

The bikie fingered the handgun.

'I wondered where you were hidin'.' He spat on the ground. 'You didn't think we'd give you that satchel and just let you walk off into the night, did ya?' The bikie sniggered. 'Well, guess what? Somebody followed you … followed you right here to the cemetery!'

Danny shook his head in disbelief. He thought he'd always been so careful.

The bikie pointed at the fresh earth. 'Good thing you dug that grave!'

He walked over to Danny and shoved the gun in his face. There was no hope of getting the shovel now.

'Get down in the hole!'

'What?'

The carnival came to life. Clowns leered at him, and a cacophony of rasping music filled his head.

'Get in the fuckin' hole!' the bikie screamed, then aimed the gun at Danny's groin.

Reluctantly, Danny climbed back down into the grave. The bikie stood over the edge and aimed the gun down at Danny's skull.

'You've got the wrong man!'

'Lie down!'

Danny remained standing.

'This can be easy for you, or you can make it hard. You don't lie down, I'll shoot you through both shoulders and then your feet; then I'll kill ya! You lie down, it's one nice clean shot straight between the eyes.'

Danny's heart sank. After all this time, and all that had gone before, from the escape in Sydney to making it safely down to Melbourne and then finding what he thought was a secure hideout here in the cemetery, now he was going to be killed by a bikie and buried in a grave he had prepared himself. Danny slowly lay down.

'Goodbye, Wainwright … you fuckin' dog. This one's for Lex!'

The bikie took aim. Danny squeezed his eyes closed and waited for the shot; he wondered how much it would hurt.

The thud and suffocating crush of the heavy object knocked the wind out of him. He grunted in agony as he was pinned under a solid weight. Slowly, he lifted one arm and felt his forehead. It was fine. He opened his eyes and peered up at Chips, who was standing at the edge of the grave and holding the shovel at shoulder level.

'You better get out of there, Danny!'

Danny felt like he was in a dream. Right now, he should be dead.

Maybe he was!

Maybe this was what it was like!

Maybe Chips was the one who was going to throw the dirt down on top of him!

'Danny, get out of there!' Chips yelled at him.

Danny was jolted back to reality. The bikie was lying on top of him. Danny pushed him aside, and as he stood up, the bikie groaned.

Danny could see a large cut on the back of the bikie's head where Chips had hit him. Blood flowed freely from the wound.

'Get the gun, Danny!'

Danny hadn't heard Chips speak like this before. His tone was authoritative. It wasn't a request; it was an order. Danny searched around under the body and found the handgun. He showed it to Chips.

'Okay, leave it in there with him, but not near his hands!'

Danny put the gun between the bikie's feet and then started to climb out. He took a step on the ladder, then held up his hand to Chips.

'Sorry, Chips … I haven't got the strength!'

Chips took his hand and hoisted him out of the deep grave.

'What you wanna do with him, Danny?'

Danny stared down at the man who, only minutes ago, would have happily shot him.

'We can't leave any trace, Chips. I don't know if his friends knew he was comin' here, but … we have to get rid of him!' He kept feeling his forehead. 'We also gotta get rid of the bike!'

Chips nodded in agreement as he glanced over at the sparkling Harley Davidson.

'It can go in the grave with him. Everything goes in there!' Chips said.

'Yeah … okay,' Danny said. Then he added, 'Chips, you don't need to be part of this. You can walk away now!' Danny pointed back at the grave. 'That's some of my past catchin' up with me!'

'Danny, I've come this far. I ain't walking away. I ain't goin' nowhere!'

Danny started breathing easier.

'Okay, Chips. Help me with the chopper, will ya?'

Both men wheeled the motorcycle to the edge of the grave and rolled it in. The handlebars scraped the sides of the grave as the bike slid out of sight. It fell heavily on the bikie's body, but there was no reaction. The groaning had finally stopped.

'Gonna have to dig another plot to make up for this one!' Danny muttered to himself.

'I'll help ya. First, let's get this done!' Chips said to him. 'Danny, get the ladder.'

Danny lifted the ladder out of the grave, and then both men began to shovel in the loose dirt. Soon, the grave was full, and there was no longer any trace of the motorcycle or the bikie known as Eddie.

45

LATE EVENING, AND Gallagher was in his office, finishing up a long shift, when the phone rang.

'Yeah,' Gallagher said, puzzled by who would be ringing at this hour.

'Mick, it's Tom … Tom Lucas.'

'Ahh, Detective Lucas, what can I do for you this fine evening? Sorry, but there are no brown paper bags ready for you or Detective Jacobs just yet!' Gallagher said in a cheerful manner.

'No, it's not that. I need to see you. Tonight. We might have a problem!' Lucas sounded worried.

'Problem?' Gallagher said. 'What do ya mean … *problem?*'

'Mick, it's urgent. I need to see you tonight, but it's gotta be just you and me!'

There was a desperate edge to Lucas' voice. Gallagher knew Lucas was always a bit skittish, but he'd never heard him sound like this. He wondered why he didn't want his offsider Detective Jacobs with him.

'You wanna meet here in my office … *by yourself?*'

'Yes, but when it's totally dark. I don't want anyone to see me!'

Gallagher paused for a moment. 'Okay. Come through the riverside entrance. I'll let security know you're coming.'

'Thanks, Mick.'

Lucas hung up.

* * *

A bit after 8:00pm, and Detective Tom Lucas sat in Gallagher's visitor's chair. He asked Gallagher for a cigarette and nervously puffed away.

'So what's the problem, Tom?'

'I've been seconded to a task force in New South Wales.'

'Sounds good!' Gallagher said as he pulled a cigarette from the packet and lit up.

'It's not so good, Mick. I was at a briefing up in Sydney this morning and flew back late this afternoon. The boss wants me to set things up here in Melbourne before him and his team get here.'

Gallagher frowned. 'So, what is it you're doin'?'

'They're searching for someone that broke out of a prison van in Sydney over twelve months ago. They reckon he could be holed up in Melbourne somewhere. Two teams of New South Wales cops are gonna be flying down here early tomorrow askin' questions and lookin' for him.'

A single butterfly took to the wing in Gallagher's stomach as he stared across at Lucas. 'So what? Why is this a problem?' he asked warily.

'The lead detective of the team I'm with, Cooper, is going to be doin' the rounds in the CBD and on the docks. I saw his running sheet; he's going to call in here in the next couple of days asking questions.'

Gallagher rocked back in his chair and drew in a lungful of smoke.

'No problem,' Gallagher said, turning this over in his mind. 'I haven't got anyone working for me that's on the run! So this shit-hot cop comes asking a few questions, and I say I don't know anyone, and I haven't seen anyone … no problems!'

'But there is a problem, Mick,' Lucas said. 'It's Jacobs.'

'What do you mean?'

'Jacobs told me he was at a pub in Carlton watching the footy and saw your men Talbot and Grist walk in. He was suspicious and watched what they were doing. He said they spoke to a man, and he thinks he gave them something. Also, there was a bit of a scuffle when they left; some bloke's in a coma in the hospital. He told me that after about ten minutes or so, the guy they spoke to left the pub. Jacobs said he followed him, but lost him in the city somewhere.'

Gallagher started getting uncomfortable. 'Yeah ... so?' he said aggressively.

'He told me the man matches the description of the bloke the task-force cops are searching for.'

Lucas took a deep drag on his cigarette and coughed as he filled his lungs with smoke.

Gallagher squinted and asked, 'How did Jacobs know who you were looking for?'

Lucas swallowed hard.

'I told him,' he said in a soft voice. 'Jacobs rang me when I was in the airport waiting for the flight back to Melbourne, and we were chatting. He asked me about the task force ... and ... and I told him who the target was ... and what he looked like.' Lucas hung his head.

Before Gallagher could speak, he added, 'Mick, Jacobs thinks the guy he saw in the pub last night might have been Danny Wain-wright ... *the guy's a hired gun!*'

Gallagher stared out at the dark night as Lucas went on. 'If it is Wainwright, Cooper will be all over it!'

The conversation stopped for a moment as a lonely ship's foghorn echoed out in the distance. 'He's pissed, Mick!'

'Who?' asked Gallagher angrily.

'Jacobs! He's pissed he didn't get the role in the task force. He said he's senior to me, so he should have got it. He says he's gonna tell Cooper all about what he saw in the pub when he gets to Melbourne. He's gonna make himself look good in front of the brass. Once

Cooper knows your men Talbot and Grist are involved, he'll tear this place apart!'

Lucas stubbed his cigarette out and helped himself to another one of Gallagher's.

'If he finds out about the money in the brown bags …' Lucas gazed down as tears started to form in his eyes. 'Mick … I could go to jail!' The sound of his high-pitched whining filled the office.

Gallagher thought about it. He saw the man in front of him was weak and close to breaking point.

'But if Jacobs tells Cooper, and they find out about us splittin' the containers, he'll also get done for taking a brown bag!'

'I mentioned that to Jacobs, but he said there's no need to say anything about the brown paper bags. Once he tells Cooper about Wainwright, he'll come here and start asking questions. He'll wanna know why your men were in the pub talking to him. He'll wanna know where Wainwright is!' Lucas paused and drew in a lungful of smoke. 'Cooper's obsessed with Wainwright; he'll do anything to get him!'

Lucas stared at Gallagher. He waited for him to speak, and when he didn't, he went on. 'It *was* Wainwright they were talkin' to, wasn't it, Mick?'

There was a moment of silence in Gallagher's office.

'Mick, provided you can finger Wainwright and tell Cooper where to find him, he'll make the arrest. Cooper will be satisfied, and the job will be done.'

But Gallagher didn't speak. Lucas dragged hard on the cigarette and then continued. 'You do know where he is, don't ya, Mick?'

Still, Gallagher didn't answer. Lucas shook his hand as the cigarette burnt down to his fingers. He sat there waiting for Gallagher to speak, and when he didn't, he stubbed the cigarette out and grabbed another one.

'I mean, if it is Wainwright, and you know where to find him, *I can make the arrest!* It'll be all over. There'll be no need for Cooper to come here at all! We'll all be in the clear!'

But again, Gallagher didn't reply. A plan was forming in his head. He leant back in his chair, only half hearing what Lucas was saying, and gazed out into the distance. There was no way he was going to hand Danny over to Lucas or Cooper. As soon as he did that, he'd need another delivery man. And what if Danny talked? Then his whole empire – the container-pilfering job, the cocaine sales, as well as the late-night drug pick-ups – it would all be in jeopardy. Gallagher leant forward and stared hard at Lucas.

'Tom, here's what I want you to do. I want you to contact Jacobs and bring him here tomorrow night. Tell him we're distributing the brown paper bags early; tell him we've had a particularly good couple of days, and the payout is bigger than normal.'

Lucas lit up and drew hard on the cigarette as Gallagher went on. 'I want you both here at 9:00pm. Got it?'

'Okay, Mick. So, what's the plan?'

'Tom … sometimes it's best not to ask too many questions.'

Lucas sat there for a moment staring at Gallagher, waiting to see if he had something else to say. But when Gallagher turned over a page of the ledger in front of him and started reading, it was clear the conversation was over.

Lucas stood up, his mind racing. He walked out of Gallagher's office into the chilled night air. The back of his suit coat was wet with sweat, and as he made his way to his car, it stuck to him like a frozen second skin.

46

DARK SHADOWS STRETCHED out across the deserted wharves of Melbourne. The sombre moan of distant foghorns rose and fell on the cool evening air. High above, a waxing moon shone down, touching everything with an iridescent glow. Bright security lights shone out into the night. Inside the dockside yard, the massive rows of steel shipping containers, piled high like a massive game of Tetris for giants, stood cold and resolute.

It was a bit past 9:00pm, and Gallagher was in his office with four other men: his two accomplices, Talbot and Grist, together with Detectives Colin Jacobs and Tom Lucas.

Jacobs smiled and spoke to Gallagher. 'So, Mick, you're distributing early, Tom tells me you've had a very profitable few days?'

'Yes, detective, I think you're gonna be surprised with what we've got for you tonight!' Gallagher said and smiled as he pointed to the visitor's chair. 'Take a seat, my friend.'

Tom Lucas stood in the background. Both he and Jacobs had arrived in Lucas' car and went through the riverside entrance as Gallagher had instructed. Talbot met them and told the security guard he could go home for the night.

Talbot stood next to Lucas at the door while Grist stood in the middle of the office behind Jacobs, who was now seated. Gallagher had a number of brown paper bags on his desk. He pushed one over to the detective, who was about to open it when Gallagher spoke.

'I understand you saw my men the other night at a pub in Carlton!' Gallagher said, the smile leaving his face.

'What?' Jacobs asked. He stared at Gallagher with a puzzled expression.

'Watching the football, at the George … you were there!'

'Ahh, yeah,' Jacobs said. 'That's right. The footy was on … so what?'

Jacobs continued opening the bag while Gallagher lit a cigarette and leant back in his chair.

'You watched what Frank and Grist did.'

Jacobs could sense a change of atmosphere in the office.

'Yeah, I saw them!' Jacobs sat up straighter in the chair and pushed the paper bag to one side. 'So what, Mick?'

'We've been friends a long time!'

'Where's this goin', Mick?'

'Friends don't talk!'

'What do you mean? I haven't spoken to anybody!' Jacobs became defensive.

'You spoke to Tom!'

Jacobs turned around and glanced at Lucas, then swung back and stared at Gallagher with a startled expression.

'I didn't say anything to anyone.'

'You told Tom you recognised someone.'

The office became silent. Jacobs started to worry; he could sense the situation had turned dangerous.

'You said you were goin' to tell a New South Wales copper what you saw.'

Jacobs hesitated and stared hard at Gallagher. 'Look … I was never going to …'

Gallagher nodded to Grist, who, in an instant, wrapped a metal chain around Jacobs' neck. He pulled it tight and dragged Jacobs backwards to the floor of the office, taking the visitor's chair with him. Jacobs kicked and struggled, but Grist held the chain in a vice-like grip. Jacobs began to grunt and fight. He twisted around in an effort to grab Grist by the head, but Talbot saw the move and rushed over and grabbed his arms. Jacobs thrashed about on the floor and thrust his legs around frantically, kneeing Talbot in the ribs.

'Ahh, shit!' Talbot yelled as he reeled away in pain.

Gallagher saw what was happening. He pushed his chair back and raced around the side of his desk and grabbed one of Jacobs' legs. He held it down while Jacobs' other leg flung around wildly. Grist continued to apply maximum pressure. Jacobs fought and grunted, heaving his body from side to side.

'Keep the pressure up, Grist!' Gallagher yelled.

But Grist didn't need to be encouraged. He loved what he was doing. Lucas stood in the background and watched. His stomach was churning. He couldn't believe how deep he was getting in – first theft, now murder!

Jacobs continued to struggle, and his grunting got louder as he fought for air. He was stronger than any of them thought. Finally, Grist managed to get a good purchase on the chain. He put his knee in the back of Jacobs' head and forced it forward. Jacobs' eyes began to bulge, and his tongue lolled out of his mouth. Jacobs dug his fingers into his neck in a desperate attempt to remove the chain. Soon, a thin trickle of blood stood out as the chain bit into flesh. Eventually, after what seemed like an eternity, the fight left his body, and he became still. Grist, however, didn't let go. He continued to hold the chain in place and squeezed as hard as he could. After a further minute, it was obvious to Gallagher that Jacobs must be dead.

'Okay, Grist, let go. We don't want too much blood!'

But Grist held on. His eyes had glazed over, and he wasn't listening. The muscles in his arms flexed as he applied more pressure; he threatened to decapitate Jacobs.

'Grist, that's enough!' yelled Gallagher. 'Let go!'

Talbot grabbed Grist's arm and shook it. 'Let go! Let go!'

Finally, Grist released his grip, and Jacobs' head thumped down on the wooden floor.

'Is he dead?' Lucas asked in a high-pitched whimper.

'What do you think!' Gallagher snapped.

It was clear to Gallagher that Lucas was a problem. He wondered how long it would be before he folded and gave away the game, here on the docks. He needed to do something about him as well, but not now.

Gallagher walked over to Lucas, put his arm around his shoulder, and said in a softer, friendlier manner, 'Tom, it had to be done. We're okay now. Nobody is going to talk, and nobody has to know what we've done here tonight, okay?'

Lucas nodded and looked up to Gallagher like a child being spoken to by a parent.

'Can I go now, Mick?'

'No, Tom, you're going to see this through, just like the rest of us!'

Gallagher stared directly at Lucas. Tears filled the young detective's eyes as they jerked around from one man to the next.

'All right, Mick … okay,' he said meekly and gazed down at Jacobs' prone body sprawled out on the bare wooden floor.

Talbot walked outside and grabbed a hand trolley and a large clothing trunk he'd left at the office door. He put the trunk on the trolley and wheeled it in.

'Tom, give Grist a hand!' Gallagher ordered.

Talbot opened the trunk lid.

'Grab his legs!' Talbot said to Lucas.

Lucas took hold of Jacobs' legs while Grist grabbed the detective's arms, and they heaved the body into the trunk. There was a dull cracking noise as Jacobs' knees were forced up under his chin to make him fit. Talbot shoved the lid down and slid the bolt into place. Grist helped manoeuvre the trunk onto the trolley's footplate.

'Where we gonna take him?' Lucas asked.

'Wharf 23,' Gallagher replied and walked out of the office. Talbot struggled as he wheeled the trolley behind Gallagher.

'Follow me,' Gallagher said to the others. 'We'll go around the back, through the dead side.'

The men made their way in the dark through the chilled night air. A light breeze picked up and blew gently along the wharves. High above, distant stars blinked and sparkled against a pitch-black sky. In the distance, night birds swooped low over the silver tops of the dark, turbulent waves out on the bay.

Soon, they were on the crumbling wooden walkway that led to the wharf. Talbot fought and grunted as the trolley wheels bounced and occasionally stuck in the rotten wooden ruts. It was slow going as he had to dodge bits and pieces of useless dock material and tangles of rope strewn about haphazardly. Alongside the wharf, rundown barges bobbed up and down on the silky black water, moored there permanently and to be used for either spare parts or for scrapping altogether. A bit further on, they came to Gallagher's tugboat.

'Wait here, Frank,' Gallagher said to Talbot.

Gallagher dragged a makeshift wooden gangplank out from under a tarpaulin and pushed it into place. Talbot struggled as he wheeled the trolley onto the boat.

'Get on!' Gallagher ordered Lucas.

Lucas was hesitant as he crossed over to the deck. Grist then followed. Gallagher crossed over, then pushed the gangplank back onto the wharf and walked into the tugboat's wheelhouse.

'Untie us, Frank!'

Gallagher waited for Talbot to undo the mooring ropes, then turned the key, and the tugboat sprang into life. It chugged away from the dock and out into the mouth of the Yarra River. Once they made the vast expanse of Port Phillip Bay, Gallagher gunned the motor, and they raced ahead, riding up and down on the smooth rolling waves. Talbot and Grist held on to the sides while Lucas, ghostly white in the face, clung grimly to the wheelhouse door and peered back longingly at the rapidly disappearing shoreline.

After a ten-minute trip, Gallagher cut the engine, and with a long slow hiss, they came to a stop. Out on the vast expanse of dark water, it became eerily quiet, the only noise being the occasional slosh of the waves against the side of the boat.

'Okay, get him out!' Gallagher ordered.

Talbot opened the lid of the trunk. With an effort, Grist and Lucas tipped the trunk sideways and Jacobs' body tumbled out on the deck.

'Grist, get the weights!'

Grist walked to the bow of the boat and brought over lengths of chain and various rusted machine parts that Gallagher had put there the night before. Talbot and Gallagher started to attach the weights to the body. Lucas stood in the background, watching, unable to speak or help. Then a groan came from Jacobs. Gallagher stood back in surprise.

'Frank!' he said.

Talbot needed no further instruction. He took a pistol out of his jacket and put a bullet in Jacobs' head. The crack of the shot echoed out across the water. Jacobs lay on his back, not moving; the red hole in his forehead slowly oozed blood. Talbot put the gun away, and without another word he and Gallagher resumed tying weights to the body.

When they'd finished, Gallagher shouted to the young detective, 'Lucas, get here. Help us lift him!'

Reluctantly, Lucas helped the others move Jacobs' body. They dragged it to the stern and, after a mighty struggle, placed it on the edge of the boat.

Gallagher spent a moment looking down at Jacobs and slowly shook his head. 'Goodbye, Jacobs,' he said, then shoved the body over the side.

There was a loud splash as the body hit the water, and in an instant, Jacobs disappeared from view. Each man peered down into the murky, black water, but all that greeted them were a few bubbles of air as the weighted body raced to the bottom. Without further ceremony, Gallagher walked back into the wheelhouse and started up the motor.

'Lucas, Grist, clean up the deck!'

Grist found a bucket and some rags, and the two men took turns to scrub and soak up the bloodstains on the wooden boards. Twenty minutes later, and they were back at the wharf. As they walked through the container yard, Gallagher turned to Lucas.

'Tom, keep your mouth shut. No one needs to know what happened here tonight … understand?'

'Yes, Mick,' Lucas sobbed and looked at Gallagher through tear-soaked eyes.

Talbot escorted Lucas out to the riverside entrance. He watched as Lucas got into his car and drove off. He locked the gate and made his way back to Gallagher's office.

Inside, Gallagher poured a whisky for Talbot and himself and opened a stubby of crisp, cold Victoria Bitter for Grist. It was time to celebrate a job well done – a problem removed.

47

DANNY SAT AT the back of Theo's Bar and wondered if she'd turn up.

He hoped coming back here after she finished work was her normal routine. He wasn't disappointed. Shortly after 11:00pm, Ebony, and another girl he'd seen waitressing at the Seven Veils, walked through the door. At first, she didn't notice him and searched around to find a suitable table. Then, just as she was about to take a seat, she saw him.

'Oh!' she mouthed.

Ebony and her girlfriend walked over to Danny's table.

'What are you doing here?' Ebony asked, and that beautiful smile appeared on her face.

Danny smiled back at her. 'I was just waiting for the prettiest girl in Melbourne to walk through the door!'

'Are you still using that old line?' she said and smiled.

Ebony sat down and said to her friend, 'Bridget, take a seat. This is Danny. Danny, this is Bridget.'

Bridget nodded and said, 'Hello.'

'Hi,' Danny replied.

'So how long have you been waiting here?' Ebony asked.

'Oh, not long. I caught a tram a little while ago.'

The waiter walked over. 'Can I get you girls the usual?'

'Yes thanks, Wilfred,' they said almost in unison.

'And, sir, light beer?'

'Whisky and Coke, thanks,' Danny said.

'Oh, you are stepping out!' Ebony remarked and smiled at him again.

The waiter brought the drinks over, and they made small talk. Bridget finished hers quickly and said she'd better go as it was getting late. She also knew that three was a crowd, and it was obvious Danny wanted to be alone with Ebony.

'Oh, do you have to go so soon?' Ebony asked.

'Yes, I'll see you tomorrow. I need my beauty sleep, you know!' Bridget replied and smiled at them as she stood up. She paid for her drink and left.

Danny waited until she was gone, then asked Ebony, 'So how's your day been?'

'Well …' she said and paused for dramatic effect, 'good, and maybe it's getting better!' She raised her eyebrows, and a smile lit up her face.

They talked for another half an hour and finished their drinks. Ebony checked her watch. 'I'd better get going. I don't want to be home too late.'

'I'll walk you to the tram stop,' Danny said.

They stood together near the corner of Collins and Spencer Streets. Ebony moved closer to him as a freezing wind blew through the city streets. Then the 96 edged its way around the corner and stopped in front of them.

'Okay, I guess I'll see you later,' Danny said.

Ebony smiled at him.

'Why? Do you have somewhere special to go?'

Danny was taken aback. 'I … ahh … um … no!'

'Why don't you come and see where I live?' She took him by the hand as she reached up and kissed his cheek.

Danny's heart began to race.

'Okay. Yeah, okay … but I don't have a ticket!'

'It's all right. It's still the Free Zone … well … most of the way!'

They talked and rode the tram back to St Kilda and got off near Luna Park; the giant white smiling face peered down at them as they passed by. She took his hand, and they walked together along Carlisle Street. Soon they reached her flat and went inside. Ebony turned on the lights and the heater. She turned to Danny and, with a sweeping motion, showed off her flat.

'So, what do you think?'

Danny stared around the flat and then back at her. 'It's beautiful,' he said, 'just like you!'

She fluttered her eyes, walked over, and pushed herself against him. He took her in his arms. She craned her neck up. His heart started beating at one hundred miles per hour. He put his face down and softly kissed her on the mouth. Their lips locked tightly as the kissing became passionate. She led him by the hand to the bedroom and closed the door. She hurriedly undressed. Danny followed her lead, and soon they stood there completely naked. She moved over to him. He picked her up, and they kissed again. She wrapped her legs around him. He walked to the bed, and she pulled back the covers while still kissing him. He lay down on top of her and moved his lips down her neck and kissed her bare breasts. She groaned and spread herself underneath him on the silky white sheets, and then, slowly and ever so gently, he entered her. The lovemaking lasted for hours. It was well past 2:00am when finally, exhausted, they fell asleep together.

Ebony's alarm went off at 7:00am. She reached over, turned it off, and felt for Danny, but he wasn't there. She searched around anxiously, then smelt toast cooking. She put on her dressing gown and walked out into the kitchen.

'You're up early!' she said and smiled. 'You making breakfast?'

'Gotta look after the prettiest girl in Melbourne!' he replied.

She smiled and shook her head. Then she reached over and kissed him.

* * *

Later that morning, Danny walked through the main gates of the cemetery and found Chips.

'Danny … where've you been?'

'I'm sorry, Chips. I've been … umm … distracted.'

'Distracted! What do ya mean, *distracted*?'

'Well, Chips,' Danny said with a smile. 'I've met someone … a girl!'

Chips was flabbergasted.

'What, Danny? You ain't s'posed to be meetin' someone! You s'posed to be here diggin' graves!'

Chips shook his head in disbelief and stared at Danny with a half-smile. 'Okay, so what's her name?'

'Ebony.'

'Ebony,' Chips repeated. 'So where'd you meet … *Ebony*?'

Danny hesitated for a moment. 'At the Seven Veils.'

Chips' mouth fell open.

'What! Are you crazy, Danny? You go hanging 'round down there, that's one sure way to get yourself killed!'

Danny didn't answer. Chips shook his head again and handed him a shovel.

'Danny, take this and finish up here. I'll start the new one on the west side!' Then Chips said with a sly grin, 'You have got the energy left to do this, haven't ya?'

48

POLICE HEADQUARTERS IN Flinders Street, Melbourne, and Detective Senior Sergeant Presley Cooper was briefing his task force at an early meeting. The plan today was to call on the docks. Cooper, who was standing at the front of the gathering, walked over to Detective Constable Tom Lucas.

'So, Tom, today we're visiting the docks ... *your* neck of the woods!' Before Lucas could say anything, Cooper addressed the others.

'Detective Lucas here was recommended to us by the Victorian Police Commissioner. Both Tom and his offsider, who we can't seem to track down, have a very good knowledge of the docks and surrounding CBD area.'

Cooper sat down at the head of the room.

'Tom, will you please give us a rundown of what we can expect to see when we get there?'

Lucas walked out to the front of the room and addressed the team while Cooper stared at him. Lucas was hesitant at first – the events of last night were still fresh with him – but eventually he got on a roll and described the layout of the docks and the shipping-container area.

'Hmm,' said Cooper, not really happy with what Lucas had to say. 'And your boss, Superintendent Whitehead, tells me you and Detective Senior Sergeant Jacobs regularly call on the shipping container manager to see what's happening there.'

'Yes, sir, that's right,' Lucas said as his stomach began to churn.

'And what is it you actually do? What do you look for?'

'Well, sir, we check the security on the docks to make sure it's all in order, and also inspect the shipping containers to make sure the seals are in place and haven't been tampered with … things like that. We give the place a good general overview.'

'Good general overview,' Cooper repeated sarcastically. 'I understand the manager of the shipping containers is a man called Gallagher. Is that correct?'

'Yes, sir. Mick Gallagher.'

'Mick Gallagher!' Cooper emphasised. 'He also recruits recently released prisoners into his workforce. Is that also correct?'

'Yes, sir, that's right.'

'I don't trust people who employ ex-cons!' Cooper said in a loud voice, making sure everyone in the room heard. He paused and waited for his comment to sink in, then turned to Lucas and asked, 'How many did you say he has working there currently?'

'Three, sir.'

'All from the same prison?'

'I'm not sure, sir.'

'How does he recruit these people? Does someone recommend them to him?'

Lucas' stomach started to sink. He fidgeted as he stood out the front. He could feel his resolve starting to buckle.

'I don't … I … I don't know, sir.'

Cooper stared at Lucas accusingly and didn't speak for a few moments. 'Thank you, Lucas. You can go back to your seat!'

He waited for Lucas to sit down, then addressed his arm of the task force as a whole. 'Gentlemen, I have a suspicious mind. I'm going to put the docks under surveillance.' Cooper turned to a red-haired man, Detective Senior Constable Jim Spears.

'Jim, you have the technology. Are the devices working?'

'Yes, Pres, all tested and working fine.'

'Good!' Cooper nodded. 'Excellent!'

49

THE PHONE RANG in Gallagher's office.

'Yeah!' Gallagher said.

'Mick!'

It was a guard at the main gate.

'What?'

'The cops are here. They wanna see you!'

Gallagher's stomach lurched, and for a moment he went quiet.

'Mick, you there?'

'Yeah, yeah. Send 'em through!'

Gallagher checked his office like he'd done a hundred times since disposing of Jacobs' body. He examined it once more to make sure any bloodstains had been successfully removed. Then he lit a cigarette and waited. Soon, four men arrived at the door.

'Mick Gallagher?' asked the first detective. He was a big guy and showed his police ID as he walked in.

'Yes.' Gallagher stood up and held out his hand.

'I'm Detective Senior Sergeant Cooper.' He shook Gallagher's hand. 'This is Detective Hunt and Detective Balme,' Cooper said and pointed to the other two men. 'I believe you already know Detective Lucas; he tells me he keeps an eye on things around here, making sure the law is upheld!'

The sarcastic remark wasn't lost on Gallagher. Lucas smiled a weak smile and raised his hand to Gallagher.

'Yes, yes, the police keep an 'eagle eye' on everything that goes on around here!' Gallagher said and smiled reassuringly.

Cooper glanced around the tiny office.

'How can I help you, gentlemen?' Gallagher asked.

'We're searching for someone … Danny Wainwright.' Cooper waited to see if Danny's name would register with Gallagher. 'He's escaped from custody in New South Wales, and we believe he may be hiding somewhere here in Melbourne.'

'Never heard of him!' Gallagher said and slowly shook his head. 'Any reason you've come *here* lookin' for him?'

Cooper pointed to the visitor's chair. 'Mind?'

'No, not at all. Have a seat.' Gallagher waited until Cooper sat down, then resumed his seat behind the desk.

Cooper put a folder on the desktop.

'We understand you recruit people recently released from prison.'

'Yes, that's right. Why? Has your man also been in the lock-up?'

'No, but you know how criminals talk, and seeing as how you employ such people, we're interested in anything you might've heard,' Cooper said and glared at Gallagher intensely.

Gallagher stared back at Cooper.

'I give ex-cons a second chance,' Gallagher said. 'I give 'em a job, you know, help 'em out like! But I've never heard them mention, umm …' Gallagher waved his hand in a display of trying to remember Danny's name.

'*Wainwright!*' Cooper said in a condescending manner. '*Danny Wainwright.*'

Cooper cast his eyes around the office walls. 'That your work roster?' he asked as he pointed at a paper roughly pinned to the wall behind Gallagher.

Gallagher turned around. 'Yeah, it's a weekly schedule,' he said and started to point out a few details, hoping to take the conversation down a different path.

While Gallagher was looking away, Cooper took a small object out of his pocket and peeled a plastic patch off the back of it, revealing a sticky substance. Before Gallagher turned around, Cooper reached under the desk and attached the bug to the wooden underside. Cooper waited until Gallagher faced him and then opened up his folder and took out an A4 photo.

'Here's a picture of the man we want to find.'

He slid a photo of Danny across the desk. Gallagher glanced down at it. It was a recent shot and unmistakably Danny.

Gallagher slowly shook his head and said, 'Nope, never seen *him* before!'

Cooper nodded. 'Okay … well, do you mind if we have a look around the place?' he asked and pointed outside.

'No, go right ahead. Got nothin' to hide here!' Gallagher replied and waved his arm at the door, happy to have them leave.

'Thanks.' Cooper stood up. 'If you do hear of his whereabouts, or happen to see him, you will give us a call … won't you?' As he said this, he slid his business card across to Gallagher.

'Yeah, sure. Of course!' replied Gallagher.

Cooper left Gallagher's office, followed by the other detectives. Gallagher watched them walk into the yard, and when they were out of sight, he got straight on the phone to Talbot.

'Yeah,' Talbot said.

'Frank, you and Grist lie low for a few days. The cops are hanging around,' Gallagher said and hung up.

As they walked through the yard, Cooper spoke to Lucas. 'Your super tells me he hasn't heard from Detective Jacobs today; he tells me that's unusual.'

'I know, sir. I haven't heard from him either,' Lucas replied and started to sweat.

'Have you called around to his house to see if he is okay?'

'No, sir, I haven't.'

'Why don't you then? Go and see if he's all right. Meet us at

Flinders Street headquarters this afternoon at, say, five o'clock.'

'Yes, sir. Okay. I'll see if I can find him.'

Cooper watched Lucas walk off. He started to form a picture of someone he didn't trust. He turned to the other two detectives.

'Okay, gents, let's take our time and check this place out. See what there is to see!'

* * *

Later that evening at Police Headquarters, Cooper ran the debriefing session. He turned to Detective Spears, who had headphones slung to one side of his head.

'Have you got a fix on the bug?'

'Yes, Pres, it's coming through loud and clear. We should be able to hear all conversations in Gallagher's office and also anything he says on the telephone.'

'Got anything yet?'

'Yes. Shortly after you left, he made a phone call to someone called Frank. Told him and someone else called Grist to lie low for a couple of days as the cops were hanging around.'

It confirmed Cooper's thoughts that Gallagher was up to no good.

'Excellent,' Cooper said and nodded. 'I want you and your men to monitor that bug night and day … twenty-four hours!'

'Will do, Pres,' Spears said.

Cooper addressed the task force. 'Good day's work, gentlemen!'

Lucas raised his hand. 'Sir, is it legal to put a bug in someone's premises without first getting the proper court orders?'

Cooper turned on Lucas.

'Lucas, it's only illegal if you get caught!' Cooper said, and the other detectives chuckled. 'If we apprehend Wainwright, something like a bug in someone's office will be ignored!' He stared directly at Lucas and said in a determined manner, 'I'll make sure of it!'

Lucas nodded weakly. Cooper continued to stare at him. He just wanted to get rid of Lucas. He was clearly a weak link.

Then Cooper added, 'Any word about your partner, Jacobs?'

'No, sir, nothing!' Lucas' heart started beating wildly.

'Hmm,' Cooper said and then addressed the other detectives. 'Did you see the way Gallagher reacted when I showed him the photo of Wainwright?'

'Yes, Pres,' said one of the detectives. 'He definitely recognised him.'

'Yes,' Cooper said softly, 'yes, he certainly did. Hunt, Balme, I want twenty-four-hour surveillance on those docks, starting tonight. Get extra men if you need to. There's something going on there, and I want to know what it is!'

'Okay, Pres, will do!'

Lucas sat silently at the back of the conference room and watched and worried. He knew he had to get word to Gallagher somehow, but with that bug in place, it was going to be difficult – maybe impossible.

PART SEVEN

THINGS FALL APART

every man for himself …

50

GIUSEPPE D'ANGELO MADE a phone call to Ben Lucizano.

Lucizano was in bed with Candy, one of the 'bar-walkers' from the Seven Veils. He reached across the naked girl, picked up the phone, checked the caller ID on the screen, and pressed the answer button.

'Yes, Giuseppe?'

'Ben, I want to see you ... now!'

'Yes, Giuseppe. I'll be there straight away!' Lucizano said, but D'Angelo had already hung up.

He looked across at the girl. 'It's the boss ... I've gotta go.'

Candy bit her bottom lip and lowered her eyes. 'Oh, Ben, just a little while longer,' she said with a sigh and ran her hand from his shoulder down to his groin.

'I'm sorry, Candy!' he said and pushed her hand away. 'I don't have a choice!' He kissed her, then hurriedly dressed and headed for the Seven Veils.

* * *

Inside the nightclub, Lucizano joined D'Angelo in the usual place at the back.

'Ben, there is a problem.'

Lucizano didn't speak.

'Word has come to me that my product is not pure.'

D'Angelo locked eyes with Lucizano, who frowned but still didn't say anything.

'I've had it tested by our people, and it's contaminated.'

Lucizano was tempted to remind D'Angelo that the cocaine is never totally clean after it's been cut in the cemetery, but he remained quiet.

'You are adding only what I tell you, aren't you?'

'Yes, Giuseppe. I measure exactly what you say and make sure it is only that!'

Lucizano's stomach churned. His head was spinning.

'Ben, I've found one source of the contamination!'

Lucizano didn't speak. He could see the fire burning in D'Angelo's eyes. 'But there could be others!'

D'Angelo paused and gazed around at the scene in front of him. The wait staff were busying themselves at tables as the diners ate and drank. Punters sat at slot machines and continually fed them with notes and coins. The rattle of glasses and burble of voices from the bar rolled across the vast room. The upstairs rooms were all occupied. The soft sounds of the band filtered through the air. It was his domain, his empire, and every part of it played a role in bringing in cash, but by far the most lucrative earner was the drugs, and if anything threatened that source of income, he would put an end to it – very, very quickly.

He snapped back to reality.

'Ben, I want you to bring Strickland and Chips to the warehouse tonight … I want to deal with them!'

'Yes, Giuseppe. I'll see to it.'

'Be there after eight, and let me know the moment you've arrived!'

'Yes, Giuseppe.'

Lucizano stood up and left immediately.

* * *

Chips and Danny had finished up for the day when Chips took a call. It was Lucizano.

'Chips, you and Strickland be at the front gate, eight o'clock tonight.'

'Sure, we'll be there,' Chips replied.

He was about to ask Lucizano why so early, but the call had already disconnected.

'Who was that?' Danny asked.

'Lucizano,' Chips said, and a worried expression crossed his face. 'We gotta meet him at the main gate at eight tonight.'

Danny looked at Chips, puzzled. 'Eight?' Danny repeated.

'Yeah, kinda strange. Usually, he says eleven.'

'Okay, Chips. But we only did the cut a few days ago.'

'Yeah, I know. You done no delivery since then, have ya?' Chips asked.

Danny shook his head. 'No, I haven't. Not for D'Angelo!'

51

A COLD WIND sliced across the cemetery as Danny and Chips walked from the unit towards the main gate. The sky above was bleak and brooding. It had been raining and the path was shimmering wet. Wispy grey clouds scudded along, sometimes showing stars, sometimes not. Shadowy headstones stood out like sentries on eternal guard as the men strode towards the front gates. Once there, they waited and peered down the deserted road. Soon car headlights appeared, and within moments, Lucizano's limousine pulled up. There was no hearse. The back window slid down, and Lucizano peered out.

'You two … get in!'

Chips looked at Danny with a worried expression as they slid into the backseat. Danny stared out the window while the limo cruised along the dark streets, away from the cemetery and deep into Carlton. Eventually they pulled up at a warehouse he recognised straight away. It was the place where he dropped off the shipping manifests for D'Angelo. The large sign out the front read:

'*Dependable Funerals – Wholesale Distributors*'

Lucizano glared at Danny and Chips with eyes as hard as marble. 'Get out!' he ordered.

Both men stood under a solitary streetlight in the cold and waited while Lucizano made a phone call. Finally, he exited the limo.

'Through here!' Lucizano said and walked ahead of them.

They entered the warehouse via a side door. Inside, the vast space was brilliantly lit by massive overhead lights. Dozens of coffins were stacked against the walls. In the middle of the room, two men were on their knees; a pool of urine had spread out underneath one of them. Danny could see Tony, the hearse driver, and next to him was Alfonso, his offsider. Both men were whimpering. In front of them stood Giuseppe D'Angelo flanked by five of his men. D'Angelo had a large gun in his hand. Behind him, a laptop computer sat open on a small wooden table. Danny and Chips stopped walking, but Lucizano turned around and pointed at the concrete floor.

'Next to them,' he snarled. 'On your knees!'

Danny's heart started beating like a small bird trapped in a net. Chips glanced at him with wild eyes as they both knelt down.

D'Angelo spoke. 'Gentlemen, you are wondering why you are here?'

'Yes, Mr D'Angelo,' Tony said, his voice quivering. The stench of his urine floated up to everyone in the warehouse.

D'Angelo walked in front of him and pointed the handgun at his head. The hearse driver started to sob.

'It has come to my attention that my product has been contaminated.' He let his words sink in. 'Someone has been stealing from me and substituting something for *my product!*'

D'Angelo shouted the last two words, causing Tony's cries to grow even louder. Danny stared down at the floor. The sweat from his brow stung his eyes as it ran down his face. He could hear Chips next to him sucking in great lungsful of air.

It could all end here!

D'Angelo shouted again. 'Do any of you have something to tell me?'

'No, Mr D'Angelo!' Tony sobbed. 'We've done nothing!' he said and glanced across at Alfonso with tears in his eyes.

'So then, Tony, how do you explain this?' D'Angelo said.

He turned around and tapped a button on the laptop, and a video started. Everyone in the warehouse was glued to the computer screen. As it played, D'Angelo pointed to his grandson, Lorenzo Jnr.

'My grandson recently installed a surveillance system for me in the warehouse. You see the cameras?' he said and pointed to a number of small, round cameras positioned at regular intervals high up in the warehouse where the walls met the ceiling.

Tony's mouth dropped open as he stared at them. Then he turned his head and looked across to Alfonso with tears in his eyes. D'Angelo continued.

'They are linked to a computer program he set up!' He smiled broadly at his grandson. 'Watch!'

Soon, the video showed Tony and Alfonso carrying a coffin into the warehouse; they were clearly struggling with the weight. Lucizano followed them in. The men put the coffin on the floor and turned to Lucizano, who said something to them, but the audio was unclear. Lucizano then left the room. Tony and Alfonso waited until he was gone and walked over to three coffins stacked one on top of the other. They removed the first two, then lifted the lid on a silver coffin on the bottom. Tony took out a briefcase and brought it back to the coffin they'd carried in. He opened its lid, and both men took out two handfuls each of small plastic bags containing the product. They put them in the briefcase and replaced them with plastic bags of a white substance each man had in their pockets. Before Lucizano came back in the room, Tony put the briefcase back in the silver coffin, and then both men placed the other two coffins on top of it.

'So, Tony! Tell me … what's that all about?'

'I'm sorry, Mr D'Angelo,' Tony sobbed. 'I'll never do it again … I promise! Please …'

D'Angelo looked down at him and shot him in the face. The blast from the bullet echoed throughout the warehouse as Tony's body rocketed backwards and started to bleed out from a large red hole where his right eye had been. D'Angelo stared at the body for a moment, then walked over to Alfonso and pointed the gun directly at him.

'Why did you take it, Alfonso?'

'He … he told me to, Mr D'Angelo!' Alfonso said. He looked across at Tony and started to cry. 'He said …'

Another massive blast split the air as D'Angelo shot him. Alfonso slumped to the floor. Part of his head slid away from his body, leaving a ragged, red trail of blood. D'Angelo stared down at him for a moment and then walked over to Danny and Chips.

'Chips.'

'Yes, sir … Mr D'Angelo, sir,' he said and sucked in short breaths.

'I brought you and Strickland here for a reason.'

Chips could hardly speak as he stared at the handgun.

'I've found out my product is not clean.'

The warehouse became deathly silent. All eyes were on D'Angelo. 'You do the cut for me.'

'Yes, Mr D'Angelo … Danny and me … we …'

D'Angelo cut him off. 'Do you take anything from me when you do it?' D'Angelo's eyes raged with anger.

'No! Mr D'Angelo … no!' Chips said, and his voice broke. 'Mr D'Angelo, sir … we … we never take nuthin!'

D'Angelo stared down at him, then walked over to Danny.

'Strickland!' D'Angelo shouted and pointed the gun directly at him.

Danny stared down the barrel, his eyes now stinging badly from the sweat running down his face. His heart started beating out of his chest, and he could hardly breathe.

'You saw what Tony and Alfonso did,' D'Angelo said and waved the pistol at the laptop.

'Yes … yes, Mr D'Angelo,' Danny said.

'Do you take anything from me when you do the cut?'

'No … no,' Danny said and prayed the lie would save him. 'Chips and I add only what Lucizano gives us … we just put a little bit into each bag … that's all!' Danny said and wrung his hands together.

D'Angelo pointed the gun at Danny, clearly deciding whether to kill him or not. He held it in place for what seemed like an eternity.

'All right,' he said in a quiet voice and stood back from the men.

Danny and Chips glanced across at each other but didn't speak.

'I've given both of you a job and lodgings. I've trusted you!' D'Angelo paced up and down in front of them.

'Yes, Mr D'Angelo.'

'But I will have my product double-checked in future. If it is not pure, or there is any missing, I will come for you … both of you! Do you understand?'

D'Angelo stared at both men and waved the pistol at the bodies of Tony and Alfonso.

'Yes, Mr D'Angelo!'

Eventually, D'Angelo put the gun away. He turned to Lucizano and pointed to the two dead men.

'Ben, see to Tony and Alfonso!'

'Yes, Giuseppe,' Lucizano said. He pointed to the other men who were standing around. 'Pick them up and put them in that silver coffin. Make them fit!'

D'Angelo motioned to Danny and Chips. 'Strickland, Chips … bury that coffin deep!'

Before they could answer, D'Angelo turned to his men. 'You and you!'

'Yes, Mr D'Angelo?' the men said.

D'Angelo then turned to Lucizano.

'Ben, these two will be your hearse drivers. They will report to you.'

'Yes, Giuseppe. Thank you!'

D'Angelo then added, 'And, Ben, you watch them better than what I've seen here!' He pointed at the laptop, where the scene of Tony and Alfonso stealing D'Angelo's product was on a continual loop, running over and over.

'Yes, Giuseppe,' Lucizano replied and gazed down at the floor and clenched his fists. He knew he'd let his long-time friend down.

Relief washed over both Danny and Chips as they realised their lives had been spared. Danny watched as the men unstacked the coffins. Lucizano opened up the silver one, took out the briefcase, and handed it to D'Angelo. Then Lucizano turned to Danny and Chips.

'Get up! Get back to the limousine!'

As they walked out of the warehouse, Danny could hear D'Angelo's men talking in low voices, and soon the high-pitched scream of a chainsaw echoed out into the night.

52

DANNY, CHIPS, AND Lucizano sat in silence as the limousine returned to the cemetery; the hearse followed close behind. Danny could sense that Lucizano was still burning up inside after being disciplined by his boss and told to watch these two new hearse drivers better than he had the previous two. He guessed that Lucizano was constantly trying to please his boss, and he'd made a bad slip-up.

At the main entrance, Chips unlocked the gates, and the hearse reversed in. 'I'll get the trolley,' Chips said to Lucizano.

Chips jogged to the unit, retrieved the trolley, and ran it back to the hearse. With a struggle, they loaded the silver coffin and wheeled it inside the cemetery.

'You two bury that coffin deep, just like D'Angelo wants,' Lucizano said to Danny and Chips, his face raging with fury.

'We always do!' Danny snarled and gave Lucizano a look of contempt.

The anger inside Lucizano boiled over. 'Don't give me an excuse to come for you, Strickland! D'Angelo might trust you, but I don't!' Lucizano squinted hard and snarled, 'You fuck up, just once, somewhere along the line, Strickland, and it'll be my pleasure to blow your head clean off!'

Lucizano stared at Danny, then turned and headed for the limousine. Danny and Chips watched the limo and hearse disappear into the dark. When they were well out of sight, Chips turned to Danny.

'Why you givin' Lucizano a hard time, Danny? About an hour ago, we were close to being executed; I don't think it's a good idea to be givin' him a hard time right now!'

Danny stared into the distance at the disappearing cars. 'Chips, people like Lucizano will always wanna stay on top of you. They think they're superior. Well, I ain't takin' no shit from someone like him, not from someone like *Lucizano* … not from anyone!'

* * *

With the moon as their only light, Danny and Chips dug a fresh plot. They secured the lowering ropes and grunted as they slowly let the unusually heavy coffin sink to the bottom. Within minutes, they had the grave filled in, and then they returned to the unit.

'One hell of a night, Danny!' Chips said and forced a laugh. He sat in his favourite chair, grabbed the remote control, and turned on the TV. 'I think we'll go easy on stealin' any more of D'Angelo's product for a little while.'

'Yeah, you're right, Chips. We'll just lie low for now!'

Danny walked to the fridge, opened the door, and grabbed a beer. 'I need a drink! One for you, Chips?'

'Yes, thanks, Danny,' Chips said.

The two men sat in the tiny room and drank in silence as the late-night TV shows rolled on.

53

DETECTIVE JIM SPEARS was hunched forward listening to any sound that came from Mick Gallagher's office, but so far, only white noise crackled in his ears. He leant back and yawned loudly, then sat bolt upright as Gallagher's desk phone rang in his headphones. The voice recorder automatically clicked on.

'Yeah.'

'G'day, Mick,' Frank Talbot said.

'Ahh, Frank, what's up?' Spears heard Gallagher say.

'Just confirming the delivery tonight. I've told Strickland to be ready.'

'Look … it's just as well you called. I've been thinkin' about it. I'm going to cancel the delivery for the time being and let things cool down. I'm just not sure if the cops will turn up again. D'Angelo is just gonna have to wait a little while longer for his coffins.'

'Oh! Okay, Mick. Do you want me to call Strickland and let him know?'

'No, don't worry. I'll call Strickland.'

Spears jotted down the names: *Frank. Strickland and put a circle around it. He also noted: Delivery cancelled tonight. Not sure when the cops will turn up. D'Angelo will have to wait for his coffins.*

In his office, Gallagher leant back in his chair, lit a cigarette, and then said, 'Only problem we've got is Biondi's pick-up. I've teed up with him to collect his tyres here tomorrow night, and it looks like it's too late to cancel it. But I've told him to tell his driver to be here around 11:00pm. We should be okay at that time of night, and perhaps things will have blown over.'

Spears jotted down: '*Biondi's pick-up. Tyres late tomorrow night - around eleven pm.*'

'You need a hand with that?'

'Yeah, I want both you and Grist here tomorrow night.'

'Okay!'

'Get here by ten. We can have a quick drink before we start packing those tyres full of whatever Biondi's importin',' Gallagher said and chuckled. 'Probably white nose powder is my guess!'

'Yeah, somethin' like that, Mick. You don't pay for a pick-up at some ungodly hour at night if the cargo is legit,' Talbot said.

Gallagher sniggered.

'Okay, Mick. See you tomorrow night.'

'Bye, Frank.'

Gallagher hung up, and Spears' earpiece went back to white noise. He jotted down: '*You and Grist be here tomorrow night by ten. Tyres and white nose powder.*'

Then Spears' earpiece burst back to life as Gallagher got on the phone again.

'Yeah?'

'Listen, Danny. I want you and Chips to lie low for a while. There won't be any deliveries for the foreseeable future.'

'I thought I was doin' a delivery to D'Angelo tonight!'

'No, that won't be happening. There's a delay.'

'Trouble, Mick?'

'Yeah, the cops are snoopin' around. Big-shot copper from New South Wales been asking me if I know you, or where you are. I've told him nothin', so just keep a low profile until this thing blows over; they'll never find you there.'

'Okay, Mick. Thanks.'

Gallagher hung up.

Detective Spears added the words: '*Danny and Chips. Lie low for a while. Big-shot copper from New South Wales been asking me if I know you. They'll never find you there.*'

Spears reread what he'd jotted down, then tore the page off from the writing pad and rang Cooper straight away.

In Police Headquarters at Flinders Street, he showed Cooper the paper.

'Good work, Jim,' Cooper said as he read the paper.

Cooper noticed the circle around Strickland. 'So, what's this?' he said and pointed.

'Not sure, Pres, but the way Gallagher was talking and the phone calls he was going to make, it seemed like Danny and Strickland were somehow linked.'

Gallagher looked down at the paper again. 'Do you think he's changed his name?'

'Could be!' Spears said and shrugged his shoulders.

54

LATE AT NIGHT and Gandolfo Biondi, the godfather of the Biondi family and owner of Quality Tyres & Repairs in Preston, stood at the bar in the Tarantulas' clubhouse. He was there to find out some very important information. Cain Trench, the president of the Victorian chapter of the Tarantulas Motorcycle Club, stood next to him.

'What are you havin' to drink, Gando?'

'Whatever you're having, Cain.'

Trench glanced over his shoulder to the barman, who poured both men a shot of sambuca. Four bikies stood nearby holding one dishevelled man. He struggled to break free, but they held him firmly. Biondi looked over at the man and then back to Trench.

'Cain, my friend, tonight we are gonna find out who has been selling in my patch!' he said and squinted as he downed the potent alcohol in one swallow.

Trench pointed to the bikies holding the man and motioned for them to push him forward.

'So, Gando, we found this one in your neighbourhood!'

'I don't know anything!' the man said. He was clearly terrified.

Biondi put his shot glass on the bar, and the barman refilled it.

'I swear … I don't know nuthin'!' the man repeated. 'I was just walkin' through there!'

Biondi took no notice of him and said, 'Someone has been selling Colombia's finest in my territory!'

'Not me. I don't even have any of the stuff!' the man said and looked at Biondi with pitiful eyes.

'You lie to me, it's not gonna be good for you!'

'I won't lie … I promise!' the man snivelled.

With that, a bikie placed four small plastic bags containing a white substance on the bar. 'Found these in his pockets.' The bikie spat the words out.

The man stared down at the bags of white powder. 'Just mine! Just for me! Personal use. I'm not sellin' nuthin'!'

Biondi stared at him. 'You're already lying,' he said and pointed at the bags.

The man didn't speak. He sniffed heavily and tried to keep the tears from his eyes.

'These boys say they saw you selling these last night … are you calling them liars?'

'No, no!' the man said, shaking and jerking his head from one bikie to the next.

Biondi took a small sip of the sambuca.

'You were there in Preston last night, weren't you?'

'Yeah, like I said, I was just walkin' through!'

'That's bullshit!' shouted one of the bikies. He kicked the man in the back of the leg, causing him to stumble forward.

'No! No, it's not. I'm not lying!' he said, and his voice started to tremble.

'Who do work for?' Biondi asked.

The man went silent. Biondi grabbed the man by his shirt and delivered a vicious headbutt. Blood sprang out from the man's nose.

'Ahh, shit!' the man yelled out.

'I said, *who do you work for?*'

'No one … no one!' the man sobbed as he slumped forward, blood running from his shattered nose. The bikies held him up. 'I don't work for no one!' he whimpered.

'I want a straight answer. This can be easy for you or it can be very hard!' Biondi grabbed the man again. 'Who do you work for?'

But the man just shook his head and didn't answer. Finally, tears ran down his cheeks as he started to cry. Biondi nodded his head at the bikies. They grabbed the man and pushed him against the bar.

'Maybe a drink or two would help you to talk?'

The man's heart started beating double time. For a moment, he wondered if he could worm his way out of this.

'We could prop you up at the bar until you decide to tell me!'

The man was bewildered. Was he going to be forced to drink alcohol? Maybe he was in luck!

Two bikies grabbed his right hand and pushed it down on the bar. Another bikie plugged in an electric drill and turned it on. He then fitted a large flat-head hexagonal screw into the chuck.

'Last chance!' said Biondi.

The man's cries grew louder. He tried desperately to pull his hand away, but the bikies pushed down hard and held it in place. Biondi nodded at the bikie, who pulled the trigger. The drill sprang into life, and the scream of its electric motor filled the clubhouse. The screw began to spin. It was placed on the back of the man's hand just enough to bring the faintest trickle of blood.

'No! No, please!' he yelled and tried again to pull his hand away.

'Who do you work for?' Biondi asked again.

But the man just shook his head and didn't answer. Biondi reached across and pushed down on the back of the drill. The screw ripped through the man's flesh and buried itself deep into the wooden bar below, fastening him to the spot.

'Oh, god, no!' he screamed as bits of his skin were flung across the bar. 'Ahh! No! No!'

The man threw his head back and forth. The bikies let him go. He tried desperately to remove his hand from the bar, but it was pinned there tight.

'Tell me!' yelled Biondi.

But the man still didn't speak. He simply screamed and screamed, consumed with pain.

'Again,' Biondi said to the bikie holding the drill.

The bikie loaded up a new screw. The man slumped halfway to the floor with his hand fixed to the bar.

'We can stop here if you tell me who you work for!'

Biondi sipped on the sambuca. The man began to sob and sucked in great gulps of air but still refused to talk. The bikie picked a new spot and drilled again. This time, there was a wrenching sound as the screw bit home. The man shrieked in agony; his forehead was a river of sweat. The bikies grabbed him and held him up once more. The barman threw cold water in his face.

'Tell me!' Biondi shouted again. 'This can go on for a long time! There are plenty of screws left!'

'Other hand!' Trench said to his bikies.

The bikies grabbed the man's other hand and forced it onto the bar. The man began moaning as he started to drift in and out of consciousness. Biondi nodded at the bikie holding the drill. He picked a spot on the man's hand and pressed the trigger.

'No!' the man shouted and tried desperately to pull his hand away from the bar. 'Stop! Please!' he said and sucked in deep breaths. 'No more! D'Angelo. I work for Giuseppe D'Angelo!'

Biondi stepped closer to him. 'How many of you are there?' he hissed.

The man started to moan. 'Four. Four of us! D'Angelo said it should be just four!'

'How long ago did you start selling in my neighbourhood?'

The man didn't answer. He threatened to faint, and this time, Biondi threw the rest of his sambuca in the man's face.

'I said … *how long ago did you start selling*?' Biondi yelled.

'I dunno,' he sobbed. 'Maybe … maybe three or four months ago!'

Biondi glanced at Trench, who nodded and downed his drink.

'Get rid of him,' Trench said to the bikies who were pushing the man against the bar.

The bikie with the drill switched it to reverse and removed both screws from the man's hand. This time, he did pass out as blood flowed freely from the gaping wounds. The bikies lifted and dragged him from the bar area to a small courtyard outside, and within minutes two muffled gunshots could be heard.

'Cain! That bastard D'Angelo has moved into my territory!'

'Okay, Gando. Now we know who it is for sure, leave it to us. He'll keep his nose out of your back yard once we fix it for you!'

'Thank you, Cain.'

Biondi put his empty shot glass on the bar and quietly left the clubhouse.

55

CREASEY GREETED DANNY as he walked through the door of the King George V.

'Hey, Danny. How's your day been?'

'Oh, just ordinary, Creasey. Nothin' exceptional ever happens to me,' Danny replied and took his seat at the end of the bar. He smiled to himself as his mind drifted back to the recent scene in D'Angelo's warehouse.

'Usual?' asked Creasey.

'Yeah, thanks, Creasey. Make it a pint.'

It was quiet. There were only two other patrons in the pub. On the TV, an English soccer match was playing in silence. As the pint was put in front of him, Danny noticed a newsflash on the screen. Fire trucks and police were surrounding a place somewhere in the city, and ambulances were ferrying people away. The reporter was mouthing silent words into his microphone when a headline flashed across the screen.

'*Car Bomb Explodes at the Seven Veils Casino and Nightclub*'

Danny could hardly believe his eyes. He took a twenty out of his wallet, dropped it on the bar, and raced to the front door.

'Hey, Danny, you gonna drink that?' Creasey yelled, but Danny had already left.

There were no cabs around, so he ran all the way to the top of Bourke Street, where he jumped on a tram. It had gone only as far as

William Street when the driver made an announcement.

'Last stop, everybody. Police incident ahead. This is the last stop … everybody off!'

Danny jumped off and ran down to King Street. There was pandemonium on the road as he turned the corner. Lights from emergency vehicles lit up the scene in reds and blues. People were milling about out the front of the nightclub. Some were sitting on the kerb bleeding while others lay motionless on the dark bitumen road. Danny could see people being carried out of the building. He strode down closer to the scene and could feel the heat from the flames. Half of the front portico of the Seven Veils was on fire and had fallen in; thick black smoke was drifting high up into the night sky. Police and firemen were inside the nightclub trying to find people. Ambulance officers were attending to the injured. He walked through the crowds of onlookers, desperately searching for Ebony, and stepped across a couple of fire hoses.

'Hey, mate, *move!*' a fireman yelled at him as he dragged the hose towards the flames.

Danny stepped back and then saw a group of people dressed in the nightclub uniform. They were standing together on the opposite side of the street, talking and pointing worriedly at the burning building. He strode over and was about to ask if anyone had seen Ebony when he saw her.

'Ebony!' he called out and ran over to her. 'Ebony!' he said and held her close; he could feel her trembling. 'Are you okay?'

'Yes, yes!' she said, breathing heavily. 'I was in the kitchen when the blast went off.' She looked back at the fire. 'Oh, Danny, it was terrible! So many people are hurt!'

She started to cry and looked up at him.

'Danny, you shouldn't be here! If Mr D'Angelo's people see you …'

Just then, a muffled blast came from inside the building, and debris and people spewed out of the destroyed front entrance. He continued to hold her.

'Oh God!' she said.

'Ebony, come with me back to my place. It'll be safer there!'

She looked around at the flaming nightclub and her other colleagues. There was nothing she could do.

'Okay,' she said softly.

He put his arm around her, and they walked up the King Street hill towards Bourke Street.

Ben Lucizano, who was standing with a group of people some distance away, nursing a badly twisted knee and scorched arm, saw them as they left.

Back at the cemetery, Danny and Ebony walked through the front door of the unit. Chips was sitting on the couch. He screwed his neck around from the TV and watched them enter.

'Danny, have you seen …' He didn't finish his sentence when he saw Ebony.

'Chips, this is Ebony. Ebony, Chips.'

'Well, hello, Miss Ebony. Danny has told me a lot about you!'

'Hello, Chips,' she said.

'Ebony works at the Seven Veils,' Danny said.

'Oh yeah, you told me! It's just on the tele now!' Chips said and pointed. 'Take a seat, Miss Ebony. Are you all right?'

'Yes, thanks. Just a little shaken.'

'Did Danny rescue you?' Chips asked with a smile as she sat down.

'Well, sort of,' she replied.

'Always the hero, hey, Danny?' Chips said, trying to lighten the mood. Then he added, 'Glad you're okay, Miss Ebony!'

All three sat on the couch and watched as pictures of the bombed-out nightclub filled the screen.

56

THE SECURITY LIGHTS on the docks shone like beacons against the dark, brooding sky. A strong southerly gusted inconsistently, sending papers tumbling and twisting across the deserted container yard. Waves slapped against the sea-stained sides of the wharves while night birds called and raced away into the darkness.

Gallagher sat in his office with Frank Talbot and Grist and finished off his glass of whisky. He checked his watch – it was 10:52pm. He felt relaxed. Tonight would be just another normal delivery night for Biondi and his car tyres, and whatever the hell they had inside them.

Down the road in the shadows, Detective Senior Sergeant Presley Cooper sat in a squad car and waited. Alongside him were three police vans and a large Police Tactical Response Unit. The butterflies stirred in his belly as the adrenaline kicked in – he was totally on edge. No one was to move until Cooper gave the order.

Gallagher checked his watch again. 'They'll be here in a couple of minutes,' he said. 'Be a lot better if those bloody bikies didn't turn up!'

Talbot fondled his glass. 'Makes you wonder why Biondi uses 'em. They're probably robbin' him blind!'

'They're the muscle!' Gallagher observed.

Talbot nodded and sipped his whisky.

Cooper shifted uncomfortably in the passenger's seat, his heart beating double time. His eyes were fixed on the entrance to the yard, where the gates were thrown wide open. He desperately wanted Wainwright, but this bust would look good on his record. Tonight would be something special.

Gallagher walked over to the door and spotted a large truck making its way into the yard. 'They're here! Frank, make sure our ex-cons are ready. Grist, follow me!'

Outside, a huge truck, surrounded by five Tarantula bikies on their Harleys, slowed to a stop. The truck driver turned the engine off, got out, and swung the back doors open before locking them to either side of the truck. The bikies, however, kept revving their motors and calling out to one another and laughing.

'Okay!' yelled Gallagher as he stepped out of his office. 'Get on with it!'

The men started loading car tyres. One of them jumped in the truck and started dragging the tyres to the back.

'Come on. Come on!' shouted Gallagher.

'Go, go, go!' yelled Cooper.

The sound of police sirens split the air as the cops burst into the yard. Cooper stepped out from his squad car as it ground to a halt and lifted a loudhailer.

'THIS. IS. THE. POLICE! Get on the ground! You are all under arrest! Get on the ground!'

Police officers quickly piled out of their vehicles. Cooper directed his men towards the delivery truck, and they started to round people up. A couple of bikies gunned their choppers and fled for the exit.

'Stop them! Stop them!' Cooper yelled.

One was grabbed by the arm as he sped past and was dragged down, his bike spitting and grinding into the dirt, while the second bikie roared out through the gates and off into the night.

'Stay on the ground! You are all under arrest!' Cooper shouted. He ran to the gate and watched as the bikie made his escape. Then he turned around and screamed out to his men, 'Cuff them! All of them!'

Gallagher and his men ran in all directions, but the police numbers were overwhelming, and eventually, Gallagher, Talbot, Grist, the truck driver, the remaining bikies, and the three ex-cons were all pushed to the ground and handcuffed. The arrests were made without violence, but finding everyone involved took far too long for Cooper's liking.

Also, much to his annoyance, the police media arm had tipped off the local news teams and told them of a likely drug bust on the docks, and soon, reporters were racing to get their exclusive. A news helicopter hovered low overhead as it filmed the scene. A young female reporter, almost out of breath, was first to get to Cooper.

'We understand there has been a large drug haul here tonight?' she asked and thrust the microphone in Cooper's face, waiting for a reply.

'I can't say anything until we've done a full debrief,' Cooper replied angrily, frustrated by her intrusion.

'Is there anything you can tell us?' she insisted.

'Yes! We've stopped a truck here in the docks tonight loaded with goods that appear to be suspicious, and we've made a number of arrests!'

'Why are there so many police here?' another reporter butted in and shouldered the female reporter out of the way.

Cooper fought to control his irritation at so many people being at the scene.

He took a deep breath before he answered. 'As you can see, there are a number of bikies involved, and we want to make sure all of our members are safe!'

'Safe from what? Did you expect violence?' the reporter asked and almost fell as he was jostled by TV camera crews as they tried to get the best shot.

'I can't say any more at this stage,' Cooper said and stumbled himself as the growing pack of reporters surrounded him. 'We'll give you a full report at Flinders Street Police Headquarters later on this evening. Thank you,' he yelled.

The reporters followed him, shouting their questions.

'There was a car bomb explosion at a nightclub in the city tonight. Do you think there is a connection?'

'I don't know anything about that,' Cooper shouted back. 'You'll have to contact police liaison,' he said and pushed his way out of the scrum.

The reporters kept firing their questions.

'Was anyone hurt here tonight?'

'Were there any shots fired?'

Cooper finally made his way back to the squad car. He wished the surveillance team had never heard of the likely pick-up of drugs tonight. The bust would look good on his record, but it wouldn't get him the promotion he so desperately coveted. He just wanted to arrest Wainwright, or Strickland, or whatever his name was now. Bringing him back to New South Wales in handcuffs would carry the ultimate reward, and then the reporters could ask all the questions they liked.

57

DANNY AND CHIPS started early next day. Six graves were needed for the afternoon. Ebony stayed in Danny's room in the unit and slept in. It was lunchtime before Danny and Chips arrived back. She greeted them as they arrived.

'Hi. How are you two?'

'More like, how are you, Miss Ebony?' Chips said.

'Yes, I'm fine, thank you,' she said, still checking out her arms and legs for burn marks – but there were none.

Danny walked over and put his arm around her.

'Why don't we all go to the George for lunch … my shout.'

'Not for me, thanks, Danny. You and Miss Ebony can go. I'll look after the fort here,' Chips said with a chuckle.

* * *

After they'd finished their counter meal, Danny sat next to Ebony at the bar of the King George V. Creasey hustled around getting the pub ready for the footy crowd that night. He walked over to them.

'Danny, you and your lady friend gonna hang 'round to see the game?'

'Nah, Creasey. We'll probably go back to the cemetery and watch it there. I've seen the clientele you get here on Friday and Saturday nights!' Danny smiled and rolled his eyes.

'All payin' customers,' Creasey said and shrugged his shoulders as he wiped a spot off the bar. 'You two want a refill?'

'No, thanks. Better make tracks, Creasey!'

Danny waited for Ebony to finish her drink, and then they left the pub and made their way back to the unit. Chips waited eagerly for Danny and Ebony to walk inside.

'Danny, have you seen this?'

'What?'

Chips pointed at the television as the afternoon news bulletin continued.

'Cops raided the docks last night. Gallagher's been arrested!'

'Arrested!' Danny repeated.

Chips nodded his head. Danny stood in front of the TV and could hardly believe his eyes. It was a repeat of the police raid made on the docks and showed the container yard he knew so well lit up by flashing red and blue lights. He watched as the swarming cops put men in handcuffs and loaded them into police vehicles.

The news presenter continued:

'*It was a big night for police last night. As well as a city nightclub being bombed, causing a large number of casualties, they also busted a major drug ring on the docks of Melbourne. A truckload of car tyres was seized, each tyre containing kilos of cocaine with a street value in the hundreds of thousands of dollars. Police have arrested a number of people involved in the drug operation including the Port of Melbourne Shipping Container Manager, Michael Gallagher.*'

A picture of Gallagher in handcuffs being put into the back of a squad car was shown.

'*Police are still interviewing Gallagher and the other men arrested at the docks with a view to cracking open this whole operation.*'

Chips stared at Danny.

'Danny it's just too dangerous to stay here any longer. It's time to go! There ain't no tellin' what Gallagher or the others might say to the cops. They could come here snoopin' around soon enough! I'm leaving, Danny, and I suggest you do too. Cops are looking for you anyways. No good you stayin' here no more!'

Ebony stared at Danny after Chips' final comment but didn't speak. Chips bent down and picked up a suitcase.

'I'm gonna pack. All I got will fit in here. Goodbye, Danny. Bye, Miss Ebony. I'm goin' tonight. I'll leave the main gate unlocked, Danny, just in case you wanna go that way as well. But I'm not stayin'. I'm leavin', Danny … *tonight!*'

With that, Chips walked into his bedroom and started packing.

58

GIUSEPPE D'ANGELO AND his grandson, Lorenzo Jnr, escaped the blast in the nightclub. They exited through a back door in the kitchen that led to an alley. D'Angelo left the devastating scene straight away and didn't bother to find out if anyone had been hurt or killed. Once he knew he and his grandson were safe, his focus on survival disappeared, and his feelings turned to anger and the need for swift revenge. It was imperative to find out who did this, and when he did, it would be bad for them – *extremely bad.*

* * *

Early next evening, and D'Angelo was holding a meeting of his people at his spacious home in Kew. It was somewhere he never liked to do business, but these were extraordinary circumstances. Each of them was told to be there by 7:00pm. He watched from a bay window as they arrived. Car tyres scrunched as they drove along the superb white-pebble driveway lined by thin poplar trees. They pulled up to one side of the house and parked, then walked to the marble staircase leading to huge doors standing at the entrance to the magnificent two-storey mansion.

D'Angelo waited until Ben Lucizano, two other high-ranking members of the D'Angelo clan, and his grandson entered the house. He ushered them into the lounge room, where they each took a seat in D'Angelo's expensive leather armchairs. No one spoke as they watched him walk over to a cocktail cabinet. He poured himself a shot of cognac, took a sip, and then turned around and addressed them.

'Gentlemen, we have been attacked and battered … but not killed!'

He eyeballed his men.

'I want each of you to find out whatever you can about this attack and report back to me. There is to be no mercy for anyone involved!' He paused again. 'I want to know the names of everyone who did this!'

All eyes in the room were on D'Angelo as he began to pace the floor.

'When you find them, you are to kill them. I want you to cut the left hand off each man, write his name on it, and bring it to me.' D'Angelo began breathing heavily. 'Then, if the man has a family, it will be presented to his wife in a shoe box. You will make sure she recognises it from the wedding ring. If she has a son, you are to kill him. If she has more than one son, kill the eldest.' He looked around at his people and, consumed by anger, he screamed, 'If there is a problem … kill the entire family!'

D'Angelo paused, took another sip of the potent alcohol, and then whispered in a harsh voice, 'Do you understand?'

'Yes!' they said in unison.

D'Angelo calmed down.

'Does anyone have any information about this?'

The men shook their heads as they stared at one another. Then Lucizano spoke. He grimaced as he shifted in the chair and held his badly twisted knee. An ugly, red burn mark ran from one side of his face down the full length of one arm.

'Giuseppe, I made it outside and saw three bikies riding away from the scene. One had a pillion passenger. I think he may have been the driver of the car.'

D'Angelo raised his voice. 'Did you see who it was?'

'No, Giuseppe, but the colours were those of the Tarantulas.'

D'Angelo stared long and hard into the distance.

'Tarantulas,' he said to himself and slowly nodded his head. 'Biondi.'

It made sense. He had started selling in Biondi's territory, and this was, no doubt, payback. Well, Biondi had picked the wrong man to attack. There would be serious retribution.

Lucizano continued. 'I also saw Strickland at the scene; he left with Ebony Taylor and ...'

D'Angelo cut him off. 'Strickland ... from the cemetery?' he said incredulously.

Lucizano nodded.

'And Ebony ... my waitress?'

'Yes, Giuseppe. They were together out the front of the Seven Veils and left shortly after the second explosion.'

D'Angelo went red in the face. He started breathing in short bursts. 'Ben, do you think they were involved?'

'I'm not sure about the girl, but I've never trusted Strickland!'

D'Angelo began to pace the floor again. 'Ben, see to this! Find out who Strickland works for; see if it is Biondi.'

'Yes, Giuseppe.'

'And, Ben, I think it's time to deal with Strickland! He shouldn't be anywhere near my nightclub or my waitresses!'

D'Angelo went quiet for a moment as he contemplated matters. 'After you find out who he works for ... kill him! If the girl gets in the way, kill her too!'

Lucizano nodded his head and asked, 'What about Chips?'

D'Angelo stood there weighing his options. 'No loose ends,' he said quietly to himself. 'Ben, it is best there are no loose ends!' He paused, then said, 'Get rid of all three of them!'

D'Angelo walked over to a window and gazed out over his beautiful garden softly lit by strategically placed solar lights.

'Ben, would you like someone to help you?'

Lucizano shook his head. 'No, Giuseppe. I'd like to do this on my own!'

'Then do it tonight, Ben … no delay!'

'Yes, Giuseppe.'

Lucizano grimaced and grabbed his knee as he slowly got up from the armchair and left the D'Angelo mansion. His mind was racing. Perhaps by killing those in the cemetery, he could redeem himself in the eyes of his friend.

But the killing would also include pleasure. He was very much looking forward to seeing Strickland kneeling before him, begging for his life. Then, after he'd heard who he was working for, he'd put a hole in Strickland's head big enough to push a fist through.

59

LUCIZANO CLIMBED INTO the limousine and gunned the engine. He wasn't used to being in this part of the vehicle; he was generally sitting in luxury in the back seat. He waited until he'd exited D'Angelo's driveway then planted his foot and the tyres squealed as he rocketed away.

The trip from D'Angelo's inner suburban home cross-town to the cemetery generally took around twenty minutes. He went easy along Lygon Street, not wanting to attract attention from a bored cop or get a speeding ticket and photo from one of the numerous hidden cameras. Once past the main drag, he accelerated, took a left, and sped up to the main gates of the cemetery. In the dark, he could see someone at the entrance carrying a suitcase. He screeched to a halt and got out. He picked up a pump-action shotgun from the back seat and limped across to the cemetery. At the main gates, he saw who it was.

'Chips!' Lucizano yelled.

Chips had waited until dark to leave and was about to walk out onto the street when he recognised Lucizano. When he saw the shotgun, he ran back inside the cemetery. Lucizano followed him. He pushed open the gates and fired a shot along the path Chips had taken. Inside the unit, Ebony jumped.

'Danny, what was that?' she asked, her voice thick with worry.

Danny didn't reply in case the answer upset her, but it was clear to him it was a gunshot. He put his head outside and saw Lucizano limping along and heading deep into the cemetery.

'Chips!' Lucizano yelled again. Then there was another huge blast.

Danny's mind was racing. He turned to Ebony. 'Stay here! Turn off all the lights! Don't come out until I come and get you!'

'Danny! I'm scared!'

'Just … just stay here! I'll come back for you!'

'Where are you going?'

'I've got to try and help Chips!'

Danny ran out into the night and along the path Lucizano had taken, but in the moon's pale light Danny couldn't see him. In desperation he stopped and yelled out, 'Lucizano! Hey, Lucizano, you piece of garbage!'

He continued to run up the path and past a freshly dug plot, then stopped dead in his tracks as, out of the gloom, Lucizano came struggling towards him, shotgun raised. There was fresh blood on his arm. Danny immediately thought of Chips. He reached for the handgun in his pocket but hesitated as he saw Lucizano lift the shotgun and aim it directly at him.

'Don't even think of that, Strickland,' Lucizano said and limped to within a few feet of Danny. 'I've been waiting for this a long time!'

Danny didn't speak. He stared into Lucizano's dark eyes and waited. Lucizano levelled the barrel at his head. In Danny's mind, the Ghost Train burst through the black doors, heading deep into the shadows where the ghouls and ghosts lurked. Then, as though the carnival was closing up for the night, and the rides started grinding to a halt, the carnival music turned eerily morbid.

A cruel wind shrieked like a banshee high up in the shadowy trees.

I think it's all over for you this time … Buddy!

A voice came from the side. 'Danny, what's happening?'

It was Ebony. She must have followed him. Lucizano turned to see who it was, and Danny took his chance. He lunged at Lucizano, grabbed the shotgun, and pushed it away.

Lucizano struggled to get it back, and a shot went off. Ebony screamed. Lucizano pumped another shell into the chamber as Danny fought to hold on. The two men began to battle for control of the shotgun. They pulled each other off balance and crashed to the ground. Danny yelled as he went down hard on the brick path. Lucizano was getting the advantage. He pulled himself up on his one good knee and started to force the barrel towards Danny's face.

'Goodbye, Strickland!' Lucizano grunted. 'This is something D'Angelo and I should have done a long time ago!'

Danny shoved his head away and moved awkwardly to one side. Lucizano slipped. He cried out in agony as he fell on his damaged leg. The men continued to fight, and for a moment the shotgun pointed at Lucizano's head – just then, the gun discharged. The noise of the blast was deafening. Blood and flesh burst from Lucizano's face and spread out across the graveyard. Danny lay there, hardly able to believe what he was seeing. He wrenched the shotgun out of Lucizano's dead hands. In the dull light he could see that Lucizano's face had completely gone; there was nothing left but blood, red flesh, and stark white bone.

'Danny!' Ebony cried out.

He stood up and staggered over to hug her. 'It's okay. It'll be okay.'

'Oh god!' she said, staring down at what was left of Lucizano's face. She shivered, then said, 'What about Chips?'

Police sirens sounded in the distance.

'Yeah, I know!' Danny said. 'We'll have a quick look around for him, but we have to move!'

His mind was racing.

Looks like Chips was right – Gallagher's probably told the cops about the cemetery and what happens here!

Then Danny had an idea.

'Ebony, help me! Strip his pants and jacket off.'

'What?'

'Just do it. We don't have much time.'

Ebony removed Lucizano's pants and bloodied jacket. Danny took his pants and jacket off while making sure the handgun and burner phone remained in the pockets. He put on Lucizano's pants and jacket, and then they dressed Lucizano in Danny's clothes.

'Ebony, help me!'

They grabbed Lucizano and dragged him to the open grave and tipped him in; the body landed hard.

'It might give us a couple more minutes if they have to haul him out of there!' Danny said.

Danny grabbed the shotgun and threw it in the grave on top of him. The police sirens were much closer now.

'We've gotta go.'

He reached into Lucizano's pants pocket and couldn't believe his luck when he found the keys to the limousine. He ran up the path in a vain search for Chips.

'Chips!' he screamed out, 'Chips!' But there was no reply.

The police sirens shrieked as the cops approached the cemetery.

'Ebony, we can't wait any longer!'

He ran back past the unit with Ebony. He noticed the gates to the Goldstein mausoleum were thrown wide open but knew he didn't have time to retrieve any of the product.

They ran to the limousine and within minutes were a long, long way from the cemetery.

PART EIGHT

A FRIEND INDEED

the long journey …

60

TWO WEEKS LATER, and Detective Senior Sergeant Presley Cooper, soon to be Detective Inspector, stood in the parade ground of the New South Wales Police Headquarters surrounded by many of his colleagues.

'Finally, hey, Pres!' one of his fellow officers said and clapped him on the shoulder.

Cooper smiled. His thoughts went to the day he brought the body of Daniel Edward Wainwright back with him to New South Wales. Right now, his remains lay in the morgue. There was no one to identify him as they could find no close friends or next of kin. It would be difficult anyway; they'd be trying to identify a person without a face.

The police tried to contact his mother but found out she had died the previous year of a chronic alcohol-related disease.

＊ ＊ ＊

The day after Cooper returned to New South Wales, the police commissioner questioned Cooper at length to make sure he'd done everything to confirm it was Wainwright he had brought back from Victoria.

'Absolutely no doubt, sir. Although it's not possible to make a facial recognition, it's definitely him. We identified him by the clothes, handgun, and the mobile phone that Gallagher told us he'd given him. It's him, all right, sir. It's indisputable. That's definitely Wainwright we have there!' he said and motioned his head in the direction of the morgue.

The commissioner nodded slightly and looked concerned. 'I don't suppose it's possible to do a DNA match?'

'No, sir. We don't have any of Wainwright's DNA to get a match with; we were going to get his DNA once he arrived at Silverwater, but ...' Cooper didn't finish the sentence, not wanting to verbalise the debacle of Wainwright's breakout from the prison van. 'Also, his mother is dead ... she was cremated. But like I say, sir, I'm totally convinced that's Wainwright in the morgue. There's no doubt about it!'

'Do we have a fingerprint profile?'

'No, sir,' Cooper said and looked despondent. 'Wainwright's prints were part of that system upgrade.' Cooper was wary about continuing. 'The one where they lost over two thousand sets of prints in the data migration to the new operating system and ...'

'Yes, yes, I know,' the commissioner said and cut Cooper off. He shook his head slightly and added, more to himself, 'We're slowly rebuilding that database. At least we can get the missing prints from those people we still have in custody ... and the tech team have promised me they'll have the database completely restored in a couple of months.'

Cooper continued enthusiastically, 'There are no hard copies either, sir. They use the finger scanner these days and capture them digitally, together with the palm print.' Cooper slowed up a bit when he saw the look on the commissioner's face. 'Have done for years,' he added, in a much quieter voice.

The commissioner didn't respond; he simply rolled his eyes at Cooper. He knew only too well how they captured a person's fingerprints these days. Prints on ink and paper went the way of the abacus and flared jeans years ago.

Cooper added, a bit more carefully this time, 'We were going to get a fresh set of Wainwright's prints when he got to Silverwater, but ahh … he …' now he was almost whispering. 'He never made it there!'

'Yes, yes, yes!' the commissioner said and shook his head. His anger bubbled over, and he said in a stern voice, 'It's just as well the public don't know half of the administrative gaps we have to deal with on a daily basis!'

There was silence as Cooper waited for the commissioner to calm down.

In a more composed voice, the commissioner asked, 'What about the juvenile centre where he served time?'

'I contacted them too,' Cooper said and licked his lips, worried about delivering more bad news. 'But they only have current records. They said they checked, but no longer have Wainwright's record. It's probably been sealed and destroyed in line with …'

'Yes, yes … I *do* know the regulations, Senior Sergeant!' the commissioner said and glared at Cooper.

Cooper bit his bottom lip, then said, 'But we don't need them, sir. I'm confident that's Wainwright I've brought back!'

'Okay, Cooper,' the commissioner said reluctantly. 'Look, we're absolutely under the pump here. We really don't have time to do any more checking. There's a new job I need you to start first thing in the morning. As an inspector, I expect you to lead the task force!'

'Yes, sir. I'll do that, sir!'

'If you're prepared to provide sign-off confirming Wainwright's positive identification, then I'll take that as being final,' the commissioner added reluctantly.

'I'll sign that, sir. Not a problem, sir!'

The commissioner sighed heavily and put his hand on Cooper's shoulder.

'All right. I'll contact Assistant Commissioner Warner-Smith, and we can put the paperwork in place regarding your promotion.'

'Thank you, sir,' Cooper said and stood to attention.

The commissioner frowned and asked, 'By the way, how is the questioning of Gallagher, the container manager, going?'

'Oh, he's singing like a bird. Prosecution have cut him a deal … fifteen years down to ten if he cooperates. Apparently, he was a critical link in the distribution of the cocaine. Looks like he was collaborating with two mafia families: the D'Angelos and Biondis.'

'Oh, really?' the commissioner said.

'Yes,' Cooper went on enthusiastically. 'Wainwright and a man called Chips were living in the grounds of the Melbourne General Cemetery and were involved in the handling and delivery of the drugs. When we got there the doors to a mausoleum belonging to a family called Goldstein were wide open. Inside was a broken cremation urn lying on the floor and a few small bags of cocaine had spilled out. We also found two baby powder containers that were filled with cocaine. Apparently, it was all to be delivered to Gallagher.'

'I take it we're looking into all of that?'

'Yes, sir. The whole operation regarding the importation and distribution of the cocaine has been handed over to the drug squad, and the State Crime Command Unit has taken control of the organised-crime aspects.'

'Good,' the commissioner said and nodded. 'This man Chips, do we have him in custody?'

'No, sir, still searching. We don't really have any solid leads yet.'

'Do you think it was him who shot Wainwright?'

'Could be, sir. He's disappeared altogether. And, what with the amount of drugs involved …' Cooper didn't finish the sentence.

The commissioner nodded knowingly, then said, 'I think there was also a man called Strickland involved?'

'No, sir, same bloke. Gallagher told us he gave Wainwright that name … probably to throw us off the scent.'

'Oh,' the commissioner said and rubbed his chin, not really

convinced of what Cooper was saying. 'So what happened with Detective Tom Lucas? I understand he's also being questioned.'

'That's right, sir. Gallagher told us Lucas was also in on the pilfering from the shipping containers; he's been arrested and charged.'

'Good thing! We don't want crooked cops in our ranks, especially those that don't do a proper job!'

'Yes, sir. I agree, sir!' Cooper said and nodded vigorously.

'Apparently Lucas also had a partner, a Detective Jacobs. Do we have any word on him?'

'Nothing, sir. We can't find him, and Gallagher hasn't mentioned him either. Jacobs seems to have just disappeared!'

'Oh!' the commissioner said. 'Well, keep an eye on proceedings and keep me up to date if you hear anything.'

'Yes, sir. Will do, sir!'

* * *

Cooper stood at attention under the hot sun waiting for Assistant Commissioner Aubrey Warner-Smith to present him with his Inspector badge and epaulettes. He took a quick look around at the crowd. His father was there, sitting in a wheelchair with a rug over his knees. Beside him, in a straight line, stood twenty policemen and policewomen, all smartly dressed in their uniforms. These were people Cooper had worked with previously, as well as a select few from Balmain Police Station. He made sure they were all there to witness his promotion.

After a couple of minutes, Warner-Smith walked over to Cooper and opened a small box. He took out the shiny new Inspector's badge and pinned it on Cooper's lapel. He also handed Cooper the epaulettes. He then took a step back and saluted. Cooper stood even straighter and saluted back. They stood side by side while the official photo was taken. Cooper's beaming smile lit up his face while Warner-Smith stood there with a stern look of indifference.

'Congratulations, Detective Inspector,' Warner-Smith said after the photo was taken and then walked off.

'Thank you, sir,' Cooper said to Warner-Smith's disappearing back.

Warner-Smith walked over to Detective Sergeant Jeremy Nickels and presented him with the Police Medal for 'Exemplary Organisation and Work Ethics' in recognition of his efforts in the running of his arm of the task force down in Victoria. There was no way he was going to give the medal to Cooper, even though the commissioner suggested he should get it as it was Cooper who had busted the drug distribution ring. But it was up to Warner-Smith to award the medal, and he couldn't bring himself to give it to Cooper. He shook hands with Nickels enthusiastically, and they both smiled happily as they posed for the official photograph.

As they walked away together, Nickels whispered to Warner-Smith, 'Aubrey, I don't believe that's Wainwright on the slab!'

Warner-Smith stared at Nickels and frowned. 'What do you mean? Cooper signed off the Arrest Report confirming it's him. He told the commissioner he'd done all the tests. Apparently, they all point to the body being that of Wainwright.'

They walked on a bit further.

'Cooper would do anything to get that promotion!' Nickels said.

Warner-Smith knew that was true. He didn't want to promote Cooper – he didn't trust him – but the commissioner had insisted. And once the media got word of the arrest and subsequent death of the convicted murderer Daniel Wainwright, it was big news. There was no backing out now. It would also be the commissioner's last big success before his retirement in two months' time. Warner-Smith knew if he played his cards right, he was in the box seat to be the next Police Commissioner of New South Wales – there was no need to rock the boat!

Warner-Smith stopped walking, rubbed his brow, and turned to Nickels.

'Jeremy, do some digging in what little spare time you have. Let me know what you find, but don't tell anyone else what you're doing … okay?'

'Sure thing, Aubrey,' Nickels said and smiled as he fingered the shiny new Police Medal pinned tightly to his lapel.

61

Six Months Later

Port Douglas, Far North Queensland

DONNA, THE RECEPTIONIST at Carl Chipper Real Estate Agents and Consultants, walked from the front desk to the office of her boss.

'Mr Chipper, there's a couple out the front who said they'd like to see you.'

'Okay, thanks Donna, but you can call me Chips. Everyone does.'

'Yes, Mr Chips. Thank you.'

Carl Chipper smiled and shook his head as he walked out into the reception area and greeted a tanned young man and a very pretty young lady.

'Danny! Miss Ebony! Fancy seeing you two here!' He walked over and hugged them both.

A look of concern crossed Chips' face.

'I was hopin' we'd find you up here somewhere, Chips,' Danny said excitedly. 'I really didn't know if you were alive or dead, but I figured if you made it, you'd head to the far north!'

'Yes, Danny, like I told you when we was back in Melbourne, I'm gonna live the rest of my days up here!'

Then Chips turned serious. 'So you got away from Lucizano too!'

'Yeah, but don't worry. He won't be bothering us anymore!'

Danny said and chuckled.

Then Danny spoke in a whisper so the receptionist couldn't hear. 'Cops were headin' for the cemetery. They were right behind us! We had to leave in a hurry!'

Chips nodded and blew out his cheeks. Danny changed the topic. 'So, Chips, how'd you afford something like this?'

Chips smiled and said softly, 'Danny, I told you I knew someone who would pay a good price for that amount of product … and, sure enough, he did.'

'Who?' asked Danny.

'Gandolfo Biondi,' he whispered. 'When I told him it originally belonged to Giuseppe D'Angelo, he laughed and was pleased to get his hands on it. He paid well!'

'So the cops never caught him?'

'Nah, Biondi was way too slippery for them. Word is he's set himself up in Western Australia somewhere, and probably changed his name.' Chips paused and shrugged his shoulders. 'But who knows?'

Danny laughed, then said, 'Aren't you s'posed to get a licence or something to run a place like this, Chips?'

'Money talks, Danny, talks lots of different languages!' Chips said and chuckled.

Danny sniggered, hugged Ebony a little bit closer, and then said, 'Don't suppose you know somewhere 'round here where we can buy a cocktail or two and watch the sunset?'

Chips smiled. 'I do, yes, as a matter of fact, I do. But I need to make a call before we go.' Chips said and retreated to his office.

Danny and Ebony walked over to the advertising boards and checked out the Houses For Sale posters. Within a minute, Chips was back.

'All right!' Chips said as he re-entered the office. 'Let's go!' He turned to his receptionist as they started to leave.

'Donna, look after the office for the rest of the day, please. I'll be back in the morning.'

'Certainly, Mr Chipper.'

Chips smiled again and then pointed to a tired white Holden panel van parked out the front. 'That your car?' he asked Danny.

'Yes,' Danny said. 'Started off we used Lucizano's limo, but I sold it for cash.'

'What? And you bought *that*?'

'Well … yeah,' Danny laughed. 'Had to do it at a 'dodgy brothers' car sales. You know, *no questions asked*. Bought an old Ford first. Then ditched that and bought this beauty! At least there's a mattress in the back,' Danny said and glanced at Ebony, who rolled her eyes and a slight smile crossed her face.

'We all fit in it?' Chips asked.

'Sure. It's got a bench seat. Why? There doesn't seem to be anywhere around here that'd be a long walk.'

'You need to drive, Danny,' Chips said seriously and walked over to the car.

* * *

The overhead fans swirled lazily in the Surf Club Bar & Bistro. On the outer deck, the three friends each took a seat and stared out at the beautiful translucent blue water. The golden beams of the afternoon sun shone in and bathed the whole area with a warm glow. A cocktail sat in front of each of them.

In the outdoor bar, a barman cleaned glasses, then casually turned up the volume on a large flat-screen TV. It caught Danny's attention as he read the heading - Crime Stoppers. He stood up and walked over to where he could hear what was being said. Chips continued talking to Ebony, pointing out yachts and sailing boats far in the distance. Danny casually leant on the bar as he watched the TV.

The announcer spoke.

'*Tonight's edition of Crime Stoppers involves a fugitive from New South Wales. Police have been searching for this man for more than a year after initially mistaking somebody else for him. Tonight, the newly appointed New South Wales Police Commissioner, Aubrey Warner-Smith, has advised of a nationwide manhunt for Daniel Edward Wainwright.*'

A mugshot of Danny appeared on the screen.

'*He could also be going under the alias Danny Strickland. If you see or hear of this man, do not approach him as he is highly dangerous. Instead, call Crime Stoppers or contact your local police station. Now back to our normal programming.*'

Acrobats started tumbling in Danny's stomach as he turned away from the television and walked back to the table. He wondered when this would all end. Surely the killing had stopped, but the endless running was wearing him down. He sat down next to Ebony and stared out over the water, lost in his own thoughts.

In the distance, the sound of police sirens could be heard.

'Danny,' Chips said. 'You and Ebony have to go.'

'What! Why?'

'I've organised something here, and you both have to leave.'

Chips pushed his cocktail to one side. 'Look over there ... the palm trees near the beach.'

Danny gazed across to where Chips was pointing. The footpaths were full of people, both tourists and locals alike, casually walking along, talking and going about their business.

'What are you talking about, Chips?'

'The tall palm tree,' Chips said and pointed.

Danny followed Chips' outstretched arm and saw the bikie with his chopper leaning against the tree in a shaded spot.

'They've watched me every day since I got here!' Chips said and sighed heavily. 'You see, when I sold the product to Biondi, I had to deal with Cain Trench, the president of the Tarantulas in Victoria. He wanted to know what happened to one of his bikie mates, Eddie

Harlow. He told me Eddie was going to the cemetery to kill you, but he figured that, as he never came back, you got to him first.'

Chips paused and stared at Danny. 'That's the man we buried … him and his bike.'

Danny nodded, remembering the day the bikie had turned up in the cemetery. Ebony stopped sipping her cocktail, and her eyes widened as she listened in on the conversation.

Chips continued. 'Trench said he'd buy the product on behalf of Biondi but that they were gonna follow me wherever I went. They reckoned you'd find me eventually, and when you did, they would take their revenge. That bikie out there is from the Queensland chapter of the Tarantulas.'

The carnival started up at the back of Danny's mind. The carousel began to turn; its music gradually gathered tempo as it staggered into life. The cars on the Big Dipper slowly reached their zenith, then rolled over the top and picked up speed as they hurtled downwards. Spruikers came out from their stalls as they called out. Carriages on the Ghost Train burst through the doors and into the darkness; girls screamed as ghouls harassed them. The Wipeout spun faster and faster. At Danny's feet, Brennan, the bully from all those years ago, lay on his back with a massive red hole in his chest. He looked up at Danny with a bloodless white face and smiled a grim deathly smile.

Chips continued. 'There's going to be a commotion here soon, and you gotta go!'

The police sirens sounded louder.

'Head back into the bistro,' Chips said.

Danny and Ebony walked back inside while Chips walked over to a young couple who were standing on the deck.

'Hi,' he said.

'Hello,' the girl answered.

'We're just leaving now, and that table near the water is free. It has a great view. I thought you might want to sit there.'

'Oh, thank you,' she said and smiled at her boyfriend, who also thanked him.

The couple took a seat where Danny and Ebony had been only moments before. Chips took his phone out of his pocket and dialled a number. The bikie under the palm tree put his mobile to his ear.

'Yeah?'

'Tell your boss I think the people you're lookin' for are sitting out on the deck of the surf club,' Chips said and hung up.

Chips strode over to Danny and Ebony.

'Come on, Danny ... *move!*' Chips said and raced outside. Danny and Ebony followed close behind.

'Leave now. I reckon you should head north,' he said and pointed. 'Find somewhere to stay for two or three days until this all blows over.'

Chips opened the passenger door of the panel van for Ebony and waited for Danny to get in the driver's side. Danny leant across the seat and peered up at Chips.

'What's goin' on, Chips?'

'I told the Tarantulas you guys were there out on the deck. That young couple gonna look like you at first, but they'll work out pretty soon they're the wrong people and then start searchin' for you. I also told the cops that the Tarantulas are gonna tear the place up. They've been banned and are not s'posed to be there. They nothin' but bad news, those bikies. Cops are on their way now! That's the commotion I'm talkin' about. But it'll give you time to get away. You gotta go, Danny ... *now!* You can backtrack through here at night in a few days and keep goin', but don't stop here, whatever you do, Danny. *Do not stop here!*' Chips looked down and then back up at Danny and Ebony with a sad look on his face. 'I guess this is goodbye, Danny ... Miss Ebony. Been nice knowin' ya ... but ... you gotta go ... now ... goodbye!'

And with that, Chips turned and casually walked away just as a dozen motorcycles started up the road towards the surf club. The noise of their engines mixed incoherently with the blast of police sirens.

* * *

Danny headed north, just like Chips told him to do. He stopped at a rundown motel in Cooktown, where he paid cash and booked a room for two nights under the names of Mr and Mrs Goldstein. Danny and Ebony only ventured out to eat and spent the majority of the time in their room watching the television news. The report of an upheaval in the Port Douglas Surf Club made the news on the first night, but there was nothing after that.

On day three, they waited until dark and then drove south until they made Townsville. Danny pulled in at a service station, where he bought fuel and a map. He headed west. During the trip, he told Ebony his life story. He told her everything and left nothing out. When he'd finished, she said it was her turn, and she told him her story. With the conversation over, they drove along in silence. After a while, she reached out and put her hand on his shoulder. He glanced over at her and smiled, then gently squeezed her soft, warm hand.

They took it in turns driving, and late the next day, they crossed the border from Queensland into the Northern Territory.

62

Epilogue

FIVE YEARS LATER a couple entered the main gates of the Melbourne General Cemetery a little before lunchtime. They made their way to a reception area and waited for the woman behind the counter to finish her phone call. Eventually, she put the phone down and smiled up at them.

'Can I help you?' she asked.

'Yes,' the man said and smiled at her. 'I was hoping to find the resting place of my great-great-grandparents. I believe they might be here somewhere.'

'Oh, okay. I can probably help,' the woman said enthusiastically. 'What was their name?'

'Goldstein ... Meir and Batya.'

She stared at him, a little perplexed. 'All right,' she said. 'It's good you know your relatives from so far back.' A bright smile lit up her face.

'Yes, we've been doing some work on the family tree, haven't we?' he said to his companion, who nodded her head towards the woman.

The woman rummaged through a set of dusty files, then checked her computer screen and hit a few keys.

'Ahh-ha,' she said excitedly. 'Yes, we have them!'

'Oh, good,' the man said.

'But they're not buried here. They're in a mausoleum!'

'Oh,' he said, feigning surprise.

'I'll have to find the key to the doors if you want to go inside.'

'Oh! That'd be great,' he said. 'A mausoleum … well, I'd really like to have a look around.'

'All right. I could be a few minutes. You can both take a seat if you like,' the woman said and pointed to a row of chairs that sat under some windows.

While they waited, the man gazed around at the surroundings, his mind racing.

What if the cops have left a note with cemetery management and want them to call if someone comes checking out the Goldstein mausoleum?

'What's the matter?' his partner asked.

'Oh nothing,' he said unconvincingly and kept drumming his fingers on the edge of his chair.

After what seemed like an eternity, the woman came back; she had an old rusted key in her hand.

'Found it,' she said triumphantly.

They walked over to the counter.

'You might have to jiggle it in the lock a bit to make it work,' the woman said. 'It hasn't been used for a very long time.'

The man smiled. 'That's okay,' he said. 'I'll see how I go.'

He took the key off her, and they started to walk out the door.

'Wait!' the woman said. His stomach lurched. 'Don't you want to know how to find it?'

His heart was in his mouth. 'Oh, sure,' he said as he turned around and smiled at her. 'I just got a little excited!'

A doubtful expression crossed the woman's face, but then she went back to the computer and hit a few keys.

'The Goldstein mausoleum is on the east side,' she said. 'There's a number of mausoleums there, but you can't miss it. Just read the headstone.' She smiled a hesitant smile and pointed them in the general direction. 'Should only take you five minutes, or so, to get there,' she added.

'Thanks,' he said, and he and his companion walked out of the reception area.

The woman watched them leave and, after a moment, went back to her computer. Outside, the couple took one of the walking paths.

'She didn't seem all that happy.'

'No,' the man replied but kept walking. The thought that the woman might ring the police was still utmost in his mind.

'Do you know where we're going?' his companion asked playfully.

'Yes,' he said. 'I believe it's this way …' He didn't finish the sentence when he saw the look on her face; he could see she was having fun with him.

At the mausoleum, he put the key in the lock, and as the woman had warned, it took a fair bit of jiggling before he could finally force it open. He then removed the chains holding the doors together and, with an effort, pushed them apart.

'So … Mr Goldstein,' she said to him, tongue in cheek, 'what is it we're searching for?'

He smiled at her. 'Something that was hidden here a long time ago,' he said as they entered the cold concrete room. 'The cops probably checked every coffin and cremation urn, but maybe not the wall itself. If it's still here, there should be a loose brick in the back.'

He knelt down and squeezed between an old coffin and the side wall. He started to crawl along until, eventually, half his body disappeared as he reached the back wall of the mausoleum.

'It should be somewhere around here … just not sure where.' His voice was muffled in the confined space.

She watched as he inched his way towards the back of the mausoleum.

'Got it!' he said.

He gently levered a brick out. It exposed a large hole where part of the mausoleum floor had fallen away. He pulled out two plastic bags full of white powder and another one chock-full of cash. He wriggled his way back out and held the bags of white powder up.

She stared at him worriedly. 'You're not goin' down that path … are you?'

Her comment stopped him in his tracks. He felt the weight in each bag of coke. It had been worth a small fortune back then; it'd be worth even more these days. But the thought of the death and destruction it had brought weighed heavily on him. He sighed and reached behind and pushed the bags back into the hole. Then he raised the bag of cash and stared at her with a questioning look.

'Up to you,' she whispered and shrugged her shoulders.

Back in the reception area, he returned the key. The woman behind the counter glanced up from her computer.

'Did you find it okay?' she asked.

'Yes. Thanks very much. It looks great,' he said and headed for the door.

The woman watched them as they left and then made a phone call.

Out on the street, he opened up the car door for his companion and walked around to the driver's side. He gazed one more time at the cemetery he knew so very well, then started the long, long journey home.

'Don't come back here – whatever you do – don't ever come back here!